Dog Days

Dog Days

AN ANIMAL CHRONICLE

Patrice Nganang

*Translated and with an Afterword
by Amy Baram Reid*

University of Virginia Press
Charlottesville and London

Originally published in French as *Temps de chien,*
© 2001 Le Serpent à Plumes, Paris

University of Virginia Press
Translation and afterword © 2006 by the Rector and Visitors
of the University of Virginia
Printed in the United States of America on acid-free paper
First published 2006

1 3 5 7 9 8 6 4 2

LIBRARY OF CONGRESS CATALOGING-IN-PUBLICATION DATA
Nganang, Alain Patrice.
[Temps de chien. English]
Dog days : an animal chronicle / Patrice Nganang ; translated and with an
afterword by Amy Baram Reid.
p.   cm. — (CARAF books)
Includes bibliographical references.
ISBN 0-8139-2534-7 (cloth : alk. paper) —
ISBN 0-8139-2535-5 (pbk. : alk. paper)
1. Yaoundé (Cameroon)—Fiction. 2. Yaoundé (Cameroon)—Social life and
customs—Fiction. I. Reid, Amy Baram, 1964– II. Title. III. Series.
PQ3989.2.N4623T4613 2006
843'.92—dc22   2005030651

Contents

Translator's Acknowledgments
vii
Notes on the Text
ix

First Barks
5
The Turbulent Street
121

Glossary
207
Afterword: *Reading around Nganang's Yaoundé* by Amy Baram Reid
211
Bibliography
231

Translator's Acknowledgments

As I complete this project, I would like to express my gratitude to the colleagues, friends, and family members without whose help this translation would not have appeared. First and foremost, I am so very thankful to Patrice Nganang for his support, his thoughtful reading of my work, and his willingness to respond to my many questions. My great respect for his writing is coupled with an immense appreciation of his generous spirit. The CARAF series editor, Carrol Coates, was both patient and encouraging at every stage of the project; his guidance was invaluable. Cathie Brettschneider, at the University of Virginia Press, helped shepherd the project from start to finish, despite my many delays. Adele King introduced me to Nganang's work, and R. L. Silver gave me feedback on an early version of the translation, which I was able to complete thanks to a grant from the Provost of New College and the New College Foundation. Caroline Reed, of the Jane Bancroft Cook Library, and Nedra Hartley, of the New College Division of Humanities, each provided assistance at crucial junctures. Finally, many, many thanks to my husband, Uzi Baram, for all the articles and references he deposited on my desk, and for being my sounding board; without his encouragement I never would have dared to begin this project. Thanks to our children, Jacob, Miriam, and Benjamin, who provided diversion and mirth, and to our dog Malu.

Notes on the Text

When the original French edition of *Dog Days* was published in 2001 (*Temps de chien*, Paris: Le Serpent à Plumes), it contained well over one hundred footnotes. These were, in the main, the result of an editorial decision, and provided French translations for some—but not all—of the "foreign" expressions in the novel, whether in one of Cameroon's national languages, in Pidgin English, or *Camfranglais*. In preparing this translation, I opted to eliminate the footnotes and, instead, to include a glossary at the end of the novel. The glossary is both more extensive than the original footnotes and more accessible, since many terms reappear throughout the novel; an asterisk follows the first appearance in the novel of a term found in the glossary. When Nganang's notes provided French translations for expressions in Pidgin English that are readily understandable to English speakers, I did not include them in the glossary. While attempting to preserve for readers a sense of how Nganang moves fluidly among languages in his writing, I have also, for simplicity's sake, glossed some terms in the text of the translation itself and, in rare instances, simply translated a word or phrase.

There were cases, however, where Nganang used footnotes to provide a sort of paratextual commentary. The tone of these notes varies considerably: from the reverent mention of the Malagasy poet Jacques Rabemananjara that accompanies the first mention of Madagascar, to the ironic aside that Mboudjak is the first dog in whom the Mami Wata have taken an interest, to the deadly serious explanation that the term AIDS has been applied to the toll taken by Cameroon's economic crisis. In these cases, all of which occur in the first section of the novel, I have integrated the footnote into the text as well as including the information in the glossary.

The glossary does not, however, aim to cover all the foreign expressions in the novel. In keeping with Nganang's desire to reproduce the effect of Yaoundé's complex linguistic medley, there are some terms—often exclamations—which are not included in the glossary and which, for most readers, will remain opaque. In a 2001 interview with Taina Tervonen, Nganang insists that tolerating a certain level of linguistic dissonance, accepting that you will not be able to understand everything that is said around you, is crucial to understanding the lived reality of Yaoundé: "Someone who grew up in Yaoundé, grew up in a universe where he will never understand everything. Just having a sense of the day-to-day is enough."[1] This is useful to keep in mind when approaching the novel, because of its emphasis on both the opacity of language and the effects of rumor and hallucination. Following in Mboudjak's footsteps gives readers a glimpse of what went on in the streets of Yaoundé in the early 1990s, but the novel refuses to provide a totalizing narrative.

Given the novel's attention to language, it is worth considering the multiple meanings embedded in the novel's title: *Temps de chien.* While *temps* can refer both to weather and to a moment of time (*le temps qu'il fait et le temps qui passe*), when used with the modifier *de chien,* meaning rotten or difficult, it becomes a common expression for really nasty weather. As a rendering of the title, however, "rotten weather" would miss both the point and the pun. As a title, *Dog Days* echoes the allusions of the original French to the weather and the novel's narrator, but with one significant difference. Whereas the dog days of summer—*la canicule* in French—are a time of stagnation, Nganang's novel is about turbulent times: the coming of a storm that seems to promise real change.

One of the first questions I had to resolve in the preparation of this translation was how to render the terms *quartier* and *sous-quartier.* There is no easy way in English to capture the relationship between these two terms. On one level, they refer to administrative sections and subsections of Yaoundé. At the same time, the prefix *sous,* literally "under," suggests not only subordination but also insufficience or lack (think of the term *sous-développé,* or "underdeveloped"). It was suggested early on that "slum" might be an appropriate rendering of *sous-quartier.* After consulting with the author, I decided against using it. Nganang emphasized that while he is writing about Yaoundé's poor neighborhoods, he is not focusing on its worst, not its shantytowns. Nganang's *sous-quartiers* are inhabited by people who may be struggling to get by, but who have some sort of income, even in times of economic crisis. Massa Yo loses his government job but is able to open up a bar, and he does not, he insists, need to rely on his wife's money to pay the bills. Using the term "slum" for *sous-quartier* would also undercut the hope that propels Mboudjak and his human fellows out on the street at the novel's conclusion, and this is something worth holding on to. In the end, I opted for "neighborhood" as the best way to render *sous-quartier,* because it fits with how Mboudjak understands the city's geography—as a labyrinth of courtyards and neighborhoods—and because it highlights the city's organization into a patchwork of distinct communities. For *quartier* I retained the cognate "quarter." While this is not common currency in American usage, it is recognizable. It is also the choice made by Myriam Réjouis and Val Vinokurov in their fine translation of Patrick Chamoiseau's *Texaco.*

Note

1. "Qui a grandi à Yaoundé, a grandi dans un univers où il ne comprendra jamais tout. Il suffit de comprendre la réalité ambiante." Quoted in Tervonen, "L'écrivain à l'école de la rue," 105.

Dog Days

This book is dedicated to a man: Muepu Muamba

Book I

FIRST BARKS

Chapter One

I am a dog. Who else but me could admit it with such humility? Since I see no reproach in this confession, "dog" becomes
nothing more than a word, a noun: the noun men use to refer
to me. But there you have it; in the end, I've gotten used to it.
I've assumed the destiny it places on my shoulders. From here
on out, "dog" is part of my universe, since I've made men's
words my own. I've digested the structures of their sentences
and the intonations of their speech. I've learned their language
and I flirt with their ways of thinking. I've even gotten used to
the arrogance of their orders. Who could ever have imagined
such a thing? I obey without the slightest bit of anger whenever
my master calls, even if I do always drag my paws a little.

It hasn't always been this way. At first I was wounded by
even the most innocuous human words. Any order made me see
red. At times I even heard my own name as an insult, mistaking
someone's call for the splat of a gob of spit. Then "dog" was
just another of the countless human things that grabbed me
by the throat, cut off my head, tore out my guts and my teeth,
covered me with filth, killed and buried me. Because for me the
word signified the arrogance with which men name the world,
assigning a place to each thing, and ordering them to be silent.
Each and every time it was used to refer to me, the word let me
know I was an object in the human universe, that I had stopped
being what I really was, and that I had no right to speak.

As I grew older, I became accustomed to this degrading term
men use for me. To make a long story short, I really got used to
it the day my master, Massa Yo, took me to the veterinarian.

"Doctor," he said tearfully, "my dog is sick. When I call him, he jumps up and tries to bite me!"

The veterinarian didn't ask anything else. He spoke for a moment, but all I caught was the word "rabies." And then he took out a long black needle. That day, I understood that I'd have to answer to my name if I wanted to survive. So I wagged my tail, lowered my ears, closed my eyes, and stretched my back. I even stood up on my hind legs and gave a little dance. Astonished, the veterinarian held back his needle. He petted my head and back. Amused by my antics, he laughed. He said I was a good dog and I purred with pleasure. He didn't give me a shot. He wrote up a long list of aromatic brews that were supposed to calm my nerves. Finally, he recommended canned dog food, which my master could buy at Score for 500 francs. Massa Yo scratched his head and thought for a minute, but then said that he could still afford to feed me . . .

"As long as my salary keeps coming," he stressed.

The name my master actually gave me is "Mboudjak," which means "the outstretched hand." I don't know why this name flatters me, or why I prefer it to just plain "dog." It ought to have revolted me just as much since, like "dog," it fails to free me from the long human leash. But doesn't it suggest that I have a hand of my own? And even that I am my master's hand? I guess we dogs have our vain streak. Anyway, I prefer "Mboudjak" to "dog" out of pure vanity: the name gives me a bit of influence over my master. It makes me not only his enlightened guide but also, and especially, his infallible hand, his right arm—the one that anticipates the path ahead, aware of all danger to come—and that makes me happy. I feel honored by my name, proud to point out to men truth's modest hiding place, and even to take the helm myself.

I may be just a dog, but I'm not stupid. I know I've never led anyone and that my master alone decides on the path and the distance we'll cover each time he takes me on a walk around La Carrière after work. He never—and I mean never—tells me where we're headed on these walks. Once we are in the woods, it doesn't matter if I prance along in front of him or run on ahead, I can already hear him calling my name if I stray from the path he has in mind: "Here, Mboudjak!"

Sometimes Massa Yo just whistles: phweet! I don't know why, but a reflex of my flesh brings me right back to follow in his footsteps. Most of the time, it's true, my range is limited by a chain that binds me to his will. Because I am his dog. Still, I'll admit that our regular walks make me the envy of the dogs in our quarter.

"Your master has money, doesn't he?" they all bark as we go by. "What've you seen?"

Amused, I reply, "Is a Big Man like a little one?"

Once when we were walking, a neighborhood dog came up to sniff my behind. His skin was scarred and striped with mange, and a swarm of flies was making his life hell. It was like they were eating him alive. My master shooed him away brutally.

"Bo-o! Do you do *that* with him?" asked the mangy dog from a safe distance. "Why does he love you like that, huh?"

His bark was full of sarcasm. I looked away proudly, but he didn't stop laughing. He said it was obvious I was my master's woman, that no man in Madagascar* ever took walks with his dog (please remember, dear readers, that Madagascar is one of Yaoundé's working-class quarters, not to be confused with the country of the same name about which the poet Jacques Rabemananjara sang). Never in all his long stray-dog memory had he seen anything like this. Only I knew the true price of my favored treatment, he said, adding that I could keep quiet if I wanted, my telltale ass was shouting what my mouth wanted to hush up: my wiggly-jiggly behind was proof of the kind of life I was leading. I knew I needed to squelch that sort of slander right at the start. I lunged forward, but my master had me leashed. I started to reply. A thousand comebacks popped into my mind, but I just shook my head and decided to keep quiet. It's true—there are things that can't be said, and sometimes it's best just to shut up. I plugged my ears and continued on my way, following my master.

Me, his "dog."

2

In April 1989, Massa Yo was *compressé,* * laid off. As if there were some logical connection, he immediately gave up his walking ways. Hunkered down from then on in the dark hole of his crisis, mortified by memories of the comfortable life from which he had been so abruptly weaned, emasculated by having to eat dry *bobolo* * with grilled peanuts morning, noon, and night, my master no longer reached out to caress my head. What am I saying: "caress"? He didn't even call me; my name had died in his mouth. I hate to say it, but if he still occasionally bought cans of dog food at Score, it was for him and his family. That meat was still affordable, in comparison with what he could have bought from the Maguida* butcher around the corner. I adapted to my devaluation. I didn't act out rabies anymore as a way of forcing his hand because I understood his problem.

Despite my silence, Massa Yo soon got in the habit of insulting me: "Parasite!" he'd say when I came to rub up against his feet. "Get out!"

Then he'd pick up one of his shoes and throw it at me.

"Get out of here you *njou njou Calaba* *!" he sometimes added.

I soon forgot the golden age of our relationship. I kept clear of him, so as to avoid any unnecessary escalation in the violence. In truth, I'd had enough of being his chosen victim, his scapegoat. When he came near me, more and more often I just took off. I hugged the walls so he wouldn't notice my shadow. I ran to hide behind the neighborhood's smelly houses. There I caught up with the strays with their bloodshot eyes and their halos of flies. I began spending more and more of my days with them. Their company wasn't always easy, however. They wanted to know what made my life with my master special. They longed to hear the ups and downs of the life of a house pet. It was the first time any of us had crossed class lines to speak to each other as brothers. They said I was lucky. And I, filled with shame, I didn't admit that my happiness was becoming more and more precarious. I didn't want to go up in flames right before their envious eyes. Sometimes, I'm afraid to say, I even sang my master's praises.

"Massa Yo could feed all the dogs in this quarter," I told them. And to my surprise, they believed me. Happily they never came and barked hungrily at Massa Yo's door. I'd told them my fiefdom was sacred and they believed me. They made do with envying my happiness from afar. To tease me, they sometimes accused me of being a "petit bourgeois" dog. They were never really mean to me, though. I took advantage of their friendship and kept quiet about my humiliations at home. When I went back to Massa Yo's, I'd be met with his ugly glare. He only barely kept from saying "So you came back, huh? I thought you'd left for good."

I suspected he wanted to give me up to the Sanitation Department, but lacked the courage to go through with it.

Once I stayed out for a good long while. When the dogs of the quarter were surprised I didn't leave them come nightfall, I told them I just wanted to try out their *nangaboko** way of life to understand them better.

"Out of canine solidarity," I added.

"Are you sure it's just out of solidarity?" asked one female dog, whose teats swept the ground.

To keep my misery from exploding in the bright sunlight, I avoided the eyes of my fellows during this stint sleeping in the streets. There was always a little something somewhere for my stomach—this part of town is really quite vast. In a gutter I'd find a chicken squashed by a car and tossed there by some human passerby. Or I'd find a rat whose cadaver perfumed everything around it. But a stony-faced dog finally wormed the truth out of me. He had guessed the depth of my suffering and gained my confidence with an offer of friendship. When I confessed, in a moment of weakness and sincerity, that I had slammed my master's door behind me, I realized he was only fishing for information. He was the one who spread the story of my disgrace to the other dogs.

One day, when I was caught up in the delightful vision inspired in me by a piece of wet leather, I heard a bark over my head. It was the mangy-coated dog who had previously accused me of forbidden acts with my master.

"Hey, Mboudjak," he howled, "you're already eating cadavers-o."

"Just to see what they taste like," I began, haughtily.

He burst out in his same old ironic laugh. "Here on the out-side, you're gonna end up eating crap!" he said. "When you had it all-o, you wouldn't even give us the time of day. Now it's your turn to be your master's scapegoat."

"*A bo dze-a,*"* said a one-eyed female who'd joined in on the surprise and amusement of the mangy mutt. "You'll be just like us."

She stared me down with her menacing eye and bared her broken fangs. I put my tail between my legs. Yes, it had come to that. I'd fallen down to the level of my fellows' suffering and run headlong into their insensitivity. They'd put up with me only as long as I seemed to represent the Other World! But why hold it against them? From then on I stoically endured their barking laughter, their whispers and their teasing. At the same time I discovered the sordid side of their world of hunger. I learned that in the depths of their shit, misery laid the kingdom of hallucinations wide open. Sometimes I listened as they spent whole days telling each other stories about dog hospitals, dog churches, television programs for dogs, meals specially pre-pared for dogs, taxes for the care of dogs, retirement homes for dogs, and even cemeteries for dogs. I listened to their foolish-ness and amused myself by imagining the beauty of the animal paradise they sketched in their efforts to drown out the all-too-loud growling of their stomachs. I struggled along endlessly in the miasma of their putrefying hell and became just another stray myself. I took on the bleak outlook of any neighborhood stray because, like them, I had nothing better on the horizon.

I'd be lying if I didn't say that their fantasies sometimes re-minded me of the sort of bliss I'd had with my master—a bliss their company would never give back to me, that's for sure.

At first I laughed at their fantasies and even said, sounding like my old sarcastic self, "What have you seen?"

I only started defending myself when they ran out of dreams and began to hold my flight from human paradise against me. And yet, as I argued with them, the image of Massa Yo's house began to change in my head. I'll admit it: the more the street sucked me down into the dark and malodorous labyrinth of its myths, the larger Massa Yo's house loomed in my memory as an island of bliss—one I ought not to have given up so easily. The more I saw of my fellow dogs' suffering, the more I regretted my hasty decision. I shook my ears violently to chase away the flies pestering me, and turned around furiously to bite my back. I was at the end of my rope and I told myself that I, Mboudjak, didn't deserve to sleep in the mud. Indeed, my companions' hallucinations kept conjuring my master's laughing face right before my eyes. I saw Massa Yo lifted out of his misery. I saw him seated once again in the civil servant's well-fed opulence. Sometimes I even saw him with another dog at his side, a dog he'd also named "Mboudjak" out of laziness. Yes, just like that, I saw him walking with this other Mboudjak along the road to Mbankolo,* as he used to do with me. I saw him walk right by me with his dog, without so much as a glance in my direction. Jealous, I barked out a thousand insults.

"Is a Big Man like a little one?" that other Mboudjak replied scornfully.

And so it had come to this: lying in my gutter bed, I thought back nostalgically to the golden age of my relationship with my master. To console myself I imagined my own spicy epics and invented the myth of the dog with a silver ring around his neck. As time went on, I forgot the bad days I'd been through with Massa Yo. A blow is easily avoided if you know how to behave, I told myself in my most cowardly moments. An insult is swallowed when you know how to forget, I said too. And spit smells no worse than muck. I even went so far as to reproach myself for having been too naive or, rather, too idealistic, for not having realized the harsh reality of life. And then one day I heard someone say in a furious debate, "What a stupid idea to walk around with a chain around your neck!"

Suddenly my feelings were divided. Life had left the dog who was speaking only three legs. Still he went on: "By Allah, I swear, even if you give me a million, I'll never make a slave of myself!"

I looked at him sadly. I knew his story. He'd lost one of his legs crossing the street, and his owner had kicked him out because his wife found him laughable and ugly. The crippled dog had only bitterness for men in his heart and called himself a communist. His fate scared me. He went on: "What's more, it's only the white men's dogs who can accept being put on a leash, or the dogs of their black lackeys . . ."

I saw a little tinge of jealousy in his eyes as he added: ". . . because they are dogs alienated from their canitude! With us, each dog jealously protects his canine condition, that is to say, his freedom."

Hearing that, I couldn't hold my tongue: "What freedom?" I howled. "What freedom? Yes, I say, what freedom! Do you even know what freedom is? Is it freedom to die and be thrown in the trash as if we had no soul?"

The other dogs burst out laughing. I stifled my arguments, realizing too late that their discussion was meant only to make fun of me. I jumped on one of them and tried to tear his eyes out, to rip up his face. All the stray dogs in the quarter needed to know that I, Mboudjak, wasn't about to let myself be humiliated by their insinuations without baring my fangs. In the end, I took a beating for no good reason. Things went from insults to blows, from discussions to brawls, from the idle gossip we call *kongossa** to slurs, and one fine day I just decided to get out of their hell. Better Massa Yo's chains than the haunting stench of those ill-mannered mutts' maws, I told myself.

Basically, I returned to my master's house for just one reason: to silence the yapping in my ears of those who really weren't my brothers. I went back to my master's, it's true, but I didn't forget to hold my tail and my ears high, and let the degraded canine population of Madagascar know that their jealousy grew out of their own misery. Shaking with laughter, the three-legged dog replied, "Don't say too much, now. You'll be back."

I stared him down and barked, we'd see about that.

3

So back I went. Once more I crouched in the shadow of Massa Yo's house. He was unmoved by the fact that I'd escaped from a thousand miseries. With my return, he grew even angrier, which left me to put up with the waves of his changing moods. *Bia boya.** I had insulted my fellows and couldn't go back to them now without being humiliated even more. By leaving them I had condemned myself to bowing down before my master's daily annoyance. To convince myself to return, I'd told my mourning pride that if I was going back to the house of that brutal man, it was first and foremost because of Soumi's friendship. Soumi was my master's son. Despite his triangular head, crowned with a record-breaking *acops,** I felt a sympathetic bond with the ten-year-old. When I saw him after my return, I put aside all the doubts I'd had on account of his father's past violence. I pulled back my ears, jumped up, and licked his face. "How you've grown!" I told him, although it was a lie.

It was really just to have something to bark out to him. Soumi washed all the dirt off me. I took this gesture as proof of his friendship, although he was only following his father's orders. I learned to lie to myself in order to survive the shame of all I had to bear. I began running through the quarter with my young friend. I exaggerated my joy for all to see. My gestures were excessive, my barking too loud. But when my fellow canines saw me bounding wildly down the road, they didn't even dare say a thing to me. They stood there, with their mouths gaping open and their tongues hanging down to the ground. This time I barked out my importance to them. When people froze with fear at my *craning**—my rambunctious bragging—Soumi told them not to be afraid. He said I wasn't vicious, and that was the truth. I'd crouch down and stretch out my hind legs when Soumi said the word. I even lay down on my belly, wiggling so he'd know I'd put myself in his hands. He threw a tennis ball off into the distance and, barking out my joy, I ran to bring it back to him. I swear by Allah that even if Soumi had thrown that ball all the way to Hell, I'd have run and fetched it, steaming between my fangs. Friendship has no limits, I kept telling myself.

"Soumi," I barked to him one day, "you are my brother." But he didn't understand. Another day, however, I heard him tell my master I was a good dog. That remark convinced me I was on the right path, and so I doubled my *choua,** my efforts for his friendship. Was there anything I didn't try in order to tame the violence the boy learned from his father? At times I came too close to crossing the thin line that separates friendship from humiliation. All my actions were dictated by my cowardly desire to escape the street, which had shown me the hideous face of its deadly brutality. Anyone who has sniffed around in the gutters recognizes the stench at a distance. For me, every game, every race, every time we got carried away was a chance to create a real paradise with the man in that child; my relationship with Soumi was sure to be the source of my salvation.

And yet, what I had too quickly forgotten in my overly hasty orgasms of delight was that I was still a dog. Yes, I accept it: it's God's will that I walk on four legs. But for Soumi, my four-legged condition defined the limits of my being; it signified that I was condemned by fate to crawl flat on my belly like a reptile. I was aware of this every time anger clouded his eyes. Then my young friend would let loose with a whole dictionary full of insults and, in just a few moments, he'd become his father. "*Mouf!*" he'd say when we were in the house. "Get out, you cockroach!"

And when a fit of anger seized him outside, he'd shout:

"Guinea pig!"

"Fornicator!"

"Ruminant!"

"Individual!"

And on and on. When I ignored him and hung around— even wagging my tail and perking up my ears to maintain the dignified pretense that I hadn't heard a thing—he'd give me a swift kick in the rear. I took these blows for the backsliding of a childish soul, blanketing myself in the illusion that he just needed a bit more training. I told myself that he was sure to grow up, and I hoped our friendship would help him to do so. In all honesty, I've never wanted to be a man, but still, I'd often put myself in my friend's place in order to understand and forgive his backsliding. Yet at the same time, I knew that Soumi would never have imagined what it was like to be a dog, not in the deepest recesses of his dreams. This difference in our souls created an invisible barrier between us that even my sidestepping of his anger couldn't destroy: camaraderie's unbridgeable gap. How can I put it? Here's an example: I was always surprised when, from time to time, and even at the end of a day spent playing together, Soumi used the cut-and-dried tone of a master to speak to me.

And that was still really nothing. Because, to tell the truth, the barrier between Soumi and me only became an insurmountable wall when our interests were at cross-purposes. Each time my young friend found his vital space in danger, the master dozing within him awoke. And his vital space, like his father's, took the shape of his protruding belly—how could it be any different for the son of his crisis-ridden father?

4

You just can't expect too much from life, I tell myself from time to time, adding and underscoring: ESPECIALLY WHEN YOU'RE A DOG. Really, how could Soumi and I ever be friends when his father's decline obliged me to share in the meal the kid considered to be just for the family? How could we be friends when I had to eat from a plate Soumi always said was his and nothing but his? How could we be friends when, each time the dinner hour rolled around, my friend came up with some strategy to get me out of the house? Or when, just before noon, he'd turn to me and say, with no shame at all: "Mboudjak, take your flies and get out!"—insisting "Out!" when I dragged my paws. Once my master asked Soumi to give me some of the delicious red and greasy *koki** that was piled high on his plate. Carnivore that I am, I would have passed up a dish reeking of spicy, greasy beans without any regret, even if it were the tastiest in the world! Soumi, however, shamelessly said his plate was already too small for him to have to share it with a dog (and he stressed the word "dog"). I was really offended by this comment from a friend. Yes, really offended. Still, in the name of our friendship, I was ready to forget this awkward exchange. "Hunger erases man's intelligence," I said to myself bitterly.

But then, boiling with rage, Massa Yo stormed out of the house and, without any warning, dumped his kid's plate of *koki* right in front of me. Cackling, the chickens threw themselves on it. "If you don't want to eat it," one of them said to me, "that's your problem-o."

I watched them noisily pecking away. My guilty conscience

poked at me. "Mboudjak," said my stomach suddenly, "what are you thinking? You're not just going to stand there like that in front of a plate of *koki*!" And it was true, even the Mami Wata*—those water spirits who, from time to time, come to torment men—would have punished me if I'd failed to get carried away by that wonderfully spicy dish spread out on the ground in front of me (please note that Mboudjak is the first dog in whom the Mami Wata have taken an interest). In any case, the food clearly could not be saved for any human. There was no reason for me not to dig right in. I gave myself a good shake, but quickly let my stomach's voice be my guide. And so as I greedily licked the ground, and Soumi's voice rose up in an endless wail, my master thundered on in the living room: "That'll teach you to be less of a glutton!" And he added, "You'll just have to go hungry!"

Was it my problem? I ate my part, knowing Soumi's mother would sneak him something to replace his meal. Why else have a mother? Mama Mado would never let her only child go to bed hungry, that's for sure. What mother has ever let her little darling sleep on an empty stomach because of a dog, can you tell me that? I told myself that peace would soon be restored to the house. The next day I even made it my duty to draw Soumi into a game to facilitate our reconciliation and remind him that he wasn't alone in his pain. It's true, I had played a part in his suffering, but he shouldn't forget our friendship. By recalling the virtues of our alliance, I wanted to calm my tearful friend's strained nerves and perhaps remind him of the obligation to let bygones be bygones. It seemed to work. Soumi soon found his usual playful exuberance. That day he played more than he ever had before. And I just let myself get carried away by the enticing intoxication of his enthusiasm.

Together we ran through the quarter's byways. There were no limits to our fun! We went through valleys we'd never seen before. We jumped over streams and splashed around in them, letting our joy bubble over. Soon we found ourselves in a forest, I think it was the Mbankolo forest. We played hide-and-seek and tag. We jumped hurdles and raced as fast as we could. We high-jumped and pole-vaulted. We dribbled balls through the trees and took penalty shots. The guilt I felt for having swallowed up my friend's delicious *koki* turned into an excessive eagerness to play. Under the pretext of a new game he'd invented, Soumi soon put my leash around my neck. Yipping away, I let him do it.

"Gallop!" he cried, "Gallop, gallop away, little horse!"

Now I'm clearly no horse, but I went along with it. We pushed on into the depths of the forest. I ran behind him, I ran on in front or alongside. Soon, holding the rope in his hand, Soumi climbed up a tree, perched on a branch, and, before I could see what he had in mind, leaped off the other side. Hop! There I was, dangling in the sky, my four feet waving in the wind. Soumi looked at me hanging there. What's worse, he burst out laughing. "*Aschouka ngangali,*"* he taunted, in a fit of laughter.

I thought I saw him dancing around my suspended body. I was blinded by the pain. My eyes bulged out of their sockets. My tongue hung down to the ground. I couldn't even bark out my suffering. Overcome by a coma, I couldn't voice my soul's distress. I was doomed to silence by that razor-sharp rope cutting into my throat, breaking my neck, slowly killing me. I struggled wildly. A mortal chill was gripping my body. My spirit sunk into darkness. I don't know how long I remained there, hanging from that tree. Maybe my cowardly assassin left me there for several days, at the mercy of the carnivorous birds picking away at my guts. Maybe he just left me there, like a vulgar *bifaga** drying in the sun. No one would dare take me down from my branch, since everyone would think I was a sacrifice offered up to the ancestors. That's the end of it: the crime to which I fell victim was lost, along with my memory, in the endless space of man's multiple and dubious beliefs. Maybe some faithful Catholics even brought a priest to pour holy water on me and say, while repeatedly making the sign of the cross: "Let the dead bury the dead, amen!"

Or maybe no one bothered to take me down from my branch because each was waiting for the people from the Sanitation Department to do their job. But, as always, they never came. You never know, maybe I'm still hanging from that tree, with my eyes fixed in an empty stare, surprised to have been caught unawares by death, and with my mouth open to the void, surprised to have fallen silent before it could bark out my pain.

I can imagine that once he was left alone to eat in peace, Soumi would enjoy his *koki* all the more. I'm sure he'd have no trouble finding a story to explain my disappearance to his father. He could say that, plagued by guilt after my misdeed, I'd decided to kill myself. But why should he lie? Yes, why lie to explain the death of a dog? He could just say straight out that he'd hanged me. I know that my master, frightened by the truth, would hold back his punishing hand. "You're worse than an animal," he'd say. "You're just like your mother!" "So what?" the little criminal would think. And he'd be right because, in any event, life would go on.

5

And yet, I'm sorry to say for Soumi, I did survive my hanging. How can I put it? I survived and returned home to his father, to Massa Yo, my master. Just between us, wouldn't you say that I'm man's best friend? Why else would I—more than once the victim of the insane rage of that man known as Massa Yo, and now the survivor of his son Soumi's murderous plot—find myself back again in that man's shadow, in that house of hunger, which had led me to my death? Do I have to be killed, re-killed, re-re-killed, and re-re-re-killed? Do I have to die once, twice, thrice, ten, a hundred, or a thousand times before I finally consider leaving my perpetual assassin? Think what you will, dear reader, but don't say I returned home to my master just because I'm a dog. No, here's why: more than anything else, it was my decision to seek justice for *myself* that pushed me back to Massa Yo's. Let's underscore the word "myself," shall we?

And so, if I sniffed my way out of the Mbankolo forest, following its labyrinth of trails and retracing the playful path toward my death, it was because I was impelled by my desire to see Soumi held accountable for his cruelty. "This'll make him shit in his pants," I kept telling myself as I made my way back. "Today's the day!" I added.

When Soumi saw me on the doorstep of his father's house, he died of fright. But he had it right before—I'm not a bad dog. Me? Mboudjak? Who'd believe it? So I let myself be convinced by his father's menacing arm which kept me away from the kid. Soumi immediately began talking about "rabies" and "possession." I howled that it was a lie; I laid out the twists and turns of my aborted assassination, but Massa Yo didn't even listen to my overly loud version of things. I heard him say I had some nerve to come back and bark at him after disappearing "yet again" without a trace. He was hopping mad and grabbed me by the scruff of my neck. I yelled that it was all a misunderstanding, but he didn't listen to me. He gave my rear a rhythmic walloping. "Where were you?" he asked with every blow. I tearfully barked my explanation, but he didn't believe me. "Where were you?" I wailed out my suffering, but to no avail. "Where were you?"

To tell the truth, words were of no use against his blind rage. I shut my eyes, let my ears droop, and gave in to his anger. His blows sent waves deep into my bones, beating out the cacophonous hymn of injustice. When he let go of me, I scurried away, but didn't stop barking. I didn't lower my voice until he mentioned the "veterinarian." I could still see that long black needle from my past and fell silent. But my master went on, saying I'd become so stubborn because he no longer had the means to take care of me. He launched into a complaint about how I was becoming a stray dog, and he damned the crisis that had emasculated him. He put both of his hands on his head to underscore all the more his distress and even his mourning. I kept quiet when he said that maybe he'd have to turn me over to the Sanitation Department because, as he put it: "Here you are back again with all sorts of bugs you picked up running around."

He pointed at my neck, which still bore the traces of my aborted hanging, as well as the many flies gorging themselves in my open wounds. I left his courtyard, indignant over his idea of justice. He hadn't even listened to my version of things. "A whole week," he said indignantly to Soumi, whose smirk I caught. "A whole week! And what's worse, this is the second time he's disappeared like that!"

Massa Yo's anger cast a shroud over the whole evening. He threatened to keep me on a leash, but there he ran into his son's inability to find my chain (Soumi said he was "sure" he had put it next to the cupboard), as well as his own inability to pay for a new one. Ah, the crisis! I hid, out of range of my master's anger but still in his courtyard. I was suffering as deeply in my soul, my skin, and my flesh as in my bones. My indignation was too great, however, for me not to concoct a plan for revenge. Yes, I said to myself, if there's going to be justice, I'll just have to count on myself to get it.

You've got Mboudjak's word on it—dog's honor.

Can you believe it? After his misdeed, Soumi no longer found the courage to come near me. Oh, you should've seen him! From then on my so-called friend fled before my shadow. When I'd lie in the courtyard of the house, Soumi would spend the entire day cloistered in the living room. And when I came to find him there, he'd perch on top of the dinner table. His parents didn't give a second thought to the reasons for this change in his behavior, the all-too-visible proof of their son's crime. But then again, did a crime really take place? I was always the one they brutally told to get the hell out. At first I'd leave the house muttering. But soon I began to enjoy seeing Soumi shiver with fear whenever I passed by. I barked out my laughter each time I saw him take off at the sight of me. I laughed, which only made him all the crazier to get out of there. He was off so fast I thought he would break a leg! My friend's cowardice condemned him to a life of perpetual trembling. *Bia boya.* So I gave up on my plan to bite his calves—no regrets. Was it even worth the trouble anymore? His own cowardice was punishment enough.

To tell the truth, once I'd gotten over my amusement, I realized that I'd come back to this criminal house less to laugh at Soumi's bumbling flights than to learn how and why a man (or a child, what's the difference!) could be so inhuman. I'll admit that I had only escaped from death because a shocked passerby had cut my noose. But I wasn't going to escape from death just to fall, stuttering out my gratitude, into the arms of the first man I met. No, not me. I had wandered through the woods and finally returned to my master's because, I told myself, if I really wanted to be safe from the evil deeds of the likes of Massa Yo and his son, I had best not flee from them. Yes, I told myself that if I wanted once and for all to escape from the rage of men,

I needed either to tremble less before their gaze or lose myself forever in the forest, or else *choua:* systematically seek out the problematic friendship of my fellows, who, for that matter, had already rejected me. But I knew that living from then on only in the forest, far from any human eyes, and preparing the canine revolution while sharpening my race consciousness wouldn't save me from the bestiality of the first hunter to come by. On the contrary! To escape from men's crimes, I told myself, I needed to muster up the courage to return to the dangerous circle of their definitions and demand justice.

OK, I'll admit it. I really came back to my master's to summon whatever humanity was in him. Yes, yes, yes! If he were really human, wouldn't he have punished his murderer of a son? If he were a man! And what of his son? If he had even the littlest piece of a man in him, wouldn't he have faced up to the accusing gaze of the dog that I am? If only there were a man slumbering somewhere in him! But then, are Massa Yo and Soumi the only ones in this wretched quarter who have hocked their humanity? Was there any way to find out without putting my life on the line? Didn't they do just what all the local men were capable of doing? *Nsong am nù.** That said, I've learned one thing in my life: getting myself killed again just to slake my thirst for justice is a foolish act no judge would pardon. What's more, I, Mboudjak, don't want to die twice. Still, each time I see my dear Soumi scurry off in fear as I pass, and his father keep silent before the stench of the crime thus confessed, and all of Madagascar let itself fall into a purr of good conscience, from the deepest recesses of my laughter, a question always pops up:

"Where is Man in all of this?"

One question and one alone.

I ask my question systematically, and every day I see men going about their business. I see Massa Yo remaining silent and Soumi running to hide from me. Yes, every day I observe men: I observe them, and observe them, and observe them some more. I watch, I listen, I tap, I sniff, I chew, I sniff some more, I taste, I lie in wait, I conclude; I come up with a thesis, an antithesis, a synthesis, and a prosthesis on their daily routine. In short, I open up my senses to their courtyards and their streets, I invite their universe into my spirit. I watch and I really try to understand just how they do it. How they do what? How they manage to be what they are. This makes you laugh? OK then, laugh. Go ahead, laugh! As for me, I know that if I want to survive men, I need to know what they're capable of.

I'm convinced of it.

6

Standing with my front legs straight, as I will from now on, with my ears erect and my tongue hanging down, panting to calm the eagerness of my hungry spirit, I suddenly become a stranger to my master. A dog who, from morning to night, night to morning, observes the street, observes his master, observes men, and does nothing other than observe. A dog who weighs and carefully considers a bone thrown to him by a passing *soya** vendor: no one in Madagascar, not even Massa Yo, has ever seen such a thing. At first my master took my focused attention, which makes me follow the trajectory of each of his movements when he eats, for an extreme form of gluttony. Sometimes, when I'd bark out my amusement, he'd get annoyed and say I begged too much. Sometimes, then, he'd throw me a bone he'd finished sucking on. He's always surprised when I don't jump right on it, but rather weigh and carefully consider the bone in question, looking at him again with laughter. Then he'd say "It's never enough for you!" and start to get violent. *"Mouf,"* he'd bellow, "get out!"

Yes, not even my return from Hell had calmed his nerves—on the contrary. Still, I noticed he was starting to be more and more tolerant of my presence by his side. My position as an observer prevented me from rubbing up against his feet, but I could lie down in his courtyard, in the shadow of the walls of his home. He didn't complain about it. I became a watchdog. As a result, I felt him grow in stature at my side, becoming someone else in the eyes of his fellows: a Man. (How could it be otherwise? With me in his courtyard, he suddenly seemed to have the terrifying stature of a tough. Feared and respected he was then.) Some of his friends even called me a "purebred." They usually added that I was a "good dog." For others, though, who were as cowardly as Soumi, I was an "attack dog." Those who believed them would start trembling when they saw me sitting in my master's courtyard, my eyes focused on the street and my tongue hanging out. They'd turn away when their gaze met mine and fearfully ask Massa Yo to hold me back. He'd say to them what his son used to say: "Don't pay any mind. Mboudjak doesn't bite," even though he really wished that, like any brave pet, and especially in this time of crisis, I would occasionally place one or two strangled chickens before his honored door to show my true canitude.

"Don't you think he's going to chase away all your customers?" his wife Mama Mado asked once.

My master just laughed.

"Mboudjak?" he said, truly amused, pointing down at my puny frame as I sat scientifically on my behind. "All he knows how to do is to disappear for days and days. Look, he can't even chase away the flies eating at his ears."

And Massa Yo was right. Since I was consumed by my new duties, open to the surprises and secrets of the street before me, I just wasn't that important to him anymore. In fact, if my master had accepted me back into his life without falling yet again into a blind fury, it was because he had discovered that I could watch over his goods, keep the bandits away from his paltry belongings, bite the calves of the parasites, and bare my fangs to those who came by in the early morning looking for a little change from him . . .

There's something I haven't said yet: my master had ended up opening a bar in order to get by, like all the local men, and to drag himself out of the miasma of misery: The Customer Is King. His bar is his pride and joy, and myself, Mboudjak, I'm just a prop for his grandeur. Yes, I'll admit it: Massa Yo was right to say that I don't bite. How could I forget that it was only because of the new status his bar conferred upon him that he tolerated my company again? I'd have to be a real idiot to put an end to the surprising sociability his bar had given back to him by biting the calves of his customers!

I'm not going to bite off my tail to spite myself, now am I?

In short, Massa Yo found a job for me in his bar. He took

me back just as I was, giving me no other task than to sit or lie there in his courtyard, in the shadow of the walls of his house, right next to his crates. All I have to do is guard his crates, that's it. When I watch the doors of The Customer Is King from my courtyard post, I see him—my Massa Yo of a master—stretching out his belly toward the street, and slowly, he becomes once more the man he was in his times of opulence: really somebody. If he hasn't yet thought of going for a walk in the woods like we used to, I tell myself, it's certainly just because his new job is making him kill the civil servant within him if he wants to survive. A bartender doesn't have fun. He has to wait there all day long for his customers. I won't say that he has now become boredom incarnate, but one thing is true: I sure feel sorry for him!

And yet, how does one escape from boredom? In their moments of deepest boredom, men usually recall the virtues of a dog. So, when I lie next to the door of The Customer Is King, I sometimes catch Massa Yo's hand on my fur. I lower my behind and scurry off between his crates. My master never insists on petting me. And I go lie down in his courtyard, reassured but on guard. I swear, never again will men catch me in the trap of their sordid sympathy and their useless games. From now on it is I who will determine the field for defining things. It is I who will give names to things and to beings. Yes, I alone will interpret the world around me. I'll do it in their language, of course, but all the same, I'll use their words and their phrases only to simplify things for myself. I alone will tell my story and that of the innumerable mysteries of daily life. Let me make myself clear: I alone will succeed in resolving the enigma of humanity.

You'll see.

7

I concede that my wide-open eyes haven't always protected me from the madness of the human world. One day, for example, when first my nose, then my tongue, then again my nose, and once more yet my nose had reassured me about a sweet-smelling liquid leaking from a bottle of Beaufort that had tipped over right in front of my thirsty mug, I couldn't keep myself from lapping up the beer. It was rather bitter, but gave me an intensely pleasing sensation as it went down my throat. I eagerly licked up this exciting water of happiness and soon the ground began to spin around me. Gigantic abysses opened up before my paws, and each time I jumped to avoid them, new abysses opened up a few meters away. The walls of the houses began to dance, too. Men turned liquid and oozed. I thought I'd crossed over—and this time by my own fault—into death's dissolute universe, poisoned by the meanness of some unknown person. But yet, the sky was still there over my head, although it had suddenly sunk quite low.

For almost an hour I was caught in that intense and uncontrollable inebriation of the universe and was able to break free only after I raised my back leg and doused the wall of my master's bar with my hot urine. Only much later did I learn that I was drunk. That I learned one day when I saw one of my master's customers—"and a civil servant, no less," as Massa Yo says—get up after he, too, had downed several bottles of the very same Beaufort. With one hand on his belly and the other holding a still-full bottle, he awkwardly began to trace the steps of an improvised *makossa** before collapsing in the middle of his song, in a crash of chairs and upturned bottles, with crates smashing and men and women laughing all around.

"Just leave him there on the ground," said my master, doubled over with laughter, to those who wanted to pick the man up. "Don't you see he's drunk?"

The crowd grew even more excited around the drunken man, and I was dumbfounded to see a pool spread out around him as his mouth opened wide in a cacophonous rendition of the national anthem: "O Cameroun, berceau de nos ancêtres."* I sniffed at the pool to be sure. Yes, it was urine. I looked at the man and shook my head. My master shooed me away, but I dodged him. Swaying, the man got up and headed off down the road, his feet marking the counterpoint as he sang, "Paul Biya—Paul Biya, Paul Biya—Paul Biya, our President." Children followed after him. For quite a while their taunts took over the neighborhood, drowning out the man's song.

And that's how I learned to recognize, even from afar, the

thousand bottled causes of the world's drunkenness. Weren't they the thousand bottles my master had opened up in front of that makossa-dancing man? Beaufort, *tritri, chômé, nsansanboy,** *quatre fois quatre, gwan, gnôle, odontol,** *petit* Guinness, and so on: in a word, *jobajo.** If only I could laugh about it! In short, I learned to despise drunks. Because when they start to lose control of their actions, most men can think of nothing better to do than grab my tail or pull my ears. Every evening in my master's bar, I have to confront their persistent stupidity; and it makes me mad when they laugh at my indignant reflex. Sometimes, I admit, I regret being a good dog. I regret that all I can do when faced with these foul-smelling idiots is bark out my canine laugh, bare my fangs, or respond with insults that, in the end, they never really get. Most of the time, when I can't take it anymore, I just shake my head and tell myself they're lucky to be Massa Yo's kings.

That's for sure and for certain.

My master has forbidden me to threaten his customers. It seems that, struck by the same deadly crisis that dumped Massa Yo into unemployment and turned him into a bartender, the entire population of Madagascar had found no other way to get by than by opening up bars. Oh yes, the bars—in our neighborhood, there's a bar every ten meters. My master would've ended up drinking his beers himself if his bar didn't have a few die-hard regulars. Doesn't Massa Yo aim to get everyone who comes into his place drunk? What other choice is there? So whatever the sins of his customers, regardless of what they do or how inebriated they may get, I'm not going to sink my fangs into their calves! I know all too well how irritable my master gets when it's late in the day and he hasn't yet taken in his expected receipts. Once, for example—at about eleven or so—a polite little old man came into the bar and offered the traditional greeting, *"Menmà, you tcho fia."** Unmoved, Massa Yo replied: "Can I eat peace? If you're just passing by, keep going on your way-o."

You could tell there'd been no customers yet that morning. I don't think it can be said any more clearly: as far as my master is concerned, only the paying customer counts.

8

From my hideaways, I observe the neighborhood's residents. I see the road in front of my master's bar open onto the city. From underneath the crates, I watch each day go by, endlessly beckoning the night. Lying in the shadows of the walls, I watch women shake their hips right and left, left and right, right and left; I see a young girl rile up all the local men by strutting around, breasts raised high. From my observation posts, I watch men on the verge of drunkenness run off to piss loudly. I see them shake their *bangalas** several times, spit theatrically on their urine, and run back to their suicidal *jobajo*. From the bar's doorway I watch children scratch their behinds through their little shorts and then stick their fingers up their noses right after. I hurry back into the courtyard of the bar, where I observe an amorous cock pursuing a hen. As I watch, he lowers his brightly colored wings, runs, and then stops short at the edge of the road, powerless as his beloved is crushed by a car. I see lizards run across the wall of my master's bar; they stop and look at all of this too, and then cock their heads philosophically, as if to say, "The world is amazing—let's live life to the fullest."

As for me, I watch and take notes.

I take in the world from below. This allows me to apprehend men at the very moment of their emergence from the primordial muck. In the same way, I apprehend the phases of humanity's annihilation. Still, I must admit, at times this position is uncomfortable. You see, most of my master's customers have really stinky feet when they take off their shoes. There are always one or two of them who, after sitting down on an overturned crate next to me, take off their shoes and point their toes right at my snout—on purpose, it seems, just to chase me away. Happily, these are a minority, but that's only because the men in the quarter can't afford to shut up their toes in shoes. Yes, happily for me, most of them only wear *sans confiance,* those cheap plastic sandals from Bata, which air out their toes! Happily, I say, because my favorite spot of all is underneath a table. Sitting under a table I am free to observe the world without being jostled, without feeling that a kick is looming. On top of that, sitting under the table always allows me to catch men in those cowardly actions they hide from the other members of their race. How many times have I seen the hands of respectful men descend into the darkness beneath a table just to scratch their nuts? How many men have I seen lose their toe under the table in the recess between the legs of their neighbor's wife and even remove the panties covering her pantry? Ask me and I'll say, "That's men for you!"

In those thrilling moments of guilty titilation when I become an unwanted witness, I do my best to pass unnoticed. I lie low on the ground. When the guilty man's foot bumps into me, I silently crawl away and, without looking back to catch his eye, hide in the courtyard of my master's bar. I avoid being caught watching the spectacle of human vice. And ever since that evening when I took one right on my nose for having watched too long as the hand of one of Massa Yo's customers, dressed up in his Sunday best, tried to loosen the resistant thighs on a real whale of a woman, I avoid laughing about it out loud, too. The man had trapped his lover in a dark corner of the bar. Too focused on following the efforts of his agile hand, I didn't notice that the woman had caught me. "*Mouf*, get out," she hissed at me, in the middle of her all too obviously guilty pleasure. "Mboudjak, get away!"

"Leave him alone," said her lover, not easily distracted from his pleasant task. "It's just a dog, right?"

"How do you know it's not my husband?" the woman replied.

And then she added fearfully, "Docta, did you see how he's looking at us?"

The man stopped what he was doing, looked at me and said: "If that's your husband, he can just watch and then go jerk off!"

Filled with shame, I left. I guess after all I've witnessed, all I've lived through, all I've seen men do, maybe I no longer have the wolf's reflexes or the hyena's wicked wit. As a result of observing men and doing nothing else but, maybe I don't even have my canine attributes anymore. Yet, to be taken for a man is the worst insult of all.

9

But hey-o, it sure is hard to be a dog! One thing had become perfectly clear to me: men don't like dogs who think. Hands down: they prefer those who follow and serve, dogs who, with their yelping silence, proclaim the eternal grandeur of all those who walk on two feet. As far as my master was concerned, I'd left his house and entered the universe of his bar a little like one joins the ruling party: to serve. Not much different from a worn-out shoe or an old pair of pants; not much different from an overturned crate or an empty bottle: I am, in a word, his dog. He himself would have happily underlined the possessive adjective "his." Not necessarily because the term highlights the grammatical and objective character of possession. As far as Massa Yo is concerned, that word is the minimal expression of the sort of power he assumes over me. And that power, however limited it may be, nevertheless proclaims his ascendancy over other humans. And so my master says to his drunk customers who are always having fun at my expense: "Hey-o, leave my dog alone!"

You see, with that one little word he lets them know what differentiates him from them. I am *his* dog, and his alone. He, Massa Yo, is privileged enough to be an animal owner, see? At least he has a dog, which, if it even needs to be said, means that he is somebody. With this sort of petty-poor neighborhood logic, my master is, I'll admit, no different from his customers and even less from other men. I'd even say that he's the epitome of what one of his regulars—an agitated and early-rising little old man known on the street as "Panther"—will one day call: "a good Cameroonian." Like his fellows, in fact, my master tends not so much to look ahead as behind himself when he walks. I see him walking down the road with his head turned over his shoulder. He gropes along, bumping into the first obstacle in his path, but regains his smile when he sees his full shadow stretching out far behind him. More than anything, he's happy to know that at least his dog is right there beside him, overshadowed by his silhouette stretched out there on the tar, following his uncertain steps and confirming his human grandeur.

What do you expect? My presence lets this ex-civil servant, of whom circumstances have made a bartender, know that he is still a Big Man. Yes, as far as that's concerned, my master is a good Cameroonian. When he says "my dog," it's like when one of his customers points to his rusted bike leaning up against the wall and says to his neighbor, "That's my bike. Where's yours, huh?"

Massa Yo says, "That's my dog," and my only consolation is that when he points to Soumi's mother, dressed as usual in a *kaba ngondo,** with a scarf wound tightly around her head, he also says: "That's my wife." So I'm not the only one caught up in his ascendancy.

Like many of the women in the quarter, Mama Mado had learned to put up with her husband. She sold fritters every morning from a stand next to his bar. And Massa Yo, who may have seen his wife's possible emancipation coming, always played the magnanimous husband. He let her do as she pleased. According to him—and once he even told her so—she ought to know how lucky she was. All she had to do was think of all the *associées** who, since the country was in the grips of a lethal crisis, haunted his bar at nightfall and she'd realize she wasn't so bad off. Yes, all it would take was for Mama Mado to see those single girls standing around in the streets of the quarter, with their slender waists, and their heads softly bobbing, sucking hungrily on one of those candies called "somebody else's sweet hubby,"* and she'd know that, with a bartender at home, she at least had made it. As Massa Yo loved to point out, it was enough already that, even in these hard times, he could still take care of "his kid." And I don't think a day went by when he didn't find a way to say he was a good provider. "Hey, even if she is selling fritters, I don't want her money!"

That's how he found within him the generosity of the macho. For there was one thing my master knew for sure and for certain, and he carefully measured his gallantry against it: Mama Mado was *his* wife. What that really meant was, since his bar had given him back his manhood (even if, in the eyes of the neighborhood, it clearly hadn't given him back the aura of a civil servant), he was free to gaze at the street. His wife really couldn't complain about it. And so while I studied the length and breadth of humanity, Massa Yo, perched atop the grandeur his bar had salvaged for him in the neighborhood, gave free rein to his gaze and calculated with impunity the field of definition, the longitude and the latitude of the hips of the neighborhood girls. No, he didn't think twice about chatting them up! His wife looked on sadly at her newly reborn husband, the one she'd seen hide away in the hole of his bed, sunk down in the emasculating miasma of unemployment, for all those long months when he was broke. "That's men for you!" she'd sigh. And I thought she was right.

"What's it to you?" I heard her say one day when one of her friends had come to fill her in on Massa Yo's adulterous urges. That's women for you, I thought. Actually, Mama Mado was one of those women who'd rather die than expose their marriage bed to the neighborhood's *kongossa*. She was one of those women who never forget their vaguely aristocratic roots in the village: in short, one of those women with self-esteem. And yet once she did complain to the vendor who sold cigarettes in front of The Customer Is King. In the end he told her, "That's just the way men are, right?"

Mama Mado tried in vain to hold her head high; she knew keeping tabs on her husband was a lost cause. She knew that a man who's trying to find himself doesn't stop halfway. And what's more, she knew it wasn't just a question of having money to burn. If a man wants to cheat on you, he won't be stopped, not even by AIDS* (by which I mean starvation wages or, as we say here in Madagascar, "Almost an Income, and Difficult to Secure")! And so, like many women in Madagascar, she forgot about her husband and decided that if she was going to work to make ends meet, it would be for Soumi alone: it was for Soumi alone that she would burn her eyes over the hot oil from her bean fritters; all her efforts would be focused on raising him. And wasn't she right? One day, just like that, Massa Yo decided to start spending most every night in his bar! He set up a little cot behind his counter and told his wife that, from time immemorial, prudence had always been man's only king. More precisely, he told her thieves had rushed in to ruin him, that in our neighborhoods filled with miserable wretches, do-nothings, and sorcerers, you need to guard what you have carefully.

"Around here," he said pointing to the whole of Madagascar, "even the Evil Eye can do you in."

But his wife wanted a more logical reason than that. "So why do you have a dog?" Mama Mado asked, pointing to my scientifically alert canine humility poised on the ground.

My master had stopped listening to her, but she insisted. Aggravated for no good reason, Massa Yo told her one of those incredible stories that circulate in neighborhoods like ours. "Woman," he said, "haven't you heard what people are saying? Thieves already have a potion that makes them invisible out here. Don't you know that yesterday they went into Massa Kokari's living room and took his television right from under his nose? *A di tell you.* Massa Kokari saw his television rise up, fly across his living room, and then load itself into the backseat of a taxi!" As if to say: "Woman, you want a logical story? Well, just what do you say about that whopper?" My master was, of course, the only one laughing. Why do men always lie so poorly?

"Just what does that have to do with anything?" the woman asked, clearly irritated by the incoherent, crazy words coming out of her husband's mouth.

Massa Yo continued, "If you have a short memory, that's your problem. But I'm not about to find myself back in hard times, *you ya*?" And he put his finger up to his temple. It was clear and straightforward. What he really ought to have said was: "Woman, just don't get in the way of a man who has finally found himself." Then it would have been as clear as *odontol*. Happily, his wife let it drop. Maybe she reassured herself with the thought that at least from then on he'd be snoring somewhere else.

But the customers who knew my master was sleeping next to his bottles, in the acrid stench of the bar, just wouldn't leave him alone. "Being a tightwad is going to kill that Bami man," they said, nodding their heads and wishing some passing cutthroats would slit his neck before robbing him. My master just burst out laughing, saying: "Don't forget, I have a guard dog-o!"

He pointed at me again, lying there on the ground. I lowered my ears and crawled off to hide well out of his customers' sight because, really, it was me they were making fun of.

10

And so now during the day, I'll watch as Massa Yo, henceforth accompanied by his catch of customers, avidly takes in the terrestrial bounty of local girls. I'll see him formulate equations for their smiles and the swaying of their hips. Thanks to the makeshift bed set up behind his counter, hadn't he magically become a man just like his cackling customers, expressing surprise at the limping gait of one girl, imagining another one carrying the weight of the whole Cameroonian republic on her hips, and then going off to urinate noisily behind his bar? Yes, from that moment on, my master was going to devour the flesh of the street with all the nervous appetite of a Big Man. I won't mention that sometimes he whistled arrogantly at a passing girl. Then, giving in to a bad habit, I'd perk up my ears in time to see the girl turn around and give him a good once-over from head to toe—from toe to head, head to toe, and again from toe to head—and then spit theatrically in his direction, as if to say, "And just where is the man-o?"

I barked out my laughter. There's one who put Massa Yo in his place, I'd gleefully say to myself. As for my master—he'd fall back into Pidgin, his dialect of disaster, cursing the whores as he tore his face into a sick smile: "*Dan sapack i day for kan kan-o.*"*

My body shook with laughter. The girl, thinking I was getting mad, would hurry on her way as my master, who thought I was defending him, praised me. Flies sang as they rose up off my ears. I shook my head in disbelief, beating my ears repeatedly against my neck. This Massa Yo must actually believe that, in time, even the most beautiful girl in the quarter will stretch out in the luxury of his little bartender's bed! No joke! I'm sure he was thinking that, with a well-stocked bar in these times of scarcity, he was all too important, all too much a player, that he was all too visibly somebody not to enjoy a certain lord's right in "this Madagascar of ours." Oh yes. Since his machete was clearly sharp, didn't he have a right to a cocoa tree, too?

In any event, he was no longer a lightweight in this Madagascar of ours. A lightweight, no, that he'd never really been, this former State official, or rather, if the truth be told, this civil servant: a civil servant who used to parade his dog around like a white man in front of the miserable wretches who today boldly set their sights on the same woman as he. That said, why should he be the only goat not to graze where he was tied up? Why should he be the only *mbout** afraid to pick up the peanuts this wonderful life suddenly throws out for the taking, right before your eyes? "Why do we have teeth if not to eat?" he seemed to say to himself.

Here's how things were: to kill time as he stood, bored, in front of his bar, my master devoured the girls with his eyes. He'd arrogantly close his eyes to the mass of *associées* who gathered in front of his bar in the evening. What am I saying, close his eyes? Massa Yo sneered at the *associées,* convinced that he was too good to waste his time with any of them! Mostly he ogled the girls—each somebody's daughter—passing by on the street. He looked at them with a wide-open eye, as if to say that these late-comers wouldn't be blind to his wealth, that was for sure. They were just *rumta**—and Massa Yo was sure he'd bend them to his will! He'd teach them who was in charge! They could be as haughty as they liked, those local kids—those *tchotchoros**— he knew how to handle them, he seemed to say, with a man's smile on his lips. My eyes would open wide: I was still looking at my master, but I sure didn't recognize him. *"Na jeune talent, non?"** he said to the customer called Docta, who was enjoying a good laugh behind my master's back for the humiliation he suffered time and again at the hands of the local girls. "That girl there got you good, my poor friend," said the cigarette vendor, with whom my master killed time each day. At least another customer offered Massa Yo some consolation. "Aaaaaahhhh," he said, "Let her go. Her and her gimpy feet!"

But my master bit his lips. In God's name, he swore—still feeling the sting of her insult on his face—one day he'd show her he was really somebody. On to the next one. That's it, on to the next one. *Essamba, essamba!* Keep it coming, Mercedes! Every day as he stood in the door of The Customer Is King, waiting for business, it was the same thing: "On to the next one!" My master had become a *cou-plié*—a rubbernecked old man—a girl gazer, girl trapper, girl stalker, girl calculator, future girl beater, silently training for the final sprint. In the evening I'd watch him get tense, and I knew his bed behind the bar was just calling out for some action. I was sure that soon I'd hear a bit of commotion, maybe I'd even hear his bottles of beer come crashing down, and then the elated, joyful orgasm of a sad fool who'd become a man. A bit later the door of the bar would open up again and out she'd come, the one whose name my master would parade in front of his jealous customers—for he was sure to tell them about it the next day—as he added her name to the still-too-short honor roll of "his" girls. Let's underline that possessive "his."

He'd do just what his customers did—what any man would do!

Caught in the trap of my observational duty, I wouldn't open my mouth to rouse his Mama Mado, left to her aristocratic pride in the conjugal bed. Well, maybe it was because, as he perfected his evident corruption, my master always knew how to buy my cogitative silence: he'd scratch the fur on my head, and sometimes even give me a little kiss on the nose. He'd have one or two kind words for me, calling me "his" puppy as he headed, singing and skipping, back into his bar. I—Mboudjak—I was his dog. Because of the girls, I'd become his accomplice.

But let's put dreams aside—here's how things really were: since Massa Yo had set up the little bed behind his bar, I'd never once seen him shut the doors of his bar behind any of the local girls. Even those that all his customers, and especially Docta, said were there for the taking—*njo**—seemed to turn up their noses at his, the bartender's, money. Let me tell you, now I'm not talking about the ones that the most cowardly of Massa Yo's customers claimed to have chased away, but even the girls who gave themselves to those customers who always wanted to put their drinks "on their tab"—even they refused to give it up to him, the bartender. But Massa Yo still didn't lose hope. He said it was quality he was after, not those *nyamangolos** who, having barely reached puberty, sold their asses at a discount in the Mokolo market, and certainly not the *associées* who hung around his bar and whom he was tired of seeing day in and day out. Full of hope, he's running after that ever distant day when, like a prisoner released from solitary, he'll finally be able to take his revenge with the tastiest little tidbit around, showing, no, proving to himself and, more important, to his customers, who all knew about his long string of bare-assed failures, that he, too, was a man. Because, according to the men of our quarter, what is a man who can't even get laid? A nothing, that's right, a zero. No, less than that—a minus. No, a . . .

As for me, as I watched my master chasing after his humanity, which the local girls insisted on strewing all over the ground, I wondered more and more if man isn't an enigma, one whose resolution is more likely to drag me through the mud than call upon my intelligence.

11

In fact, my master could feel free to harass the girls on the street. As of yet, no woman had really shown him up. And when I say "really shown him up," I am mostly thinking of that man who shook up The Customer Is King with his pain one day. He was a small-framed man; his brown suit coat alone set him above my master's regulars. What caught my attention, though, was the speed with which he downed his bottles of beer. In fact, he'd made himself stand out in the eyes of all my master's customers by buying a whole crate of beer. Seated on his treasure, he drank his *jobajos* in silence, ignoring the begging voices that surrounded him.

"You're not really gonna drink all that beer, are you?" asked the Panther Nzui Manto. "Hmm," said another, "that crate is even bigger than you!" And a third, strategically solicitous, "Careful, my brother, there's a fly!"

Nothing had any effect. The man emptied his bottles, one after the other, paying no attention at all to the flies. As their hopes of *gnôle njo,* a free drink, faded away, my master's customers shifted from thirsty remarks to snide comments. Say, have you ever seen anyone in Madagascar drink a whole crate of beer alone? Noooo! And is anyone ever going to do that? Never! They said the man with the brown jacket hadn't seen anything yet. But he just looked at them, biting his lips and making gestures with his arms that grew ever broader, ever slower. He was getting liquefied, becoming sip by sip just another of the innumerable drunks I'd already seen dance in my master's courtyard, pissing and even shitting in their pants. I was already barking out my laughter in anticipation when suddenly I saw him hide his face. Every drunk has his quirks, it's true; this one enveloped the stupefied street with his grown man's tears. Astonished, my master's customers stared at one another. Where did this asshole come from? Rather than drowning it once and for all, the alcohol seemed to have roused the all-too-visible disappointment lying in the belly of this babyish adult. Even my master left his counter to see the spectacle of a grown man crying. He quickly went back in the bar, though, shaking his head and smiling. A man more compassionate than Massa Yo went up to the unhappy fellow and asked: "*Tara,** did they sack you?"

The man didn't answer.

"If they did sack you, you know you're not the only one," the other man began.

The compassionate man had, I'm sure, his own long rosary of misfortunes, which he immediately began to recite. A voice next to him interrupted: "Leave him alone."

Another voice agreed: "Don't you see? He can't even take his own pain and here you come and tell him all your problems."

Then the crowd of laughing men suddenly jumped back in a gesture of terror. Some threw themselves into my master's bar. I protected myself from their hurried steps by hiding under Mama Mado's fritter stand. In just a short second, an empty circle had been traced around the man with the brown jacket. He was standing at attention on top of his crate of beer and holding a small black thing to his temple. A stupid grin crossed his lips. His gaze gleamed. Emotion ran high all around, a number of voices shouted out, "He has a gun!"

"He wants to kill himself!"

"Brother, don't cover us with blood-o," cried one man.

"Wombo-o," screamed a woman, "get the kids out of here!"

"Stop him!"

I saw my master rush out of his bar, and then pull up short at the sight of a smiling man who wanted to kill himself.

"Bo-o, no do that," he begged, moving slowly toward the soon-to-be victim. "A beg no do that, bo-o."

Someone else added, as if the suicidal man didn't know it already: "*Tara,* you're only gonna kill yourself, you know!"

"Precisely," said the man, placing the gun barrel between his eyes.

A loud rumor rose up from the crowd. My master stopped his cautious advance and silenced his dialect of disaster.

"I want to be done with this," said the man, "I'm fed up with being treated like a slave. And besides, what's it to you if I croak? You all come running as if you cared, but you don't give a shit!"

Straining, as if there were an arm holding him back, the man stuck the pistol barrel in his mouth. The crowd started, like it was going to do something, but fell into dead silence. Many of those gathered put their hands on their heads. The suicidal man's arms trembled, his eyes went dim. His knees knocked together, and he seemed to be dancing there on his crate. I raised my voice. I barked out my indignation. I barked out my amusement, too, but I must admit, mostly I barked out my shock.

"Think of your children," a woman's voice ventured.

There was a long moment of silence. The man pulled the gun out of his mouth and said, "I have no more children."

Then he put the gun back in the hollow left by his words.

"Think of your brothers," the woman ventured once more, following up on the brief victory of her first phrase.

There was the same long silence, at the end of which the man took the gun back out of his mouth and gasped, "I have no more brothers!"

Immediately a voice in the crowd called out, "Think of us, then, won't ya?!"

The man didn't even have time to put the gun back in his mouth. "Do I even know you?" he asked.

"So what?" said a woman's voice. "We're all your brothers, right? Give us your gun."

"Think of your mother," called out another woman's voice, which I recognized as Mama Mado's.

Hearing that, the man paused, firmed up his gaze, and, still clasping the gun, sadly let his arm fall down. His was the face of misfortune. His mother's inaudible words seemed to be spinning around in his head. Yes, it was as if suddenly his mother were right there in front of him, a poor peasant woman trapped

in the shameful poverty of the city, uncovering her head to in-
tone her tribal mourning song, and savagely lifting her dress to
show her son the dark and wrinkled vagina of his origins and
to curse him before his suicide. And suddenly I saw the isolated
man start to argue, most certainly with his invisible but tearful
mother, who was cursing him, cursing him, cursing him, and
who never stopped cursing him. His knees knocked even faster.
He got down off his crate, as if pulled by invisible arms. Soon
he again lowered the hand holding the gun and let his wail
sound out once more across the night. "My mother is already
dead!" he said in an altered voice. "She's dead!"

Taking advantage of the confusion caused by the suicidal
man's sudden indecision, some men moved toward him. He
didn't let them get close. He jumped abruptly back on his crate
and put the gun to his temple again. "Don't come any closer!"
he said, holding up a desperate hand.

The men who'd moved toward him raised their hands in a
gesture of goodwill. The suicidal man seemed to have lost his
mind. He was dancing there on his crate of death. His knees
were like rubber. He seemed unable to keep his balance any
longer. He had seen his mother's ass. Or maybe the alcohol
had taken control of all his actions. The hand holding the gun
trembled wildly, waving over the heads of the crowd. "If you
come any closer, I'll kill myself!" he screamed in his madness.

His weapon turned dangerously toward the faces of the quarter. Was this suicidal guy becoming homicidal? People threw
themselves down, some on the ground, others in my master's bar.
Soon a man's voice cut through the air with an unexpected command: "Just what are you doing, you *anti-Zamba ouam**?!"

Immediately, the wide-nostriled face of the man who'd spoken stood out in the crowd. It was the cigarette vendor. "Do
you want to kill yourself or kill us? Do you want to kill yourself
or don't you? If you can't kill yourself, give me the gun. Or give
it to me so I can kill you myself and be done with it. Good God,
what kind of melodrama is this, eh?!"

This unexpected "Good God" put an end to the suicidal
man's confused gestures. The cigarette vendor's threats seemed
to do the trick. The crowd relaxed. Everyone froze again,
though, when the suicidal man threw in their faces, like some

tragic curse: "The only one who can take this gun from me is Mini Minor!"

If he had said "Mami Wata" instead of "Mini Minor," the reaction would certainly have been less terrifying. Mini Minor was the queen of the *chantiers*,* yes, the queen of the dilapidated neighborhoods. She was the only one around with a car—an R4, a Renault, let me tell you. She never stopped in front of my master's bar, except to give orders to the men killing time there or to put them to work carrying packages for her. No one spoke her name with impunity, although she lived closed within the walls of her house and never attacked anyone directly. She never even spoke to anyone in the quarter. But the thin man in the brown jacket went on, undeterred, as if unaware of his blasphemy: "She's the one making me suffer like this. Yes, even if I kill myself, I want you to know she's my killer. I gave her everything I had. I left my family for her. I abandoned my wife and kids for her. My mother died and I didn't even sit in mourning, just because of that woman. I've been keeping her *chantier* running since she opened it. My family cursed me, but that didn't mean a thing, as long as I was with her. What didn't I give her? When we were still getting paid, she's the one who got my paychecks. And now, since the government put a freeze on salaries, she's playing hide-and-seek with me. I ask her to marry me and, now that I'm in hot water, she turns me down. When I go to her house, who do I find sitting in her easy chairs? The police commissioner!"

When he heard "police commissioner," the cigarette vendor burst out laughing. An uncontrollable laugh shook the crowd around the suicidal man. I barked out my laughter, too. Yes, the pole had been placed a bit too high this time. The only thing left was for this comical whiner to say he was one of Biya's young friends! Why not even his little brother, ho ho! Everyone was staring at that man in the brown jacket, each wondering, apparently, just who he was to tie up so many myths in one twist of the tongue. But there he stood, on an upside-down crate of beer, trembling in his miserable jacket, with an indecisive gun in his hand: a real loser, to put it bluntly. A *nathin*. Then, in the middle of a laugh, the cigarette vendor made a real joke of the whole affair: "So it's just because of *them* and *only them* that he wants to kill himself-o!"

Pointing at the man in the brown jacket, he encouraged everyone to have good laugh. Maybe because he was unsettled by the amusement of these men who'd stopped taking him seriously, the guy with the gun didn't see the ploy of the cigarette vendor's hand as it pointed at him, and then bam! The weapon fell down at the crowd's feet. A thousand hands rushed to grab it. Thus freed, the crowd rose up in one boundless wave of confusion and threw itself on the man.

The suicidal man could have been killed.

"He deserves a lesson!" a voice said.

"Where's that gun?" asked the cigarette vendor's voice amid all the confusion.

"Hit him."

"Leave him alone."

"Give me the gun!"

"The police commissioner!" said a voice filled with fear.

No one paid any attention. My barks added flavor to the human chaos. I didn't know what I was saying anymore. I was caught up in the rush of it all myself. And then an authoritative voice made the crowd freeze: "Stop all this commotion!"

The fear-filled crowd opened up before the silhouette of a dark black man with eyes of fire. It was the very man whose name had just been spoken. He stared at the crowd around him and, without addressing the suicidal man, asked of everyone and no one in particular: "Where's his gun?"

Whoever had ended up holding the gun in the chaos of the crowd handed it over, no questions asked. And then the commissioner bent over the defeated whiner with the gun, over what remained of the suicidal man lying there on the ground, his head covered in dust. The commissioner grabbed him by the collar of his jacket and spit his ferocious anger right into his face: "You fool! Where did you get this gun?"

He pointed the gun right between his eyes, as if ready to blow him away at the least resistance.

"Let me through!" said a woman's voice. "Let me through!"

The only response to this was a puddle that spread out next to the coward who hadn't been able to carry out his threats against the quarter. The man in the brown jacket was pissing in his pants. The crowd shook again with amusement. The urine made a little river that ran straight to my hideaway. I sidestepped it and ran inside my master's bar. Just then a little woman with those glaring baldspots we call a *mon vieux** made her way through the melee. When she reached the suicidal drunk, she bent over him and put her hands on her hips: "So, mister," she said, "you want to tarnish my name!"

This was Mini Minor herself. "It's all over now," the commissioner said to her, having regained his calm. "He's drowning in alcohol, as you can see."

Having spoken, he tried to restrain the angry woman. But, small as she was, she wasn't easy to keep quiet. She angrily pushed away the hand of the representative of law and order. She was brimming with rage. Boiling like a volcano, she kept spewing out haughty, formal phrases. There was no holding her back. With each of her sentences she'd turn toward either the commissioner or the crowd. "No," she said, "he gets what I'm saying. He says I fucked him over? *Bèbèlè.** Do you all hear that? This raving lunatic here, who can't keep a woman satisfied, this guy who pisses in his pants, says he was engaged to me? Me, Ateba Zengue Marguerite? Mister, do you even know what you're insinuating? Look at me. Do you know who you're dealing with? Do you think a woman like me could live off of you? You, with your paltry little civil servant's salary, you heard that some of your friends have 'second offices'* and you want to be like them. You're a man too, right? But the rest of you, just look at this raving lunatic, who comes into a bar like this where people respect me and says he is keeping me, *anti-Zamba ouam*! He even dares to say he wants to marry me. Take a look at Mini Minor's husband. Now tell me, you all who know me: do I deserve a polliwog like that?

And the crowd replied, "No-o!"

The police commissioner just let her go on. He even smiled as he spoke into his walkie-talkie, asking his men to come clean up the puddle of pee in the street. Mini Minor stomped in the puddle of pee, "Reeeeally, even nightmares have limits! Me, the wife of this cockroach!"

The peppery little woman turned back to the squashed cockroach. "So go ahead and kill yourself, you cuckold. Are you drunk? What are you waiting for? Did somebody take your gun?"

Again she turned, this time toward the police commissioner, and spoke to him in an intimate tone: "Etienne, did you stop him from killing himself? Did you? I'm asking you to give him back his gun."

"You know that's impossible, don't you?" said the commissioner with polite wave of his hands. "His weapon is State property now."

Then Mini Minor spoke to the cockroach: "You raving lunatic! You dare to come and sully my name right here in my own quarter! 'Mini Minor, it's Mini Minor who killed me.' From now on, mister, I forbid you to utter that name."

With that she abandoned our poor civil servant right there. She went back through the crowd and disappeared into the rumor of the quarter. Her indignant voice split the sky again with one or two choice expletives. A *Big Woman* is no little woman, I thought, and I was the only one who dared bark out my thoughts on the matter. My master's stare made me shut up, but what did it matter anyhow, really? Mini Minor could walk off just like that. She knew her lover would take care of everything else. The silence of the neighborhood's thousand staring eyes followed her. A real *small-no-be-sick,** she was! Meanwhile, the commissioner kept smiling as he had his rival shoved into the police van he'd called. Maybe he'd only lock him up for the night. Surely he knew that, after having taken such a cold bath in public, the poor fool would never again have the courage to get drunk with Mini Minor on his mind. It was in his best interests not to! Oh yes, the man in the brown suit coat would crawl like a rat, he'd creep like a lizard, he'd grovel like a pebble, and then go hide away at home. He'd go hide, far away from the neighborhood that was the scene of his humiliation.

Once the *sans payer** had disappeared in the distance, the police commissioner dusted off his hands and dispersed the crowd with his threatening voice, before disappearing himself in the direction of his mistress's *chantier*. I never again saw his rival with the brown jacket in front of my master's bar. And yet he left behind him the mortified mask of his face, which remained intact in the discussions of the neighborhood bars, as the definitive example of what you must not do, or of whatcha gotta do, to be a man. Because, as my master's customers said, with a smile and a crook of their ring finger, he had tried to catch a shark with a tiny, little hook. The details were etched in my memory. Beyond the scandal, what this surprising event taught me, along with the rest of the quarter, is that the police commissioner of Mokolo, the one with the terrifying reputation, was going out with Mini Minor, and his first name was "Etienne." I could lift my muzzle and howl at the moon, I still knew one thing for sure: that wasn't the end of the story.

12

The failed suicide of the man in the brown jacket fed the commentaries of The Customer Is King for quite a while. It wasn't just that Massa Yo's customers used their eyes to imitate the poor soul, frozen at attention there on his crate of death. Their laughter also enveloped Mini Minor's small self in a garb of threatening vitality. Even the police commissioner seemed to have come into Madagascar's daily routine for no other reason than to furnish the street's uncontrollable laughter with the sympathetic shadow of a lover relentlessly smiling as his rival pissed or—to tell the whole truth—shit in his pants. The men laughed at the orders he quickly repeated once his mistress appeared, at the bright Colgate smile he put on for the woman who "had him wrapped around her little finger." The terrifying police commissioner had disappeared into the darkness of the *chantier,* but he lived on as a magnanimous caricature in the vernacular of the bar, as a verb that could be conjugated at will: "Etienne*: to have a hold on or control someone." In the present indicative: "I tell you, she sure 'Etiennes' him."

The imperfect: "No-o-o, he was 'Etienning' her."

The future tense: "I'll tell you something—that 'Etienning' will stop tomorrow."

In the end, the suicidal scene added a little smile to the respect each one had for Mini Minor, a little smile I saw on people's faces from then on whenever she passed by. The little woman would park her car in front of the door to The Customer Is King, and as the street's gaze fixed on her, all my master's customers would fall silent and follow her with their eyes. When she had disappeared in the distance, my master would say, still dreaming of her ample behind: *"Dan tendaison for dan woman na big big, huh?"**

And one of his customers would reply: "Is a Big Woman a little girl?"

Whoever could have spoken to that woman like that without being told off? Who, I say, what man? And yet one morning when a laid-back customer, the very one the neighborhood called "Docta," whistled at a girl passing by in the street, Massa Yo himself called him to order, with a shake of his hands. "Bo-o, are you looking for trouble, too?" said a frightened Massa Yo.

That's because it was one thing to dance around behind Mini Minor's back, to hold her up for hidden sarcasm, to conjugate the verb "Etienne" in every tense—yes, to laugh at the deep "Etiennicities" and the limping "Etiennations," the "fucking Etiennates" and the "random de-Etiennations." It was quite another to actually try taking Etienne's place in the Queen's shadow. It was one thing to talk about her and laugh; it was another altogether to be flip about it or, rather, to be too familiar with her offspring. For the girl in question was none other than Mini Minor's niece, Virginie. But Docta wasn't put off in the least. He regarded the street with the skepticism of a legal mind impelled by the Ideal; still, everyone in the neighborhood knew he was a bottom-feeder. I knew that for this Docta from a poor part of town, as for my master and many of his customers as well, the street was nothing but a long, deep river. To kill time, you had to pull as many fish out of it as possible. For Docta, though, and this I knew for sure, fishing for girls was also a matter of life or death. Maybe that's why, unlike everybody else, he wasn't afraid of getting burned.

"My dear friend," my master asked again from the back of his bar, in a voice both hushed and prudently insistent, "just what are you looking for, huh?"

"Psst!" called the carefree Docta, wholly focused on his chance to win the jackpot.

Virginie turned around, saw our Docta standing in the door of the bar, smiled, and came toward him. "So, *my dear,* you would have gone by just like that?" he asked, adding commas to his accent and stressing the "my dear."

Smiling, the girl replied, "I didn't see you."

It was obvious she was lying. My master scratched his head. He was surprised to see the two were on familiar terms. He retreated into the shadows of the bar. Docta knitted his lie around the girl's. "Oh, that makes sense," he said, "I don't come here often. And so where are you off to?"

"My aunt sent me on an errand."

"I just wanted you to greet *your future husband.*"

"Hello, then."

And as the girl set off down the road, my master's head re-emerged from the darkness of the bar. The cigarette vendor came up, thousands of questions clearly burning on his lips. Docta let his authority grow in the ensuing silence. He didn't launch into the explanation the whole bar was waiting for. The "future husband" remained arrogantly silent before the numerous ears yearning to hear the story. That whole day he kept quiet about his "Etiennations" with Virginie, although the entire neighborhood was hanging on his every word. Yes, I said to myself, that was his revenge! Because, really, was there anyone in the quarter who didn't know Docta's story? He'd finished his engineering degree just when the State was recruiting one final group of fifteen hundred graduates with bachelor's degrees. It was his one and only chance to become a civil servant, to have his own little place in the system. But here's the thing: he was an engineer and the State wanted students in the liberal arts. And fifteen hundred of them all at once! At the personnel office, it seems, they just told him that "It wasn't the engineers' turn yet."

He hadn't understood what that meant. He was still waiting. He kept waiting. And now most of the time he chose to wait in front of my master's bar. As he waited, he drowned his days in alcohol, strategically adorning them with that horizontal sport. He never failed to let each and every one know that his days in The Customer Is King were numbered. He usually had something on him to prove the transitory nature of his situation. Sometimes it was an old copy of Césaire, or a newspaper, or a briefcase, or even some story about a woman. What he wanted this time, I knew, was to show my master, the cigarette vendor, and all the other customers of The Customer Is King that this story with Virginie put him out of their league. Suddenly, he struck a pose like a statue; he shook his head mournfully, turned up the corners of his lips in a hint of a smile, and, staring at my master's customers, said, "I will get her in bed."

He smiled, snapping his fingers to make his point as he added, "I have to get her in bed!" knowing full well what fireworks that statement would set off in the heads of everyone around him. And Docta couldn't stress it enough—this was a question of his human duty. He added, "There goes the most strategic scam in all of Cameroon, shaking her ass just like the Virgin Mary in front of God's eyes, just before she got herself knocked up!"

Docta stressed "the most strategic scam" as if it were the quintessence of the theory he'd derived from his long struggle to survive. He bent over my master's counter. "Do you know who's scamming on her?" he asked Massa Yo and the cigarette vendor.

Let's let him tell us, since he was the one to know. "A *mangemille,** that's who!"

What a letdown for the whole bar! The cigarette vendor offered a knowing correction. "Do you mean to say a gendarme, one of the State Police?"

"What's the difference? Doesn't the State dress them all right down to their shorts? Since his commissioner is keeping the aunt, he's making a move on the niece. I tell you: 'Cameroon is Cameroon!'"

Hearing that conclusion drawn out loud, my master grew cautious. "And in this Cameroon of ours," he asked, "you're not afraid of butting heads with a *mange-mille?*"

Massa Yo underlined his "this Cameroon of ours" as if he were scared out of his wits. And suddenly I saw the man in the brown suit coat again. What's worse, neighborhood stories I knew all too well filed through my head: stories of failed "Etiennations," of "Etiennations" trampled in the mud, on the backseats of tiny little cars, stories of guts ripped out in the night, of customs officers' pants seized for lack of liquid assets after they'd gotten a piece of ass, yes, unbelievable stories about the limping affairs of pot-bellied politicians, all those stories that come by the thousands in waves of rumor to expire in front of my master's bar. I opened my eyes wide, shook my head, and let my tongue hang down, saying to myself, so as not to quote anyone else, that if Cameroon is Cameroon, then that Cameroon was history.

"I must really have hit rock bottom," said the learned Docta, "if I'm fighting a policeman, especially over a local girl. You there, didn't you see her come when I called? I told you, I will get her in bed, regardless of who's keeping her now."

He beat his chest: "It's a match on my home field, fellas!"

My master burst out laughing. "What home field?" he said. "So now you have a home, do you?"

With that, Docta assumed a professorial air but remained evasive. "My good friend, it's clear you just don't know anything. Let me tell you, since the dawn of time a woman's bed has always been man's home—the home of a real man that is."

And the cigarette vendor added, archly: "Aaahhh, which woman's bed? Admit it, you're after the aunt, aren't you?"

"So what?!"

My master kept quiet. The cigarette vendor burst out laughing. And I, yes, I barked out my laughter, too, for my thousand stories were still bubbling up in my head. Like this one, for example: many times I've seen Docta with women six times his size. Next to them, he was nothing but bones, just a *longo longo fil de fer.** To put his arms around their waists, he had to arch over like a bow. I'd also seen him once or twice with a woman who was too tall. To speak to her, he had to tilt his face up to the sky, like a rooster trying to drink. Oh yes, he practically had to scream at her. Our Docta really didn't seem to place much importance on the size of his lovers' beds. He always seemed to enjoy showing off his lovers' excess in the streets of the quarter. One day he actually said: "As far as I'm concerned, neither length, nor breadth, nor even depth matter."

"Are you sure about that?" the cigarette vendor had asked, quite amused.

Docta thought for a minute and then added a correction: "To be precise, the only length, breadth, or depth that matters to me is that of their purse!"

There, in short, was his strategy for scamming. Everyone in the quarter knew it was women who made it possible for our strategist of an engineer to survive his interminable wait outside the system. And it was surely women who would help him get his foot in the door—into its *circuits* and *chantiers*. So now he'd set his rapacious sights on Mini Minor's virginal niece. It couldn't be just a coincidence. What did their volume, their age, or their fragility matter to him? The girls, the young girls, the women of the neighborhood—Docta knew them all. They were his road to Damascus. He gobbled them up with a carnivore's appetite. But a hungry man is never satisfied. Docta was still chasing after the most strategic scam in Cameroon, the ultimate scam itself, the one last scam that would save him once and for all. That was the founding myth behind all his actions. And I, Mboudjak, was a witness to it all. How many times had he thought he'd found that scam in the young things, women and girls passing by on the street, only to come back the next day and admit his mistake to the cigarette vendor. How many, just how many times? Let's drop it for now.

"And so what did you do then?" the cigarette vendor always asked, each time he came in with more of his stories about the girls.

"Well, I still did it, that's for sure," the engineer replied, bolstering his reputation as Docta, the ladies' man: a man of action. And this time—like all the other times—my master didn't waste too much time with him discussing the odds his scam would work. He went back behind his counter, as if to say that, in the end, Virginie or no Virginie, he still needed to sell his beer.

13

Then it hit me: What? Docta is what kinda ladies' man? Let's not exaggerate, come on! Let me tell you, I remember the day when our strategic, scamming engineer slumped down at my master's bar and ordered a beer, which he drank immediately in one long gulp. His mouth was swollen with a story: another story about a woman. His eyes gleamed as he saw all my master's curious customers looking at him. He began: "Let me tell you, women are nothing but baisedroms*! A place to fuck, that's it!"

And off he went in his own inimitable style! From behind

his bar my master let out a crazy guffaw, interrupting the sad storyteller. "So women are already baisedroms for you?"

The customers burst out laughing, too. A sightly drunk guy sitting at the corner of the bar repeated "baisedrom" several times, as if to savor its flavor fully. But Docta wasn't about to be interrupted by that digression. He continued in an unexpectedly familiar tone.

"Here's the thing," he said. "I was sitting there in the Abbia Cinema, just minding my own business. I was watching my movie with my Mami Nyanga-o. Not the fat one, you know, but my one and only Rosalie. My one and only. And then, when the lights go on, after the previews, who do I see walk right by me? An ex-girlfriend with her husband, the airport manager. To be specific, I should add, I met this girl when I was a student, but we didn't really have a chance to do things up right. I dumped her because I was fed up with always having to hide from her husband. And yet, my brothers, when a woman really loves you, you've just gotta give it to her. Or else it's going to eat at her for the rest of her life. So then, after the break, as the film was starting up, all of a sudden I feel this foot jabbing me in the arm. I move my arm away. A little later, the foot jabs me in the neck. So I turn around to tell the stubborn jabber what's what. And I swear, the girl had convinced her manager of a husband to change places! There they were, both of 'em, sitting right behind me! So I swallowed the insult and pretended nothing had happened. And then, right after, the same foot jabs me in the head."

"So what did you do then?" interjected the impatient cigarette vendor.

Docta paid him no mind. He just went on setting the stage for his story. "So here's my situation. Here, right next to me, is my own Rosalie, whose thigh I'm caressing. After all, I went to the movies with her!"

He pointed to his left side with a theatrical wave of the hand. "And there behind me, my ex-girl, who just keeps on jabbing me."

Then he pointed to his back. "And there, of course, right next to that little she-devil, is her airport manager, who, like my own girl, is just watching the film, not suspecting a thing. You know who he is, right, the airport manager. At any rate, he's a real *aloga*, you know, a huge Bassa-man, with muscles like a gorilla. As for me—well, just look . . ."

And the engineer showed his skinny chest to my master's customers, pointing out his bony little hands, his figure of a starving intellectual. ". . . Do I measure up? Especially since, sitting there in my seat, I have my back to my rival! I tell you—women are baisedroms! This woman knew she had me trapped. So I get up and go out of the theater, to settle things once and for all. I know I'm caught in the girl's plans. The only thing I can do is to settle on the terms of the scam. So I tell my girl I'm going to the bathroom. A little later, my ex gets up, too. We just look at each other. I don't say a thing. 'Docta,' she begins, 'it's been quite a while, huh?'"

Here Docta took on the intonations of a naive girl, someone right off the plane (let's be clear: right off the plane from Paris). He held his hand up in the air. Then, switching back to his own voice, he acted out his reply. "So I said to her, just to cool her off, 'Yeah, it's been quite a while, but so what?' But she goes on, 'I just wanted to see you.' And so she saw me, the bitch. I was standing right there in front of her, in flesh and blood. 'You don't even kiss me hello anymore?' she asks. And you think it was for just a little kiss that she made me get up and leave my Rosalie, and that she left her regular rhythm man? Me, I'm thinking my girl must be getting impatient with me taking so long. I'm thinking about the airport manager, who, I'm sure, didn't come just to watch the movie alone. So right when I'm trying to cut this melodrama short—'cause the only thing I can do to avoid the worst is to make a date and put an end to the thing—right then, the door to the theater opens wide: slam! And who do you think I see right in front of me?"

My master interrupted with a burst of laughter: "The airport manager!"

"No, worse. Rosalie! And you know how mad she can get!"

Docta raised up both of his hands, to show his surrender: wombo-o! My master was laughing even harder. The other customers laughed right along, too.

"So what did you do then?"

Docta paused before going on. "I kept my cool and introduced them both. But then, to make things worse, I tried to lie. I told Rosalie that my ex was an old school friend. Now Rosalie, despite her crazy side, is still a civilized woman, so she didn't say anything. She let me go on and acted as if she believed me. I'm so naive, I actually thought she'd forget about the whole thing soon. So then, when we get back to the house, the only thing on her mind is taking all my stuff and tossing it out the window. Right in the street, I'm telling you. And do you know what she said to me? That she's the one who pays the rent! She even had the balls to call me a parasite! I tried to explain, to sweet-talk her. Nothin' doin'! Just try to reason with a woman who's got some idea in her head—especially if that woman is Rosalie!"

"*No way* my woman could throw me out!" my master noted drily, to get back at the man with the large appetite for the ladies.

As Massa Yo spoke, his eyes grew small. His lips emphatically stressed the "No way" in true Cameroonian style. Docta, who'd just realized he'd humiliated himself with his story, quickly tried to fix things. "In any event, good riddance. Rosalie can leave if she wants to. She's still got my name written all over her in indelible ink: she's got my kid!"

A customer's anarchical voice piped up: "Are you so sure that kid is yours?"

"If women are . . ."

". . . baisedroms . . ."

Docta's only reply to the generalized laughter was a sudden silence. As for Massa Yo, he again hit his bar with the flat of his hand and repeated, loud enough for the whole street to hear, that no woman would ever throw him out of his house: "*Ma woman no fit chasser me for ma long, dis donc! Après tout, ma long na ma long!*"*

14

It's true—his house really was *his* house, as he so loudly proclaimed. I'd even add that since he had a house, he was a man. A real somebody, you know! If my master made a point of eating at home each morning, it was surely because he wanted to

show, no, prove to his heart so hungry for status that his broad
shadow was always bowing down behind him and loudly pro-
claiming his humanity. In the half darkness of the morning, I
often followed him around the living room of his house where,
to tell the truth, he'd ended up becoming a real stranger. He'd
settle into the one armchair in the tiny dining room and stretch
his legs out wide. There on the table, right in front of his gluttonous eyes, was the plate of fritters ("the first batch of the
day") his wife had his son bring him on the double. Sometimes
his voice, muffled by his full mouth, sounded out across the
living room. Usually it was to order Soumi to bring him water:
"cool water." Soumi would come running into the living room
with a goblet full to the brim and dripping. He'd hand it to his
father and wait while he drank. Then he'd take back the empty
glass and run off, disappearing on the far side of the courtyard.
Soumi would be back soon, though, asking his father for his
daily pocket money. Grumbling, Massa Yo would ask, "Don't
you have any? What about your mother?" Scratching his head,
the kid would reply, "She told me to come see you." As he
searched his pocket for money for his son, Massa Yo would
shake his head and rail: "Ask your mother just what she does
with all her money, huh!"

This response of Massa Yo's was a daily ritual. I saw this
as the regret of a deeply egotistical man: the regret of a man
who felt his ever-lengthening shadow suddenly turn into a cannibal. Wasn't he the one who once bragged he'd never touch a
cent of his wife's money, that it was his humble contribution to
woman's liberation? Oh yes, my master really could take pride
in that meaningless liberation. After all, Soumi was *his* child.
What's more, he was sitting in *his* house; Mama Mado was *his*
wife; I, Mboudjak, was *his* dog; and soon we'd go into *his* bar.
And yet, every morning, when he gulped down his breakfast of
fritters as his son watched in silence, he clearly regretted that
his oversized shadow suddenly made him feel responsible for it
all. He'd take twenty-five francs out of his pocket and put them
in his son's hand. He'd patiently wait for the smile and grateful
"Thanks, Dad," and then, with a nod of his head, go back to
his breakfast.

Then Soumi would run outside to embrace the morning—

once he'd tricked his mother into rounding out his pocket money that is. He left his father his illusions of grandeur, there in the silent living room of the house that the man only saw empty. It's true. Massa Yo ate alone, alone in his big, empty house, and he was alone still when he left to go to his bar. Leaning over his plate, he'd catch my observer's gaze. "You, too," he'd say. "You want me to give you a piece of my flesh!"

With a threatening wave of his hand, he'd send me outside. I'd get up nonchalantly and shake myself, grumbling my amusement. Then my master would repeat his angry gesture: "Get out!"

Sometimes he'd even get up and, with a swift kick, send me flying right into the street. Oh yes, when he was eating, Massa Yo wanted to be alone in his house. "Everyone in this house is after my head!" I'd hear him say.

I'd run outside, my tail between my legs and my rear low to the ground. Once a good distance away, I'd stop. If you want to survive and complete your observations, my dear Mboudjak, you must avoid all confrontations with men, I'd say to myself. The biggest battle is always over the defense of one's vital space, you know! A starving man is worse than an animal—don't ever forget that! And in the morning, you know quite well, your master's vital space is always his plate of bean fritters! There's one thing my relationship with Massa Yo has certainly taught me: although he could no longer do without my services as a watchdog, he still wasn't willing to feed me as he did during his times of opulence.

"A dog you feed isn't really a dog," he said one day, when he couldn't take it anymore. "It's a child!"

But I, Mboudjak, was not a child. That I knew for sure. I was never one for sticking too close to Massa Yo, it's true, but I kept an even greater distance at mealtimes. Why do the men in our neighborhoods get a dog if they're always shooing it away? My relationship with my master was based on a profound contradiction, and I had always wanted it that way. I'd leave his house running, but I stopped in his courtyard, when I should have kept going and disappeared down the quarter's narrow little streets. Sometimes I'd stop in the malodorous place behind his bar. I'd close my ears to the endless buzzing concert of the flies.

I'd plunge into the aromas of the leftovers. I'd dig in the ground with my muzzle and my paws. I dug down deep, into the depths of my own nausea. I always managed to find a little something to tickle my taste buds, at least a bare bone. I'd lay into it with concentration. It was my breakfast.

I must say that most of the time, when the quarter was waking up, instead of following my master in the egotistical solitude of his house, or breaking my teeth on a meatless bone, I preferred to sidle up to my mistress's noisy customers. Sometimes there were high school students jostling each other around Mama Mado's stand. The neighborhood was never so animated as when the middle and high school students left their houses and gathered around my mistress to fight for their breakfast. Their young voices mixed with the hurried horns of the threatening buses, the insults of the stubborn taxi drivers, and the rumor of Madagascar waking up. It was the most stressful part of my mistress's day. Her hand moved deftly above the heated oil. One by one, she'd let drops of batter fall. A student's voice would say, "The usual, Mama Mado," and my mistress knew just what he wanted. Another's voice would order, *"Put oya soté, for jazz must do sous-marin,"** without needing to say it twice. The kids jostled each other around the hot oil. With my tongue hanging down, ravenous in the early morning, I'd watch them from a distance. Once, I remember, an impatient student stuck his hand right into the big pot of boiling oil. I saw him hop on one leg, his hand, dripping red with blood, held up to the sky. One time another let his new book bag fall into the pot of beans; soaked by the flood of his cohort's laughter, he ran away, disappearing between the houses to hide his shame. Another time, in the general confusion, a third kid tipped over the plate of already cooked fritters Mama Mado had set out on her stand. Oh yes, however hungry I was, in those moments of early morning chaos, I preferred to stay well out of reach. Forced by my outraged mistress to pay for the damage he'd caused, the clumsy student would certainly blame the accident on me. "It's because of that dirty dog!" the mischief maker would cry, pointing at me.

Poor Mboudjak!—I couldn't defend myself when faced with the accusatory gazes of a hundred starving students. They'd have my head! Men, and especially children, I know what they're like! Yes, that's one thing I can say for sure. Even my barking wouldn't help me against that crowd of kids whose murderous hunger I know all too well. And my mistress, well, she'd have nothing better to say than "Mboudjak, get out of here!"

To tell the truth, of all my mistress's customers, the ones I prefer far and away are the civil servants. Not because their "I don't give a damn" arrogance always reminds me of my master's former opulence, that moment in paradise when we'd take walks in the woods around La Carrière. On the contrary! The contingent of civil servants usually arrives at Mama Mado's at around eight, nine, or ten o'clock, when the streets have been swept clean of students. I prefer the civil servants because they—unlike the students—are much more generous. They're the only ones who throw me their leftovers from time to time. Besides, they're never mean to me. If I'm still on my guard around them, it's only because of my pure scientific principles as a social scientist. And so if I sniff, turn over, and check out the fritters they toss me, it's so I don't fall for the umpteenth time into the trap of human cruelty. Actually, those civil servants, they're always too wrapped up in their day to even think of harming a puny little thing like me. Once they're served, in fact, they always take the time to pop the first fritter into their mouth, to chew and swallow it, to digest and wash it down with one or two spoonfuls of soup, and only then do they start in with their never-ending stories. How could they even plot against my canitude in such moments of grace?

The civil servants are, without a doubt, a separate breed in the disorder of Madagascar. I've seen some of them spend two, three, four hours in front of Mama Mado's stand, quietly chewing fritter after fritter and telling each other stories. I've seen others stay there with my master's wife, long after she had sold her whole stock of fritters, just because they needed, at any price, to finish telling her a story they'd started too late. Clearly, I always told myself when I saw them lazing about like that, these civil servants are nothing like the workers, who are forced to rise early by the brutality of their supervisor. They are different, too, from the children who are hustled on their way in the morning by the strictness of a teacher or monitor. Seeing them kill hours, hours, and hours in front of my mistress's fritter stand, seeing them finish their breakfast only with the midday sun, and sometimes then end their day bellied up to Massa Yo's bar, I always say to myself: "How fortunate you are, men who have no master!"

15

At around eleven o'clock, on those days when he didn't have any customers to serve, my master would come sit down next to the cigarette vendor. The two would start their daily round of gossip, interrupted only by the arrival of a customer. Unlike Mama Mado's civil servants, they never chatted because they had a story to tell. No, they jabbered to pass the time as they waited for the next customer. Though he was an ex-civil servant, my master always chatted with one eye on his bar. As for the cigarette vendor, he told his stories as he watched the street, hoping each passing taxi would stop in front of his display. And when a taxi really did stop, he'd break off mid-sentence, immediately going over to stick his head in the car window.

When the taxi left, the cigarette vendor would return to pick up his story where he'd left off, but my master wouldn't be sitting there any longer. So he'd move on toward the bar. Sometimes he'd find Massa Yo serving a customer. He knew that, for the bartender, the customer was king, and so didn't dare distract him with his tall tales. He'd just go back behind his little stand and swallow what was left of his tale, bones and all. Often, though, he'd wait, with his story hanging on his lips, until my master finished serving his customer. But sometimes Massa Yo just gave him a sign. Then I'd see the cigarette vendor turn and run back to his stand crying, "Dear customer, wait for me!"

When he'd come back again later, my master would say, "We're not here to chat, you know!"

Then the cigarette vendor would return to his stand for good, waiting in silence for the next taxi driver to stop. Yes, nailed down to his roadside post, the cigarette vendor could only ever tell my master bits and pieces of stories. I understood why: tormented by memories of the misery that he never ever—and

I mean never, never, never, never ever-o—wanted to sink back into, Massa Yo simply couldn't afford to be a carefree smooth talker. He was always too worried about his business. Some of his customers said he was too much of a cheapskate, that he was a "real Bami," but they didn't know his story. They knew Massa Yo only as a bartender, a bartender who was always standing in front of his bar, with his paunch sticking out toward the street and its uncooperative girls. They had never seen him as an officer of the State, a civil servant like those who ate breakfast till noon. Nor had they ever seen him walk on the road to La Carrière like a white man, killing time at the State's expense, with me on a leash, of course.

Just then, a peanut vendor passed by. One of my master's customers signaled her to stop. The cigarette vendor kindly helped her set her tray down on the ground. He took advantage of the situation to grab a couple of nuts which he shelled with his teeth and tossed into his mouth. "Just to taste," he said, chewing.

The woman protested. "So now you have to pay for a taste?" asked the cigarette vendor, who was obviously not going to buy anything from her.

The man who had called the woman over took a handful of peanuts to taste too. He froze suddenly and made a face. He turned as ugly as a fetish priest and kept spitting a reddish mix of peanuts and kola nuts on the ground. "Ugh, your peanuts are biiiitter!" he said. "Did you piss on 'em?"

My master burst out laughing. The girl didn't wait to be shown the door. She just picked up her tray and placed it back on her head. She even refused help from the cigarette vendor. But when she turned to leave, letting out a string of curses in her own language, the cigarette vendor reached out and grabbed a few more nuts, upsetting the girl's tray in the process. She spun around, ready to let go with another explosive curse. She caught my master's obvious smirk, assumed he was the guilty party, and let him have it with a whole mouthful of insults. "You damned thief!" she spat out, unconcerned about whom she was addressing. "Paying for peanuts is too much for you, huh?"

Massa Yo protested. His customers found that hilarious.

"Me, a thief?" said my indignant master, pointing to his well-stocked bar. "Do you know who I am? *A fit buy am tout ton plateau,** huh!"

"So then buy it!" said the girl.

"Buy it?" repeated Massa Yo. "If I buy it, will you do *it* with me?"

The girl burst out laughing and took the whole street as her witness. "And just where is the man-o?" she asked, pointing to my master. "You want me to give *it* up and let you do me with your little finger?"

"Just give him a little sample," said the cigarette vendor, shaking with laughter. "You'll see what kind of man he is!"

The girl answered him without missing a beat: "*Mouf*, was I talking to you?"

She made this last comment as she backed out of the circle of cannibalistic males. Yes, she knew full well that all those men sitting in front of my master's bar just wanted to waste her time. She knew they were only killing time, devouring the girls' behinds, and that they saw her merely as a source of amusement, a possible scam, or an "Etiennement," not as a business woman. Because they were always undressing the girls with their eyes, and never buying any of the goods they got the girls to show them, the bar's regulars had earned a sad reputation with the quarter's female vendors. As for my master, all the women knew that when he had them display their wares, he just wanted to take advantage of the situation and get an eyeful of the breasts offered up at the same time. Unable to screw the girl of his dreams on his little bar cot, more and more often Massa Yo made do with getting an eyeful in these shameful peep shows. None of this enhanced the bar's reputation! Sometimes when one of the regulars of The Customer Is King called out to a woman selling peanuts, dried manioc, or grilled plantains, I'd see her hesitate a minute and pretend she hadn't heard a thing. The man would repeat his order and only then would the vendor come display her wares at his feet. "Have you given up on selling?" he'd ask, fingering her wares.

"I didn't hear you," the girl would lie.

"Did you even cook these things?"

The endless games of hide-and-seek between the regulars of The Customer Is King and boredom, their games of cat and mouse with the women only stopped when Panther came in. That's right, the Panther Nzui Manto, as he was known on the streets. I am always excited to see him emerge from between the houses. Most of the time, in fact, I get up and run to meet him. I jump up on his chest to welcome him. The courtyard of my master's bar only really comes to life with the arrival of this little old man. He lifts his hands up to the sky so that his voice, hoarse from too much palaver the night before, carries into the distance, far off into the neighborhood. His Medumba* rolls off his lips with shameless delight. When he speaks, his eyes close a little and his eyelids flutter. Most of the time, he takes it for granted that everyone in the streets of Madagascar understands his language, which he clearly doesn't consider foreign but an authentic part of Yaoundé culture. In the movement of his body, covered with the furrows of age, in each of his words, in the childlike surprise of his eyes at the slightest contradiction, and in the energetic gesturing of his arms with each new argument, I see the confidence of a man who knows that he is the Chief in this bar's courtyard, in the streets of this neighborhood, and in the very vibration of the city itself.

Panther has a thousand, ten thousand, a hundred thousand, a million, even a billion stories in his head, and they're always incredible. Most of the time you have to throw logic away to make sense of them! For example, one day he shook up the cigarette vendor by telling him that Sitabac* was so powerful that if it bought tobacco from a grower and, in the end, wasn't satisfied with the taste of the cigarettes it made, it only had to put the cigarettes into the machine again and run the production line in reverse to get the tobacco back, just the way it came. Then the company would return it to the grower, saying "Here's your tobacco. Get the hell out with your bad luck!" The cigarette vendor had shaken his head in disbelief at that story. But that wasn't anything. Another day the little old man told one about a woman he said he'd met whose vagina had been stolen by a little mouse when she'd washed it and hung it out to dry after a fateful romp. Another time, there was the story of a woman with three sets of genitalia, and two of them were male.

"So what proves she was a woman?" my master had asked, thinking he had caught the devil by his tail.

"Her breasts," said the unflappable little old man. "Yes, her breasts!" he insisted, as if that made it all clear. My master shook his head, clearly recognizing Panther as the Chief of the Quarter. His stories outdid those of everyone else. So it wasn't just what people said: Nzui Manto really was the master storyteller.

16

Yes, Panther spoke as if someone had put him on a leash. He kept speaking until white foam gathered at the corners of his mouth. Since his stories were always beyond belief, he always struggled to impress their truth on the quarter. Most of the time, to cut short the arguments he was always stirring up, he said he'd seen *the thing* "with his own eyes." That was supposed to prove it was true. But for Panther, truth was as malleable as the imagination of rumor itself. And to be honest, if Madagascar was rumor's riverbed, and my master's bar its shore, then Panther controlled its flow and fixed its swells in cement. Even the civil servants from Mama Mado's stand were still greenhorns when compared with his oversized mouth. Besides, Nzui Manto wasn't looking for their company. He preferred to tell his thousand tales at The Customer Is King. It's just that he never figured out how to make Massa Yo happy.

A billion tales, I said, this Panther had a billion tales to tell, and that made my master impatient. Sometimes Nzui Manto would start his first story when my master hadn't sold even a single beer yet. So tell me, how could the two men be friends? What my master hadn't understood is that the little old man wasn't really a customer.

"Panther," he said one day, as the man finished his tenth story, trying to provoke him and prod him into buying at least one beer, "you're nothing but a world-class freeloader!"

Now Panther just wouldn't be the Panther Nzui Manto if he let such an insult pass without a reply. First, he didn't buy the beer Massa Yo's rapacious mind was pushing on him. And then he put the bartender in his place with just one sledgehammer of a sentence: "Really, Massa Yo," he said, "your head is filled with nothing but *jobajo*!"

And he was right. Clearly no one in the quarter was more of a bartender than my master. Still, Massa Yo thought he could even the score: "And you, just what is your head filled with, huh?"

He had clearly forgotten one thing: if there was any field in which the little old man was clearly unbeatable, it was that of the mouth. If there was one space he mastered, it was that of words. If there was a kingdom he ruled, it was that of speech. Yes, Panther wasn't just a smooth talker, he was someone who loved talking: a *paroleur,* a wordsmith for the poor neighborhoods. The little old man's face lit up immediately at my master's insulting words; he leaned his body forward, like a distance runner. He didn't explode, no, but he gave the street a glimpse of the earthy depths of his stories: "A little imagination, Massa Yo," he said, sparkling with anger, "a little imagination, *nchoun'am.** Oh no, life is unlivable if it's not reinvented. Look at this day passing by, look at this street that disappears in the distance, look at life, which never stops. *À me ben tchùp,** soon, night will fall. Even workers running to earn their daily bread will soon be retired like me. And that beautiful girl waiting for a taxi . . ."

"She's your own daughter, right?" said Docta, threateningly.

". . . soon she'll be a faded rose. This muscular young man here (Panther held the cigarette vendor's arm up in the air), will soon be nothing but a pile of wrinkles . . ."

"Like you," said another voice.

People burst out laughing. The little old man was livid. "And even you, Massa Yo, you think you're so smart there in front of your bar, but you're just out to take advantage of your brothers' suffering. *Lèn mbe,* the money you work for will just end up in Biya's pocket. (He pronounced it "Mbiya," though, like others of his generation). That's why, my friend, only imagination can add some spice to your life. So think about something other than your beers. Look at how ugly the day is. Make it beautiful with your imagination!"

"Leave Massa Yo alone," a customer said.

Someone else drove home Panther's point, "What imagination? It's his cheapness that'll kill him. He puts all his imagination into *stealing* our money, right?"

Undoubtedly enraged by the word "stealing," my master

grew threatening. He left his counter, counted out a few coins, and handed them to the man who'd just spoken. "Since I'm a thief," he said, "give me my beer and take your money back!" The customer had already drunk half his beer. Clearly that was a problem. But Massa Yo didn't give him time to interrupt. "No, no, no, no," he said, categorically, "I don't want his money anymore!"

A customer came to his assistance. "Panther," he said, "do you see what you're doing? This is how you trick people with your crazy stories. If you have so much imagination, go tell your stories on television and leave us alone!"

Voices were raised. In the chaos, the customer who had said "stealing" said "Bami." He had clearly forgotten he was in a Bamileke* neighborhood. Immediately, a man stood up and let go with a verbal Molotov cocktail. He was talking about tribalism. His noisy arguments were seconded by all the others, who immediately turned on the man they had just been defending against my master. The misspoken drinker left the bar, with everybody's insults trailing behind him. His insulting word had inflamed the conversations of the customers. The retort was ready, but the guy who had thrown down the verbal gauntlet hadn't waited to hear it. And as he disappeared in a taxi, voices got louder, hands waved, and excited gestures grew violent in the bar. The energy produced by all those bodies threw sparks in the air. All of a sudden, The Customer Is King came alive, and the little old man multiplied his curses, crying at the blindness of the new generation. He said he wasn't ashamed, no he wasn't, that there was no one more Bami than him in all of Madagascar. No, there wasn't, because he, Panther, was the founding ancestor. He insisted on "founding," as if to give roots to the refuse all around.

"Give the Chief a beer," a customer said to my master.

At the sound of "beer," the old man's eyes lit up. He didn't even hear another guy concluding a snide remark with: ". . . as if you can eat that?"

Panther was jubilant at the visible effect of his words. He started an impassioned speech, launched into a scandalous thesis, and opened his bag of words, but fell silent as soon as my master put the bottle of beer between his legs. I had already realized that if the little old man never bought a drink, he always found a way to get at least one offered to him before he reached the end of his arguments. Now he preferred to let the commentaries he'd awakened in the bar continue on without him for a bit. People were talking about the man who had insulted everybody. He must be Nkoua,* they said. Panther wasn't listening anymore. He put out the fire in his wordy mouth with the quiet glug-glug of a drinking man. Yes, the drinking mouth does not speak. Then he wiped his lips with the back of his hand and spoke, nodding in the direction where the man with the killing words had long disappeared: "The *nkaknin** run off to their jobs but don't know they're working for nothing. If I don't have a pension today—am I right?—it's because the Mbiyas have *stolen* my money and stashed it in Switzerland!"

He stressed the word "stolen" as he looked at the men around him. "Just drink your beer," my master said in exasperation as he returned behind his counter, "and leave Biya alone."

"Hey Panther, about that," said a customer, trying to help out the little old man, "you're the only one who thinks Massa Yo's got no imagination. Doesn't he scam on the girls every night?"

The customer turned back to my master, who was hunkered down behind his counter, and addressed him loudly. "Tell us the truth, Massa Yo. What do you tell women so they follow you and leave the rest of us alone, huh? Just don't tell us you put that bed behind your counter for nothing."

Hearing "that bed," the men, in a chorus, burst out laughing. My master kept quiet. Clearly he accepted his defeat, one to nothing. He didn't even move until one of his customers craned his neck to see the bed they were talking about, there behind the bar. "You see your mother back here?" Massa Yo snapped, which only added to his customers' delight. It was the first time I'd seen my master's frustration explode in public—the frustration of a man whose secret virginity is revealed. I looked at him standing there behind his counter, offered up to his customers' mirth, and suddenly I felt sorry for him. My sympathetic barks filled the bar. He turned to me and said, threatening as he showed me the street, "Mboudjak, get out!"

Chapter Two

Then I turned into a poodle. Mama Mado took me to a beauty salon. She sat right behind me, done up from head to toe, wearing a multicolored dress, with her lips blood red and her feet elegantly crossed, one over the other. She was leafing through a brightly colored magazine; one side of its cover showed a white couple kissing on the mouth, and the other, another couple, whites as well, staring into each other's eyes. *Nous Deux*—"Just the Two of Us"—it read above the couple gazing at each other. Delicately touching her finger to her tongue, my mistress would lift each page of the magazine with just a touch, as if by magic.

Looking in the mirror in front of me, I'd see her lift her head from her stylized reading every now and again to flash me a plastic smile. Or maybe it was that other face of hers she scrutinized in the mirror, only catching my gaze by chance. For there I was—a real little nothing of a dog, a *tchotchoro*, if truth be told—sunk deep into the easy chair of my metamorphosis. Three women sat on my left, in chairs just like mine, their heads swallowed up by giant helmets; they, too, were reading magazines. My eyes lit up when I realized that the one closest to me—a fat woman whose breasts poured out of her plunging neckline like water from a basin—was reading her magazine upside down. That shocked me, so I craned my neck over a little more, just to be sure. My eyes met hers—they flashed red with indignation. She readjusted her shirt over her breasts and glared at me angrily. "Dogs shouldn't be allowed in here," she grumbled.

Without missing a beat, my mistress put her in her place. "Ma'am, leave my little doggie alone, will you?"

And I, the "little doggie" in question, just slunk down further into my chair. That woman is a racist, I told myself as I glared at her and her overflowing breasts. Then I turned my attention back to that little body of mine reflected in the mirror. The two women on my right, each wearing a similar helmet on her head, stared into the mirror as if they'd never seen themselves before. The first practically devoured herself with her eyes, while the second cruelly moved closer to her face in the mirror, as if she were going to jump right in, but then stopped and popped a pimple sticking out on the end of her nose. Terrified, I turned back again to my own little body. An overly perfumed girl was busy with my fur. She was dressed all in blue. In the mirror I saw her bend over and shear off my coat with a big pair of scissors. Then she ran a comb repeatedly through what fur remained on my back before wrapping it in little tufts around a rainbow assortment of curlers. Working this way, she covered the whole of me in blue, white, red, yellow, and green curlers. Her task complete, she stood up gracefully and, without turning around, looked at my mistress in the mirror. Her eyes wide with wonder, Mama Mado got up and came to stare at the multicolored dog I'd become: a real phenomenon. I noticed the two women whispered silently to each other as my mistress bent over and caressed my head, emitting little sounds I was supposed to understand. "Doggiedoggiedoggie," she said in a strange voice, "*we'll* be beautiful before long."

Proudly she added, "*We'll* walk with our heads held high today!"

As for me, I was looking at this "we" she spoke of, this little "we" slouched down in a beauty salon chair, this "we" she hoped to render presidential: my little body covered with a bright coat of curlers. I stared at myself in the mirror and died of shame. My wavy coat terrified me. I hid my eyes from the horror I'd become. Was beauty really born of ugliness? I really was ugly. I shook my tail, which was tied up with a bow, and wondered, was it possible to escape from one's own image? I barked out my suffering. My voice filled the salon, much to the indignation of the overly sensitive women around me. I heard my mistress's voice. "Now *we* will be brave."

This new sympathy of Mama Mado's made me tremble right

down to the depths of my flesh. I turned around and realized that the helmeted women on my left and right were laughing behind their magazines. I was ridiculous. Yes, I was comical and ugly. One of the women freed her head from the helmet and came toward me. Terrified, I realized that she had not one single hair left on her head. She twisted her lips into a great big laugh, only stopping after she walked out into the street. She looked like a witch. Her laughter kept shaking the walls and mirrors of the beauty salon for a long time. My mistress tore me from the enchantment of that lugubrious laugh by petting my curlers and repeating her "we" a few more times. The feel of her touch ran through me, and for a moment I was reassured to have her there by my side. I was trembling. I lost the courage to bark anymore. If only I could grab a magazine, too, *Nous Deux* or anything at all. Even if I held it upside down, I could bury my head in it, yes, bury my head in it forever. If only I could disappear into the letters, the words, the sentences of a magazine. Alas! Soon the hairdresser came back toward me. She doused me in a perfume so heady I had to close my eyes. I felt her hands moving busily over my body. When I opened my eyes again, I saw myself in the mirror: I was now a dog with wavy fur. The hairdresser was making furrows on my back. My mistress's face beamed with pleasure. Once liberated, I jumped off my seat, running and barking. I quickly realized my mistress had me leashed. And she was in no hurry to leave.

Soon, however, we did leave the beauty salon. On the street I felt the weight of all eyes on my back. The quarter's unanimous opinion weighed me down, condemning me to walk on all fours; no, it outright condemned me to crawl. Laughter pealed out here and there. Sometimes there was the squeal of an admiring voice, but I paid it no mind. I saw myself naked and exposed in the street. But my mistress must have been on cloud nine. It was her revenge on all those who'd never seen her as anything but a fritter vendor, I told myself. She let me hurry on at the end of my leash as she exulted in her newfound grandeur. And I, filled with unspeakable shame, looked back at her from time to time to bark out my pain. There she was in her instant royalty. Even Lady Di would have been taken in by it. She shook her hips, swaying her head right and left.

Mama Mado wasn't walking, no, she was dancing in the street. And the whole road was looking at us. Old men stopped puffing on their pipes. Young men stopped mid-stride. Ludo* players paused mid-roll. Peanut vendors stopped mid-measure. Kids suspended their soccer game and followed us with joyful shouts. Some taxi drivers even began to honk out their joy: beep-beep-be-beep-beep. With a hint of a smile, Mama Mado turned sprightly back toward the assembled crowd, but didn't stop. I heard some passersby, roused by the picturesque spectacle of our passage, say, "What a woman!"

My mistress smiled at them. Others said, in the very same voice, "What a dog!"

My mistress smiled just as nicely at them. And yet there were some critics—Afrocentric intellectuals, to be sure—who said, "That poor dog, alienated from his canitude!"

My mistress pretended not to hear them. She held her head all the higher. She held it even higher still when a voice cried out: "Dirty hussy!"

I'm sure Mama Mado attributed these outbursts to the jealousy born of misery. Once she turned back toward a man who had insulted her. She stared at him hard and then, with great dignity, spat on the ground. As for me, Mboudjak, I dragged my body on, crawling at the foot of her grandeur. Yet I knew that I was the first dog in all of Madagascar ever to go to a hairdresser. I was an event, and my mistress, who had orchestrated it all, was reaping the rewards of her audacity. Some stray dogs dared to come sniff at my behind. And I swear, it wasn't I, it was my perfume that convinced them I was no longer of their class. They shied away from me, ashamed of their dirt, humiliated by their miserable state. Faced with their newfound respect, I felt myself joined to my mistress by the grandeur of beauty, by the grandeur of Inaccessibility. Mama Mado let it be known throughout the quarter that I was the dog of the future. No more starving dogs. No more dogs chased by flies. No more dogs with their teats sweeping the streets. No more cadaverous dogs. No more vampirish dogs. No more three-legged communist dogs. No more dogs scarred with mange. No more dogs left blind in one eye. Me, Mboudjak, my time had come, and so had that of this other Mama Mado, who suddenly roused

something other than the need to be mothered in all the men of
the quarter. "Come here, sweetie," said one man. "I'll take care
of you like your poodle." With a determined gait, my mistress
moved on toward The Customer Is King. I saw Massa Yo frozen like a statue in front of the door to his bar. His eyes were
watering. He was speechless, caught in the admiring gesture
of a man who stupidly shoves his hand down into his pants
pocket to squeeze his *bangala* right in front of a woman. He
saw his wife, whom he suddenly no longer recognized, walk
past the empty fritter stand that had always been her field of
definition and that had come to define the borders of her very
being. He looked at her with the same cannibalistic eye he used
to stare at the local girls. Massa Yo smiled idiotically at this ter-
rain he no longer recognized, and whistled, as he would have at
any girl going up the street. Mama Mado shook her head with
dignity, but didn't respond just yet. My master whistled again.
Then, all of a sudden, he recognized his wife. Even worse, he
saw that dog crawling along on the ground, clothed in beauty,
it's true, but a sham all the same. And in that moment, alas! I
suddenly became ridiculous in his eyes. I couldn't protect his
bar; I couldn't frighten robbers; I could only make his customers laugh: that's what the wicked gaze he locked on me seemed
to say. Then my master burst out laughing. Overcome by his
own laughter, he slapped his head. He was laughing so hard I
felt his spasms run through me. "Is that a dog?" he asked his
wife as he shook with laughter.

He leaned against the door of his bar to have a really good
laugh. "A ground squirrel," he said, pointing at my puny self,
lying there on the ground. "Yes, a ground squirrel, not a dog!"

The cigarette vendor and all his other customers ran to see
the ground squirrel in question. All of them looked at me, some
even sniggered. Docta, who wasn't laughing, squinted and said
I looked strangely like Mini Minor's dogs. Hearing that name,
I jumped up and barked, rousing myself from my dream. I went
over to the cigarette vendor's stand and, in my sleepwalker's
daze, lifted my hind leg to relieve myself. "Get the hell out!"
said the cigarette vendor's voice, and I saw the shadow of his
threatening foot rise up. "Dirty mutt!"

I heard my master's voice, "Hey-o, don't kill my dog!"

I ran to hide back behind his bar. There I relieved myself against the wall, happy to be just a plain old dog.

2

In order to understand men better, I made it my duty to stop dreaming about their lives. Yes, I made it my duty always to solidify the world around me: I would not fall into the intoxication and uncontrolled dance of things, I would leave the metamorphoses of their universe aside, and above all I would not sink into the sulfurous labyrinth of their hallucinations. I made it my duty to keep my four feet fully anchored to the ground at all times. I am a bar dog—so be it—but I must absolutely be realistic as well. I know my life depends upon it. And yet, do you have to be drunk to sink into the universal inebriation of the neighborhoods? Must I have swallowed alcohol to see the streets of Madagascar dance in front of my paws?

Day in and day out, the commentaries of my master's bar continually skew the insulting reality of the street before me and call my intelligence into question. Panther's fertile imagination—but is it just his imagination?—tramples on my logic each and every day. Rumor flies on the words of that old man. It's not only Mama Mado's faithful regulars who get carried away by rumor. No, once it's sugarcoated by the civil servants, who always know a little too much about what's going on with the government ministers, it also turns the reality of the streets on its head right before my eyes. Yes, I say, rumor dreams up the world all over again. Rumor isn't just fueled by Panther—no it's not—but by Docta, the engineer, too. He has already jotted down in his notebook all the details of the affair between Mini Minor and the police commissioner, but he still can't give a straight answer to the only question the cigarette vendor keeps asking him about Virginie, "Tell us, *tara,* did you win her over yet?" Or rather, he can only ever whisper, "*Mola,** leave me alone. I'm still working out the strategy for this scam! But believe me, the hen is already pecking at the corn, you heard it from me. It's coming along, coming along."

Rumor also inflames the alleyways that snake between the

houses in Madagascar. Sometimes I console myself with the thought that, here in the neighborhoods, reality is actually just a long dream, and, with my eyes wide open, I'm the one starting out with false assumptions. Yet my problem is quite clear: in my confusion, I can no longer accurately taste what my judgment might take to be true. Once in the hands of the ghetto's raging magic, even the hardest of bones turns into cartilage. What I mean is that the rumor of the neighborhoods, the speech of the slums, and the chattering of the men in front of my master's bar trample on my ability to judge for myself. Rumor liquefies, dissolves in acid, and grinds into dust. Yes, rumor reinvents the world around it, and it is forever making me the dumbfounded victim of its trickery. So I gaze at men, my mouth wide open and my tongue hanging down in surprise. I even let my tongue drip—what else can I do?

One morning, for example, Panther shook up Mama Mado's stand, saying that a well-known member of the opposition had been arrested in Europe, stuffed into a crate of corned beef, stamped, and mailed back to this country. It didn't matter that I perked up my ears, perked and reperked them again. It didn't matter that I kept my mind sharp. How could I tell if this was just another of those many commentaries fabricated by the human mind to frustrate my efforts to see through their dirty tricks. But all my master's customers believed the story.

"That's what Biya should do to all those opposition leaders hiding overseas," said one man in all seriousness. "At least then the Parisians would quit barking," added his neighbor.

Another of my master's customers said, "So you think if they come back, we can make them shut up?"

"At least if they come back, they'll be of some use. Instead of wasting their time criticizing, they'll build the country with us."

Panther's voice said, "*Mbe ke di? Ou mbe ke di?** What are you saying? That you're building Cameroon, sitting there behind your *jobajo*?"

Standing by the door of The Customer Is King, he dotted all of his i's. The men shouted their responses to his criticism.

"If a *jobajo* is too much for you," said Docta's voice, "then leave us alone."

Panther put him in his place. "At least I worked all my life, you do-nothing. Just what have you done in this country of ours?"

I shook my head, sending my crown of flies into the air: a battle was brewing. I took it all in, willfully opening my eyes to the street in front of my paws: a battle would take place. I stifled my misgivings and determinedly opened my spirit to the blurry evidence of the street that disappeared off into the distance before me; I opened myself up to the lie it told itself. I stifled the echo of the neighborhoods' crazy speech in my gut. In desperation, I turned my ability to judge on my master and his customers, whose every word, after all, I needed to weigh. What job, I asked myself, what kind of work could Panther have done in his life that would let him look down on Docta from the height of a former Father of the Nation? What kind of work, can you tell me? I watched him shake his wrinkles and said to myself, "He's always just mouthing off! Oh yes, always more *web-web**!" But we'll let that pass. Without pausing in his argument, Panther soon went back to lean against the wall behind the bar. I heard him urinate noisily. Only his words rose above the sound of his urine hitting the ground. The arrogant Docta had responded by asking if he thought just being retired was a feat. I heard him clear his throat and spit on his urine, then his voice again filled up the bar's courtyard. "*We're* the ones who built this country, huh!" he said.

He made a show of zipping up his pants and struck his chest three times, proudly insisting upon that "we." I looked at his feeble body, eaten away by age. I looked at his face, eaten away by life, and asked myself: Where is the truth in all of this? Didn't this Panther go on a bit too much? Once I told myself that if I wanted to get close to the man himself, maybe I just needed to stop listening to his overflowing stories. In the world's fleshy carcass, I was looking for the hardness of a bone, for the best morsel life's feast had to offer, and he was making his hallucinations dance in the street. Realistic: I must be realistic. He was obviously inventing the reality around him to suit himself! A manipulator of reality, that's what the little old man was. But then, *bia boya,* what else can you do? When that little old man was there, yes, especially when he was there, the courtyard of my master's bar became a braid of words, an interweaving of commentaries, a whirlpool of emphasis, a continuous explosion of superlatives, a perpetual contest of one-upmanship. Yes: thousands of insanities all jumbled together. And to my despair, rather than leaving man's solidity behind as it followed its muddy course, this endless flood of rumor soon became the bar's background noise, its *kwassa kwassa** ambience. From then on, whenever I saw Panther fabricate the world with his words, I just shook my head and said to myself, "The world is really something. Let's just get on with life!"

3

One day Mini Minor stopped her car in front of my master's bar. She got out and, using her most polite and formal tone, as usual, ordered a few of the loafers killing time beside my mistress's stand to give her some help. They hurried to comply. The little woman whose receding hairline cut a path as wide as a highway opened up the back of her car and pointed at a little box peeking out from it. One of the loafers burst out laughing and asked if he'd really been called for just "that little thing." He loudly declared he could carry the box all by himself. It was his way of shoving his friends aside so he could have the reward promised by the little woman to whoever helped her all for himself. But when he tried to get the box out of the car, he was surprised to find out how heavy it was. He strained his veins, tightened the muscles in his butt, stuck out his tongue, and splayed his legs, but to no avail. His eyes bulged out of their sockets and sent drips down on his feet. He shit and pissed right there, but the box, anchored in the back of the car, just kept staring at him mysteriously. Mini Minor laughed. It was shocking to see her laugh. "Just what's in that box, huh?" the loafer asked.

"That's none of your business, mister," she replied.

And with a determined gesture, she ordered the other loafers to help their buddy. It took four of them to carry the little load. I followed them. Posted on the wall around Mini Minor's *chantier* was a sign: "Beware of Dogs." Another sign declared, next to a thunderbolt: "Warning: Premises protected by electric alarm." A third proclaimed, in capital letters, "CHANTIER

DE LA RÉPUBLIQUE." Still a fourth added, "Members only."
Everything on the walls was designed to keep me away. Soon
the tumultuous voices of a pack of dogs convinced me that
the interior of the *chantier* really was off-limits to me. With
their strident barks, they showed how happy they were at their
mistress's return. The little woman raised her voice and ordered
Virginie to hold them back. The petrified porters asked if they
could just leave the box there. Mini Minor replied, "They don't
bite people who are with me."

But when the *chantier*'s gate was opened, a pack of dogs ran
out, barking wildly and jumping all over. Virginie ran after
them, shouting threats. Terrified, the porters let the box fall. I
heard their terrified screams and then saw one, then two, then
three, then four, then all the dogs come at me. They surrounded
me menacingly. They each sniffed my fur and my rear. One
howled insults at me. Another expressed surprise that my ears
were so fly bitten. A third laughed at my behind, asking if I'd
just farted. I told him he stank of rotten beans. The other dogs
immediately barked out their laughter. They said I was the one
with the bad breath. They asked where I ordered my heady
perfume. Right when I was getting ready to give the one who
just wouldn't stop sniffing my behind a good bite of revenge,
Virginie showed up and ordered the dogs back into the *chantier*. She chased them away from me, waving her arms and repeatedly yelling "Go!" Even as they ran for cover behind the
closed door of their brothel, the dogs didn't stop insulting me.
"So many flies!" they said.

"Whose dog is that?" Mini Minor asked, pointing at my
frustrated humble self, barking in front of her gate.

Her voice burned with rage at the scandal caused by my presence. One of the porters said, "That's Massa Yo's dog."

"Get him out of here, and far away from my house," she
ordered.

The loafers turned on me as the woman continued, "Keep your
dogs at home, will you? Really, it always ends up like this. Don't
you know how hard I work to disinfect my house every day?
Who can be sure your mutt doesn't have rabies? Who knows for
sure he isn't contagious? Then he'll contaminate my *chantier*.
Don't you know this is a restaurant? Really, what filth!"

She said something to Virginie in their language and then, waving her arms, ordered the loafers to pick up the box they'd dumped on the ground and carry it into the house. One of them said something about the dogs, and the little woman replied, "I've already said they won't bite you!"

Later, when the porters came back to the courtyard of my master's bar, I listened as they let their shock explode. "That woman is awful, huh?" said one man. "Did you see what's in her *chantier*?"

He made a lot of gestures, but couldn't come up with the right word to express the truth of *just what* he'd seen. Then suddenly he shrugged his shoulders and said, simply, "They're the ones screwing the country, *Etienning* it, right?"

He sadly insisted on the word "Etienning." Another loafer replied, "Leave it at that. The crisis isn't for everyone, you know!"

"So what's she doing with all those dogs there, huh?" a second wondered.

"They're there to keep us out, right?" was the response he got.

"Just what was in that box after all?" wondered a third.

"Who knows?"

Sometimes I wandered by the impenetrable walls of the Chantier de la République. It was not so much the mystery behind the brothel's closed walls as the presence of so many of my fellows within that piqued my curiosity. The gate violently proclaimed its "Members only." I consoled myself, saying the little woman wasn't just shutting herself off from my eyes. She was cutting herself off from everything, and by that I meant from life itself. Her *chantier* was in Madagascar, it's true, but she had turned her back on all of us. What a scandal! In the end, though, rumor forced open the Chantier de la République's closed doors.

One day the streets, bars, and shops began saying that in one of the city's best-known *chantiers* they were serving human flesh. Panther, who'd brought this bit of information to The Customer Is King, spoke of a certain Mami Ndole as the source of the evil. He was surprised no one knew this Mami Ndole, and said her *chantier* was right at the second intersection in Mokolo. Yes, he'd been there himself. He swore the police had found three human skulls in Mami Ndole's refrigerator, along with hearts still dripping with blood.

"They only found them by chance," he stressed, his eyelids fluttering as he stared at my master's customers.

The wretched woman, he said with a shrug, had made the mistake of turning a police commissioner who'd wandered into her *chantier* into sausage. She had seasoned and cooked up the poor guy, but in her rush she'd forgotten his cap. It was his cap that betrayed her.

"You're lying!" everyone shouted in disbelief.

"If not for that, no one ever would've known!" said one man.

"I swear to God, there's no such thing in this whole world as a perfect crime," Panther added knowingly, with another shrug of his shoulders.

"Those guys are afraid of nothing, huh," the cigarette vender noted. "Making sausage out of a police commissioner, I tell you!"

And Panther concluded his story.

"The investigation is still underway. Mami Ndole wasn't acting alone, you know. There's a whole network of *chantiers* they have to bring down."

As I listened to this story, I remembered the strange box the little woman had had carried into her *chantier*. All my master's clients were staring off in the direction of the Chantier de la République too. The fate awaiting the police commissioner was beginning to make all of us feel for him. His end was too obvious not to be alarming. That evening Mini Minor stopped her car in front of my master's bar and offered a round of beer to everyone there. Licking her fingers and lifting them innocently up to the sky, she said she was just an honest businesswoman. "Hey-o, I don't want to lose any customers," she said.

That day she smiled at everyone and gave up on the overly formal turns of phrase. She had no choice. I knew that all it would take was for Panther to say she was a Mami Ndole and her case would be closed. After that it wouldn't matter if she threw the doors of her *chantier* wide open, none of her customers would ever set foot in it again. That day I learned the full extent of the power of the street's crazy words, the regicidal power of rumor.

4

Yes, rumor is a dangerous music. Its crazy reality is born of man's drunkenness, in those moments when words grow loud, fears too obvious, and gestures uncoordinated. I was discovering its power, but still had questions. I must be honest—in the neighborhood, it was always difficult, oh so difficult, to protect myself from the dance of the world around me, to remain objective when faced with reality's hallucinatory magic. Yet, was it really necessary to remain lucid if I wanted to understand men? Didn't my will to survive prevent me from seeing life?

One day, the nonstop commotion of the streets, the nauseating odor of the serpentine alleyways, the sinister side of the ghostly *chantiers,* the rumor circulated by haphazard tontines, the *kongossa* whispered in devilishly raucous bars, and the insistently loud music of the *circuits*—the very ambience of Madagascar itself—conspired to concoct a full-blown man. He just popped right out of Panther's big mouth, of course, leaving my mind baffled and bewildered. "It seems," he said, all caught up that day in one of his interminable mid-afternoon revelations, "it seems there's a guy going from quarter to quarter, making men's *bangalas* disappear."

"Keep on telling us your lies!" my master exclaimed.

But the cigarette vendor had already heard about this scandal. His taxi-driving customers had let it slip as they bought a Delta menthol: "Yeah, he just shakes your hand and then zip! your thing is gone."

To be on the safe side, he grabbed his testicles through his pocket as he spoke.

"Well," said one of my master's customers in all seriousness, "I'd just like to know what he does with all those *bangalas.*"

"Maybe he sells them to European collectors?"

"What a twisted idea!"

Hearing that, the learned Docta informed the common folk: "It's quite possible. For medical transplant."

"Those whites are really something!"

"'Really something,' that's for sure!" said the little old man, who was certainly remembering the colonial era, which he alone among all those gathered had seen. "You know, most whites can't even get it up. That's why they come and buy African *bangalas.*"

Once again I listened to the little old man creating reality with his stories, I saw my master's trusting clientele build it, brick by brick, along with him, and I just shook my skeptical, scientific, canine head. Stubbornly I told myself, "Mboudjak, don't forget, you decided that to stay alive, you'd look at the world with objective eyes." I didn't want to get caught up in the magical tricks of crazy words. It didn't matter how skeptical I was, though, I still knew one thing for sure: if the *bangala* thief were to show up one day in Madagascar, it would be just his dead body, I swear, just his dead body that the city would come and haul away. Just hearing the violent threats and curses raining down on the back of that fictional man was enough. If my master promised to scalp him, Docta swore he'd burn him alive. And the engineer added, laughing, "But before I burn him, I'll grab his loot for myself!"

According to another rumor, one circulated a few days later by Docta himself, a member of the opposition was going from neighborhood to neighborhood stealing *bangalas.* You just needed to wave at him and zip!

"You owe me royalties on that," Panther insisted. He swore the engineer had stolen his story; he even called him a "plagiarist." Docta didn't give in to the old man's fussing. He said it was just another of the Chief's strategies for getting himself a free beer. As for me, I wondered which of the two was the biggest liar? Since then, however, I've learned how much fear the words "member of the opposition" unleashed in the streets of Madagascar.

5

One morning a man dressed all in black came into my master's bar and ordered an ice-cold Guinness. He tried to pet my back. I jumped up and then saw his cadaverous smile. He smiled at me like no other customer ever had. I moved away from him and barked out my fears. I waited until I was in the bar courtyard, far away from him before I started barking. I didn't want to be caught in the shadow of his evil aura. Talk about fictions, that man seemed to be ripped straight out of a rumor. It's true, the word that had invented him quickly spread its evil throughout the paths, alleyways, and streams of the neighborhood. He became a regular at The Customer Is King, but never quite managed to have the same chattering routine, the exact same insignificant gaze, nor, even less, the same squashed-under-the-thumb-by-life look of many of my master's customers. I soon noticed that when he arrived, my master's customers would whisper slanderous things about him. They called him "the Crow."

Those who were curious would look up when the Crow arrived. As for me, I'd stand up tall, stretching out my legs. Even the hens would stop playing and cry out in fear. The man in black would quickly fall into his usual studied arrogance: he spoke to no one. He was at least forty and looked every bit the priest, minus the black robe. Except too, perhaps, that instead of going to church, he folded up his lugubrious silhouette and came into my master's bar. This secular priest sat on the benches and upturned crates like the others. He always ordered an ice-cold Guinness, but never said anything else.

Soon, though, he started taking a small red notepad out of his pocket and jotting things down. I've got to make one thing clear: he would have been forgotten in the courtyard of my master's bar, he'd have faded into the background, like just another civil servant sitting there at 11 a.m., if he hadn't gotten into the bad habit of silently taking notes. Commentaries were flying full force, arms were raised for the daily verbal challenge, words were becoming incendiary: and there, right next to the big talkers, a sinister man sat silently. But even that didn't turn people against him. No, the poor wretch pushed it even further: he took out his notepad and started taking notes. One day Docta went up to him and asked straight out: "Hey, Brother, what are you writing down, huh?"

Surprised, the writer stopped his scribbling. He lifted his face and saw the mob of my master's clients waving their threatening fists over his head. The inhabitants of Madagascar knew something about spies. Panther often spoke about the fifties, about the freedom fighters hiding in the neighborhoods, the fire at the Congo market, the death train. And I had heard the cigarette vendor tell the story of one of his big-mouthed clients, arrested on April 6, the day of the failed coup d'état back in 1984. Maybe it was because of those old fears that the whole neighborhood had ended up looking suspiciously at anyone who wrote down its words. Recorded speech frightens everyone who is used to playing with words. You never know. Everybody's frightened eyes locked on the man in black's notepad as voices inquired, with a laugh, "Brother, are you are journalist?"

One man declared, "What do you mean, journalist? He's a spy."

As the voices in his bar's courtyard grew angry, my master's voice pleaded from behind his customers, "Hey-o, we're not into politics in this bar." Commentaries catch fire all too quickly in front of the neighborhoods' bars. Fists are always raised fast amid rumor's convulsions. So the man in black unwittingly turned into the *bangala* thief everybody was waiting for, with one hand shoved down into their pants pocket and the other clenched in a deadly fist. The Crow didn't back down from the threat surrounding him. An accusatory voice said, "Show us what you've written," and without hesitation he showed everyone his notepad. The cigarette vendor read out loud so the whole street could hear the words that summed up the strangeness of the character for everyone in Madagascar. "Just listen to this, will you: 'The neighborhoods are the forge of mankind's creativity. The wretchedness of their surroundings is but an illusion. It conceals the profound reality of the unknown which remains to be discovered: the truth of History in its creation!'"

Docta came up with the words that made everyone burst out laughing: "History with a capital H. Oh, oh, oh, the gentleman is a philosopher!"

"A philosopher." Aha! Feeling a little let down after reaching the high point of their rage, some of the men shook their heads at this new enigma, then went right back to their beer and picked up their commentaries where they'd left off. Docta made a big gesture, as if to say, "Ha! Who cares?"

The day after this revelation, as a show of goodwill, the man in black came with a book he'd written. The title of the book was—who could forget it?—*Dog Days*. He said he'd tried to write a story about the present, about the day-to-day, to seize history in its creation and put the reins of History back into the hands of its true heroes. He said, in short, that in his book he wrote about "people like all of you here around me." Only then did the drinkers at The Customer Is King start looking at him differently. "No way! People like us in a book?!" they exclaimed. But while everyone else suddenly looked at the Crow's book in wonder, scanning its thousands of letters for a familiar face, Docta backed away, shaking his head with disdain. The scamming engineer seemed to think he'd found an even bigger failure than himself.

"Can you eat that?" he said when the little old man asked him if, since he'd gone to school, he could write books too.

After the revelation of his peculiar project, some of my master's customers sidled up to the sinister man. They suddenly seemed to have secrets to share with him. For example, a man with a big round belly got the conversation off to a bumpy start, saying he used to write too and then adding, as he scratched his head apologetically, "Yes, when I was young."

He laughed to himself, a little like a kid caught misbehaving. He went on in a conspiratorial tone so his fellows wouldn't hear of his sins, "I wrote poems . . ."

Then suddenly he puffed out his chest and proclaimed for the whole street to hear, as if it were an obvious source of grandeur, ". . . Love poems."

I looked at him in shock. I just couldn't believe that his filthy, shriveled silhouette, that his carcass, now leprously perched on an upturned crate, had once housed a poet. As if roused by the memory of his very different youth, this poet of ours who'd been assassinated by life ordered another Guinness for the man in black. It was as if he'd suddenly discovered the camaraderie of the literati. He took a long swig of his own beer and finally found the sentence that for me explained his current loss of the song: "I lost my inspiration the day I married my wife," said the sad man.

He shook his head sadly and added, "Since then, I drink to drown my sorrows."

6

According to Docta, the man in black had a reputation in neighborhood bars all across town. He was first recognized in Melen, where he'd shown up with a camera and made the suicidal error of pointing its lens at an unremarkable bar. He said he wanted to "capture moments of reality." What he'd gotten—and he was lucky that was all too, added the engineer—were two big lumps on his face, because no one wanted some stranger to go and sell his shadow to Famla.* That's when our man made the switch to "spying on people." I was more and more certain that Docta only told these stories to undercut the sympathy my master's customers had suddenly felt for the Crow. But it didn't matter that he spiced up his words of warning, saying the sinister Crow's notes were written in code, or that he insisted the Crow's words were nothing but metaphors, the residents of Madagascar saw it only as jealousy. "Just what is a metaphor?" asked one of my master's customers.

The engineer struggled to stammer out a reply.

"If someone's leagues ahead of you," said the little old man, "just carry his bag."

Much to our engineer's despair, even more people kept coming to confide in the writer. They came to tell him about the reality of their lives. I quickly learned that all of them nurtured the strange dream of one day having their crazy life published in a book. I learned that each one of the neighborhood drunks harbored in his belly the dream of becoming famous: of becoming the main character of a book like the one the man in black had shown them, a book thousands of people would buy; of becoming, maybe not the hero of the story, but at least the book's main character. I never figured out who had told them keeping company with the gloomy, silent man would give them that honor. Even the Panther Nzui Manto decided he no longer wanted just to stir his crazy stories into the daily flood. No, now he wanted to put them down for posterity, in a book everyone would read. One day an orange vendor, clearly captivated by the same dream, marched with determination into my master's bar and asked, "Where's the philosopher who's often here?"

"He hasn't come in yet today," said my master.

"I'll come back later," the woman said in a rush, as if wracked by a sudden bout of diarrhea. "Whatever the cost, he's got to know what *they* have done to me."

She said "they" with a shake of her head, and already I could see her accusing the cannibalistic customers of Madagascar's bars. She went off, leaving her undefined "they" dangling before the street's thousand questions. And when she finally did meet the man in black, she sat down in front of him and said, quite matter-of-factly, "Brother, people told me you're not like the men from this quarter; they say that you think. Well, listen to this . . ."

Yes, the all-too-sudden familiarity between the Crow and the residents of the neighborhood bothered the engineer. He, too, knew how to read, write, add, and subtract. Of course, he hadn't written a book, but he developed ideas and laid out his theories for everyone to see. What's more, he had a prizewinning record with the girls. But from up there on the high horse of his arrogance, he'd never been able to establish a real feeling of familiarity with the residents of Madagascar. Too focused on the feminine path of his eternal salvation, he had never looked on the other regulars in the courtyard of my master's bar with anything but disdain. With each of his silences, the man in black—this stranger who had known how to become the confidante of the *soya* vendors, the orange vendors, the unemployed, and the ever-present ludo players—made it clear that he had the support of the residents of Madagascar that the engineer had never been able to earn. Still, I think Docta didn't really hate the man in black. At first he'd been amused by his bizarre profession ("How can you be a writer in times of crisis like these?"), but he soon grew uncomfortable with the continual presence of the man's overly astonished gaze locked on the reality of life in the neighborhood. Then he'd sunk into reproach, accusation, and now slander.

In fact, there was a simple reason behind the accumulation of Docta's reproaches against the man in black. Yes, causality works, even in the neighborhoods, especially at those moments when hatreds are born. Here's what happened: one day Docta ran as if pursued by the Devil himself and hid behind my mistress's empty fritter stand, in the corner where I was hiding from the onslaught of the day and its flies. He motioned to me to keep quiet. "Hide me," said the engineer to the cigarette vendor, who, like me it seemed, understood nothing of this whole act.

I poked out my curious muzzle and I saw *her*: Rosalie, yes, Rosa Rosa Rose herself. A young girl got out of a stopped taxi, leaned nonchalantly over the door, and paid her fare. She held a child by the hand, a kid of about the same age as my master's son. So she was the accursed witch making Docta run! Her kid looked at the street with the childish surprise of a poor devil in way over his head. His eyes turned toward me. Then I saw Docta sink even further down behind the crate, even though he was already hidden by its shadow. The cigarette vendor looked at him with surprise and said, "How long are you gonna hide there, huh?"

So that was Rosalie, the very Rosalie who had previously thrown him out into the street. The engineer didn't move until the cigarette vendor assured him she'd really disappeared between the houses. "But she's headed to your house," he added.

"Why is she coming here?" railed Docta, as he got up from his hiding place. "Women are impossible. She screams, she screams, she screams-o, and when I leave, she chases me all the way here."

He was just mouthing off, that was clear. The truth he had hoped to conceal in the shadows next to me soon burst out all over his face. He was just as frightened of the girl's words as of the eyes of the kid she held by the hand. Yes, that child's eyes said loud and clear that Docta had run away, that he was a coward. His responsibilities, which the girl had obviously come to throw in his face, had him quaking in his boots. A professional womanizer, that's what he was. A child rearer, he certainly was not. Besides, just where would he find the necessary money? Chômecam*—the unemployment office—was his realm and my master's bar was his field of definition.

"Women are awful," he said again, wiping his brow. "Give me a Delta menthol."

Oooh, yes, I thought: once they're no longer a baisedrom! But when Docta turned around to catch his breath after his close call with the eyes of that girl and her kid, when he turned around to greedily and freely gulp at the cigarette he lit with such relief, he was horrified to find that the man in black had witnessed the whole humiliating scene. Sitting in the doorway of my master's bar, the Crow smiled discreetly. Worse, he pulled out his notepad and scribbled something down. I saw Docta mutter an angry word, an insult for sure. He nervously stamped out his cigarette, although it wasn't finished, and said out loud, "We should run that owl right out of this quarter."

That was the worst thing ever said about the writer of the city's dregs. Like a deer in the headlights, I realized just what the scamming engineer—that very one who'd just escaped from his life by cowering in my master's courtyard—just what he would have had in mind for me, if only I were a man. For I, too, was always observing men and doing nothing but. I was on the philosopher's side, if only out of pure professional solidarity among observers. But then, what else could I do? Running that man out of this quarter soon became the engineer's obsession; he tried repeatedly to convince people he was right. Once I heard him confessing to my master, "I just don't like that guy. He's always sticking his big old eyes into things that aren't any of his business and he never says anything."

"He has the right to keep quiet, doesn't he?" replied Massa Yo, clearly more amused than anyone else by the idea of chasing off one customer when another batted his eyelashes.

Panther added, "Besides, why do you want him to talk anyway?"

The cigarette vendor burst out laughing and said, "Yeah, why should the Crow have to say anything when Panther already speaks for all of us here, huh?"

"Let him speak . . ." stammered the engineer. "Damn, just let him say something . . . , anything at all. Like everybody else . . . I tell you, his silence is driving me crazy. But mostly it's his eyes. Yes, his eyes. He can spend his whole life in the cemetery if he wants, as long as he stops haunting us."

"You mean haunting you."

"He's not haunting anybody," my master corrected. "He drinks his *jobajo* and watches the street. That's all."

"Precisely, he *watches* the street," said the scandalized engineer, tragically stressing the word "watches." "He's always watching and never says a thing. Everybody comes to tell him their story, he takes down notes and never says a thing. If he's mute, then he should be blind and deaf as well. I tell you, that man is dangerous!"

Nobody took the engineer's warnings seriously, for I suspect that, like me, everybody in the quarter knew for just what sort of person the eyes of the man in black really were dangerous.

7

The day after his humiliating game of hide-and-seek, the engineer made an ostentatious and unashamed appearance in front of my master's bar, holding the hand of the kid the girl had left with him the night before. He must have told himself it was the only way to wash the shame from his face. As he stood next to his child, his eyes expressed a pride I couldn't explain. He was laughing like crazy, like someone who'd won the lottery but stupidly sent the ticket through the wash in his pocket. I didn't bark out my amusement, though, because I was happy that our man—who only the night before hid there in the shadows of the crates, swimming against the current, running from his destiny in the form of a woman and child—had been able to reconcile so soon with his humanity. He pointed out his kid to my master's customers, saying, quite seriously, that he was a father, yes he was. And I understood that. Some of my master's customers patted his kid on the head. The cigarette vendor gave him a piece of candy and asked his name. The child stared at him with his naive eyes. Docta was the one who replied. "Takou," he said smiling. "Takou, just like his dad."

Some said the kid's face was the spitting image of his father's. Docta just shrugged his shoulders all the more. "What do you expect? I'm his father, after all."

Hearing that, the Panther Nzui Manto burst out laughing. "Yesterday you were hiding and today you're his father?" he exclaimed with surprise. "No, no, no, we're really gonna see it all in this quarter, huh?"

The little old man shook his head, adding, "*Menmà*, you have to do more than just make a baby to call yourself a father, huh!"

Imitating the engineer's voice, he went on, "'I'm his father.' You even dare to say that out loud, after you ran and hid when his mother came around. Now that your parents have agreed to feed him, all of a sudden you're his father, huh? Do you think I don't know? You're the ones filling up this quarter with little delinquents and, with no shame at all, you call yourself 'fathers.' But then, *bak a yùn**—we'll see whether this kid doesn't do you one better. Do you even really know what a father is?"

"And you're gonna tell me, right?" interrupted Docta, arrogantly.

Later he'll say that he, Docta, the scamming strategist, had decided to break it off with his kid's mother. She thought she could hurt him by leaving the kid with him when he'd already decided to take on his paternal responsibilities. "So take 'em on!" was the reply he heard. "It's your duty, after all." Panther couldn't believe his ears and shook his head repeatedly. "What a generation of failures!" he said, dumbstruck. "What a generation of irresponsible fools! What a generation of do-nothings!"

And off Docta went with his kid, parading a pride he alone saw. Off he went, a troubled man, according to the little old man's myriad words of indignation. To tell the truth, the humiliating episode I told you about in the last chapter was nothing much. Just the second act in the full-length drama of his humiliation. Rosalie's real entrance into Madagascar had come before the Crow's stare, and it was much more spectacular, too. Let me give you all the details.

It seems that the *kongossa* on the street had told Rosa Rosa Rose that her Docta in heat was now chasing after a certain Virginie and that he wasn't yet ready to learn his lessons from the long dry spell she'd orchestrated for him. The girl came to Madagascar to "see with her own eyes," but hadn't been able to find "that do-nothing Docta." She sat down next to the cigarette vendor and waited. She had waited a long time, stewing in her anger. Then, suddenly, there was Virginie, coming up the road. The cigarette vendor bent over and whispered "that's her" in her ear. Immediately I saw Rosalie's eyes burn red. "Ah ha!" she said, "so you're Virginie, huh?"

She got up out of her seat like a lioness ready to pounce. Virginie didn't know what to say. The poor girl didn't yet understand what was going on; or maybe she was a great actress, pretending not to understand anything. She just ignored her attacker and continued on her way. But could she? The other one had jumped in front of her and blocked her path. Some of my master's customers came running, as if they'd just been waiting for it to happen. A few men tried to separate them. But who could calm Rosalie's anger? The rage born of her disappointment, a rage compounded by her exhaustion from having waited too long for that "do-nothing Docta," yes, her explosive rage set her eyes aboil. Rosalie pushed away the dozens of hands holding her back. There she stood, Woman herself—yes, a crazy woman, who burst out laughing. And Rosa Rosa Rose said to everyone, her voice full of contempt, "So *that's* Docta's new conquest-o!"

No one had laughed with her, because everyone in this quarter knew just who the "that" she was talking about was. Mini Minor's mysteries and the police commissioner's threats were all still fresh in everyone's mind. But that Rosalie, clearly she just didn't give a damn about the neighborhoods' myths.

"And there I thought she was some kind of Miss Universe," she screamed, "or maybe a Miss World, or even a Miss Cameroon, or at least a Miss Yaoundé, *bèbèlè*. Just look at her will you! She's not even Miss Madagascar-o!"

As she spoke she gave Virginie a once-over, from head to toe, toe to head, and again from head to toe. Arrogantly, she turned up her nose and asked, "That's all he could find? A *rumta*!"

The crowd, which had grown even larger around the verbal protagonists after hearing the irate girl's fighting words, jumped and rumbled with enthusiasm. Virginie, who shared her aunt's peaceful tranquillity, still hadn't replied. Women crossed the street so as not to miss anything of the scene playing out in front of my master's bar. Their voices rose up, trying to forestall the worst. And yet near me I heard some—who were too eager to take Virginie's side or else were casting themselves as apostles of peace—mutter "that spoiled child turns up her nose whenever she passes by here, like she was some kind of queen," and that she needed to be taught a lesson. The *kongossa* started rolling. Soon, from the voices of all those gathered, chaos was

born. A punch was thrown. I heard a faint cry and then a brouhaha exploded around the fighting women.

The hands of the girl with the kid were now grabbing her
rival's hair. With an authoritative hand, the cigarette vendor
pulled them apart. He was quickly joined by the little old man,
who proffered a plethora of proverbs that clearly neither of the
girls wanted to hear. They kept shouting insults at each other
over everyone's head. The crowd, already brought to a boil by
their blows, grew more animated with each word. Some voices
said they should let the women fight. "Just try to touch me
again!" threatened Virginie.

She was holding on to her own hair, just as determined as her
foe, although she was clearly still in pain. The other woman's fury
had taken her by surprise, but her seething face revealed her growing rage. Rosalie's mouth just wouldn't stay shut: "Try again, 'just
try to touch me again,'" she parroted in a theatrical style that
amused the crowd. "What are you gonna do to me, huh?"

"Just try and you'll see!"

"See what you are?"

"Wha-wha-wha-what!"

"That's just what you expect from young things. They steal
somebody else's husband and then play the innocent. Just know
that when you crossed me—Rosalie-Sylvie-Yvette Menzui, Rosalie for short, or even Rosa Rosa Rose—you made a big mistake."

As she declined her multiple names, she hit herself three times
on the chest.

"Besides, you should know I'm Docta's legitimate woman.
I'm his home base, you hear me? Yes, I had his kid and he's
going to marry me, you stuck-up sleaze!"

Hearing the word "stuck-up," Virginie tried to free herself
from the hands of the men holding her back. Rosalie hiked up
her clothes and assumed a fighter's stance. The little old man
flexed his muscles. He swore up and down, but his words were
ineffectual. He had put himself on the battlefield. The crowd's
thousand arms were of no avail against the rush of the two
angry girls. Soon there was no one but Panther keeping them
apart. Their blows blinded him. He took too many on the head.

Once again the crowd's voice rose up into chaos. I saw the little old man try to protect his head. It was as if the two battling women had turned on him. Clearly his white hair didn't impress them. The cigarette vendor had to pull him out of there and flex his own muscles in front of the girls to bring their anger to a halt.

"Let go of me," said Rosalie, finally restrained by a number of arms. "I'm gonna kill her!"

"I'll show her!" said Virginie, who'd finally burst out of her timid shell. "What a witch!"

*"Bi fang nda-a!"** insisted Panther, "Let it be!" But no one was listening to him.

When Virginie's rage began to cool off, she exclaimed: "People are really impossible! So now you're claiming Docta is yours? But didn't you throw him out, saying he was a real loser? And now you're chasing after him? Let me tell you, he doesn't want you anymore, dearie!"

"Uh, uh, don't forget I'm the one who paid for his school," the other stammered.

"School? Your mama! Just tell me what he's doing with all that schooling, huh! Besides, he might just as well burn that diploma now! If he doesn't come and kiss my ass, where is he gonna find work in this country?"

"That little Virginie sure has a mouth on her, huh?" more than one remarked. Rosalie's rage was reaching its highest point. A movement in the crowd held her back. I heard her begging everyone to let her teach "that *tchotchoro*" a lesson. But that wasn't going to happen. Fortunately, her voice soon became condescending, as if she'd suddenly realized her own true stature.

"And just who am I quarreling with, anyway-o?" she asked the crowd. Then she turned to Virginie and added: "You should know, you're at least three levels beneath me!"

The other woman's unstoppable voice immediately replied, "'Three levels beneath you'! So you're coming to argue about a man with someone 'three levels beneath you,' is that right?"

But looking down from the heights of her newly discovered grandeur, Rosalie finally decided to leave. She gave in to the old man's words and to the pleas from the crowd restraining each of her violent gestures. She agreed to get in the taxi someone stopped for her. Virginie's voice savored the unexpected victory of her foe's retreat. "Hey, you're leaving?" cried Mini Minor's niece, jumping so she could peer over the shoulders of the people holding her back.

Rosalie wanted to get back out of the taxi. But the little old man said, "*Menmà,* just let it be."

Then he shut the taxi door again. After she had left, the quarter heard Virginie rant and rave about the woman who'd come to provoke her in her own quarter. She had her aunt's temper. Once they'd begun to flow, her words seemed endless. And now that her adversary had left her the field, there was no stopping her. Even after the taxi had whisked Rosalie off into the distance, Virginie shouted at her absent foe, "You can be sure I'll wipe my ass with that Docta of yours!"

It was the day after this historic brawl that Rosalie had returned, determined to abandon her kid with the engineer and the quarter. Ah Rosa Rosa Rose! She would let Docta scrape rock bottom, if that's what he wanted. In the meantime, he could just take care of his kid himself!

8

Docta's repeated humiliations were on everyone's lips. Most of all, the street remembered his repeated groveling, which Virginie broadcast widely. Docta was hit with the nickname "la Torche," short for "torchon," or ass-wipe, and sometimes even called "Totor." He wasn't proud of the name and swore at everyone who called him that. A while later, Mini Minor herself came and screamed in front of my master's bar, too. Returning to her overly polite turns of phrase, she swore she'd have any "ranting lunatics who bothered her girl thrown in the slammer." She'd shown up a little late, if truth be told, so once she'd gone, my master's customers laughed behind her back. The memory of the jousting match that had swirled around the niece of the "small no be sick" with the record-breaking receding hairline was still too vivid; yes, too vivid were the images of the "torchon." Yet let me say this: the rumor sawing away at the little woman's grandeur might well be insidious, it was in no way irreverent. That's why, when a voice rose above the quarter's whispers one day and called out "Etienne!" as the police commissioner was passing by, all my master's customers were surprised. Who had called out? What treacherous voice had dared to call Power by his private first name just when the police commissioner wanted to lose his silhouette in the neighborhood's tortuous shadows so he could finally get back to his "second office," his mistress's *chantier*? Maybe it was the uncontrollable voice of rumor itself? Or perhaps the perfidious voice of those with guilty consciences? Maybe it was a voice torn from the endless dream of these jabbering streets? Whatever it was, when the man, hearing his name called out, stopped and turned his smiling black face to greet his mistress (the only one around here who'd ever called him that), he found the courtyard of my master's bar staring at him with the naive fear of an innocent kid. Immediately the eyes of the man of order turned blood red. His face lit up like a flame. His rage zeroed in on the trembling cigarette vendor, who immediately became the guilty party. "You wretch, you dare call me 'Etienne' as if I'm your equal?" he screamed, grabbing him by the collar and hitting him on the back of the neck.

With my master's customers as his witnesses he screamed, "So you're the one causing trouble in this neighborhood, huh!"

"It wasn't me who called you, chief!" said the man, pleading.

"So who was it?"

"I don't know, chief!"

"I'll show you just who this Etienne you dare to address so familiarly is!"

I saw the cigarette vendor's knees cross into a capital X, as if he were trying desperately not to piss in his pants. His voice grew even more pleading. "Forgive me, chief!" he begged, almost in tears.

The police commissioner's face lit up.

"So it was you who called me!"

"No, chief!"

"Then why are you saying 'forgive me'"?

"Just because, chief!"

"You want to be a wise guy! You're the one up to tricks in the quarter, trying to give everyone a bad name, huh! You're the one causing trouble! I'm gonna throw you in the slammer!"

As the scene played out, instead of moving closer to where the arrest was taking place, my master's customers made themselves scarce, slinking into the shadows of The Customer Is King and leaving the guilty cigarette vendor to face his destiny alone. He'd pay the price for the thousand whispers that had been following Mini Minor for some time now, and Virginie too; it was the cigarette vendor alone who'd pay for Virginie's clothes, tattered in the brawl with Rosalie. He was the scapegoat who would wash clean the *chantier*'s trampled honor, the wretch chosen to answer publicly for the suicidal boredom of Madagascar's streets. He wrung his hands and begged in vain.

"Uh, forgive me, chief, even if it was me, I won't do it again."

The commissioner was jubilant, "There, you've confessed! First you wanted to be a wise guy. You know I can confiscate your stock of cigarettes?"

"Yes, chief!"

The commissioner undid the handcuffs hanging from his belt. He had a prisoner, a man he could teach a lesson. I barked out my indignation, but couldn't rouse the local men from their torpor. One or two voices were raised, but not too loudly. To tell the truth, they just grumbled and left it at that. In the profusion of his pleas, the cigarette vendor may have made a gesture of surrender, which the commissioner immediately took for an attempt to escape. Before I could even realize what had happened, the cigarette vendor's face was already in the dust, his legs spread wide in a V. The man in the suit kept the vendor's mouth to the ground as he violently cuffed his hands. I barked out for all I was worth. A lot of people came running, curious bystanders. "So, mister, you wanted to escape," said the commissioner.

"What did I do, chief?"

"Resisting arrest."

Only once he was cuffed was the cigarette vendor allowed to get up. His face was a mask of dust that made his sad eyes stand out. Just then, with a murmur, the crowd let the Crow through. As if he refused to see what was going on right in front of his eyes, he walked right up to the cigarette vendor's display and ordered a cigarette. The commissioner took it upon himself to inform him, "There'll be no more cigarettes today."

You've got to believe me—it was as if he'd been drawn out of his silent shell by the overly flip remark from this representative of the State in person. Suddenly, the ever-silent Crow asked the one question I had been waiting for, "Why?"

Yes, why? And the commissioner, who obviously wasn't used to answering whys with becauses, let loose with a "For no good reason, so go tell your mama about it!"

And he added, to end things once and for all, "Get out of here, you polliwog, or I'll throw you in the slammer too!"

But as his hand was rising up to intercept the next passing taxi, it was held back by another question from the man in black, this time a clearly sacrilegious one. "Tell me, sir, do you have a warrant for his arrest?"

The quarter's crowds were gathering around the event. I watched the eyes of the men all around echo the difficult questions of the man in black. It seemed that one last dose of courage was born in each person's gut. I even saw my master come out from behind his counter to see what was happening. Voices grew even louder. Latent complaint turned into overt protest. Rumor turned into questions repeated right out in the open. I heard the term "arrest warrant" several times. I also heard the term "judicial review," which I didn't really understand, but it seemed to be an important element in the general argument. And then I heard the word "justice," then the words "injustice," "dictatorship," and "new deal," the name "Biya," and finally the sentence, "Cameroon is Cameroon." Maybe it's that sentence that made speech explode like a bomb, for all of a sudden people pulled back in fear, as if the sky had suddenly been torn apart by a thunderbolt only I hadn't heard. Yes, it seemed the sky sent its truth crashing down on the street. Suddenly an empty space cleared out around the commissioner and his two prisoners. When I, Mboudjak, saw the little black thing that had made all the neighborhood men back up, I couldn't stop myself from barking out in surprise: the police commissioner held a gun in his hand. It seems his overloaded cop brain exploded under the pressure of too many questions from the crowd. He spat out a reddish mixture on the ground and bellowed at the Crow, who curiously hadn't budged, "You're a member of the opposition!" Then he added, "I'll show you!"

That day I learned that being labeled a "member of the opposition" was worse than being accused of a crime. Our man in black didn't seem overly impressed by it though. For him, "opposition" was nothing more than a word in the French language.

"You're coming with me to the police station!" bellowed the commissioner.

Aiming his little black gun at his two prisoners, he hailed the first passing taxi; it stopped immediately. He ordered the vehicle's two passengers to get out. The street just let him do it. I barked wildly. I really didn't yet understand what had brought down the thunder, but mostly I was outraged that all the men in the quarter let themselves be dominated by one man, even if he did have a gun in his hand. Yet my barks seemed to resonate in the street and the courtyard of my master's bar only to emphasize their emptiness and underline even more their mortal silence. That's when, carried away by the volcano boiling in my belly, I threw myself on the commissioner's left calf and sank my fangs into it. The man in the suit screamed like someone having his guts torn out and sent a bullet flying through the air over the quarter.

Life froze. Chickens squawked out their surprise. I lifted my head and locked onto the round and threatening eye of the gun pointed right at me, as the voice of the commissioner roared overhead. "Get this mutt out of here or I'll put him on ice right now!"

His eyes rolled back into his head. Even with the gun pointed right at me, I started barking again. I stood up tall and bared my fangs. This time I hurled insults at the esteemed commissioner, insults he surely didn't get. But I didn't give a damn. I barked and leaped forward on my front paws. I was a pure ball of anger. Truthfully, at that moment I really didn't give a damn about death. I would've even bit the smoking muzzle of his little black gun, if a big kick in my behind hadn't sent me flying into my mistress's stand like a sack of sweet potatoes. I blacked out for a moment and soon opened my eyes to an orchestral ballet of stars. I shook my head to make sure I wasn't dead. I saw the sun go red and dance; the street's brothels sagged over even further and clouds fell from the sky at my paws. I heard the syncopated sound of invisible spirits, the otherworldly call of the muezzin, the endless cry of a waterfall, the uninterrupted hum of passing limousines, then the multiple voices of the ever-chattering crowd. One voice alone, which I recognized as my master's, convinced me I was still alive. The voice was cruelly giving me an order I already knew by heart: "Mboudjak, get out!"

When I shook off my torpor, my first reflex was to flee. Without knowing why, I ran and hid in my master's bar. It was only once I was behind the counter that I realized I had escaped from my death a long time before. I stumbled back out. I tried one final bark that elicited only another threat from my master. His bar was empty. His customers were still gathered in front of the frightful road, gazing together off into the distance, where the commissioner had long since disappeared with his two prisoners. So they had all just let them go without moving a muscle, I thought, feeling let down. One of Massa Yo's customers even found the courage to say, "If you look hard enough, you'll find it."

My master ordered me to stay in his bar, not to budge. He hit me several times on the head, as if to drive home his lessons for survival. "Do you even know? That man could have killed you!" he said, adding, "Really, dogs are sooooo stupid-ooooo!"

One man said dogs don't recognize guns, that dogs don't even know what death is until they're already dead, adding that we're like chickens who've never caught on about the hand that rings their neck every Christmas. He concluded by saying my master shouldn't hold it against me because I was just an animal. I lowered my ears. The men's conversation quickly turned back to the cigarette vendor and the philosopher. I took advantage of my master's distraction to go hide in the courtyard of his bar. I saw him lift his hand; I sidestepped the blow. I heard his voice curse me. Once at a safe distance, however, I didn't hesitate to bark out just what I thought of his behavior: a coward, that's what he was. Yes, nothing but a coward! I saw him shake a threatening finger at me, promising to tan my hide if I didn't come back right that instant. To tell the truth, at that moment I didn't give a damn about his threats.

I barked out my disappointment for the whole quarter to hear!

9

If the residents of Madagascar did nothing, as far as I know, to free the cigarette vendor, they did less than nothing to free the Crow. Having been labeled a member of the opposition right there in broad daylight condemned him to oblivion. That crazy word had roused a common fear in each person. Was it just a fear of politics? I think it was worse than that: pure and simple cowardice. Yes. Had my master even closed his bar to run and help the cigarette vendor, the man he killed time with each and every day? Like everyone in the quarter, he had very quickly washed his hands of it and went on selling his beers, calmly and without shame. In his defense, one might say he didn't close up shop because little groups of commentators had sprung up, quickly filling his overturned crates—and giving him his receipts for the day. He wasn't going to let a ripe sale slip by like that, right in front of his nose. He had simply closed his neighbor's cigarette stand and gone about his business. I realized with horror just what a friendship born of shared misery is worth to men.

"Didn't I tell you?" Docta pointed out, when he learned the man in black had been arrested.

Without too much grumbling, the regulars of The Customer Is King adjusted to the absence of the cigarette vendor and of the Crow, who had flown to his defense. A few hours after their arrest, Panther's voice cut through the guilty whispers in the bar courtyard. *"Mbe ke di?"* he screamed. *"They* arrested the writer-a? *Sè?* When? Why? Which way did they go? How? I don't believe it! *A tat'te!* It's a lie!"

The Panther Nzui Manto hadn't been there at the fateful moment. His late appearance in the shadow of my suffering gave me a sudden hope of courage. In the midst of everyone's silence, he multiplied his questions in Medumba. As the little old man said "they," his eyebrows shot up in surprise. With his eyelids fluttering, he angrily scanned the crowd, which immediately rediscovered its own shock and starting telling what had happened. Panther seemed thunderstruck, and I hoped to see a man born at last in the courtyard of my master's bar. The little old man shook his wrinkled body and exploded in even more questions. He turned back toward my master. "And you, Massa Yo, what did you do?"

"I don't get involved in politics-o," he replied.

A man's voice shot back, "Isn't everybody afraid of their 'big brother' the gun?"

"Aha!" screamed a young man, "just what gun, anyway?" He lifted his arm, revealing the dark circle spreading beneath it, and waved the air around in front of his face. "Cowardice has a thousand excuses," he said scornfully.

The voice of another of my master's customers interrupted, "So even those who weren't there can bitch about it now-o?"

I watched these men, who began and ended their days chatting in front of my master's bar, suddenly realize they had a lot of responsibilities. Their faces, molded by their habitual boisterous laziness, suddenly took on the seriousness of a thousand duties. One after the other, they screamed,

"What do you mean, cowardice? Hey, I've got kids to feed!"

"My wife's expecting a baby."

"I'm not into politics."

"I couldn't go to the police station. I still haven't paid my taxes yet. You never know."

"What do you mean, you never know?"

"Do you want me to get arrested like the philosopher did?"

On that extraordinary day when the cigarette vendor and the writer were arrested, I learned that my master's customers were actually all businessmen, to put it politely. Most of all, I learned that men are not brothers.

"Besides," one man said, "it's just *siscia,** threats. All he had to do was give him a little something and he would've been set free. Everything the commissioner did was just to get a *tchoko,** am I right? It was just a bunch of noise. But what do you want? Cheapness is gonna kill the people in this quarter. Instead of giving his share, he holds back."

Panther was outraged. "*Ye maleh,** just look at this country of Mbiya's, eh!"

He turned back to my master again and said, "What I don't understand, no no no, is that you, Massa Yo, just keep selling your beers as if nothing happened."

My master didn't answer. He stood there, comfortably ensconced in the bed of his cowardice. His eyes even avoided mine. The little old man didn't stop at that. "He's your friend, isn't he?" he said. "Didn't I say you had nothing but beers in your head? Money's your only friend, right? I'm sure one day we're gonna hear you've sold Soumi to Famla. Here's a guy you spend all your days with. You see the police haul him off, and you stay calm. As for the rest of you, didn't you all come tell your stories to the writer? He was arrested right in front of your eyes, and why? Because he wanted to defend one of you. You let him get hauled off and did nothing about it. Yeah, and *you* call yourselves men!"

He said "you" almost like he was spitting in disgust on the street's tar, almost like I, Mboudjak, would have lifted my hind leg and pissed on the door of my master's bar. Finding himself stripped bare by the insult, Massa Yo came to, shook himself, and pointed his threatening finger in the little old man's face. "And you, just what are you waiting for to go and free him, huh? Always sticking your nose into things. Always mouthing off, doing the *web-web*. You know the police station he's at, right? So what are you waiting for? Aren't you the Chief around here? Am I right? Let me know if you need money for the taxi!"

He finished his tirade in the darkness of his bar. His angry, wounded voice thundered in the courtyard of The Customer Is King. Soon he came back and held some coins out to the little old man. "Take it, here's money for the taxi," he said. "What are you waiting for?"

Panther looked at him with disdain and, for an instant, fell silent. Then, as if the sky had just revealed something obvious to him, softly and deliberately he said, looking my master straight in the eyes, "*Menmà,* if I still had your strength, I'd have done something other than sit behind my counter and watch life go by!"

Ah! I said to myself, men do like to hide their cowardice behind foggy theories. In the end, I realized this little old man wasn't made of anything different from my master. His big mouth, which invented such incredible stories, only stuttered out his silence when faced with life's tragedies. He told stories of the superfluous so he could keep silent about the essential. A chatterer, that's what he was, nothing more. A big mouth, like all Massa Yo's customers. Someone who built castles in the air with words. At best, History would have to be made without him, or rather, with just the strength of his words. A wizard of ineffectual words, that's what he was.

A few hours later, everyone was relieved to see a taxi stop in front of my master's bar and magically spit out the cigarette vendor. Yes, it was a revelation! The joy of Madagascar's residents would have made you believe that words alone had unlocked the cigarette vendor's handcuffs. But the cigarette vendor wasn't taken in by this newly invented, and unmerited, pride that quickly took over the street. He walked right by the thousand curious faces that surrounded him, went into my master's bar, and ordered a beer. He uttered not even one word to appease all the avid eyes, which reflected too clearly the thousand questions exploding in everyone's hearts. He paid his bill with dignity and, as he left, said to the street, as if he'd learned from his troubles to appreciate the smallest gestures of man's humanity, "Thank you to whoever closed my stand in my absence."

10

For a long time the writer stopped coming to watch the languor of the streets in front of my master's courtyard. I didn't hear anyone worry about him either. Docta no longer kept quiet about how relieved he was. He waxed on like some kind of visionary: with the bad seed cast out, the health of the community had been restored. For Madagascar's lively street, it was the Crow who had caused his own downfall by asking iconoclastic questions. Some even insisted he'd been the one cocky enough to call the police commissioner "Etienne." Who else in the quarter would have done it? Listening to the endless *kongossa* of these men of short memory really made me sick. All I saw when I looked at the courtyard of The Customer Is King was the face of betrayal and the acceptance of fear. "Ah!" I wondered, "Why do men have to be so inhuman?" Most of all, I barked out to the street—which, for its part, wasn't listening—my one and only question: "Where is Man?" Each and every time I barked, my master's foot rose up to silence my muzzle. Sometimes my master went so far as to pick up a crate and throw it at me, as if he wanted to do me in. I dodged it instinctively. As I reached the end of my questions, I found myself moving further away from Massa Yo's bar.

One day, without really thinking too much about it, I put one paw in front of the other and found myself behind the Party Headquarters. Seeing a mountain of garbage rising up before me, I suddenly felt hungry. I touched, I sniffed, I tasted. The scent of garbage soon hung heavy around my head. I rediscovered my joie de vivre. All of a sudden, it was like I'd escaped from the prison of an overly small bar courtyard and from the restrictions imposed on me by science. I let myself get carried away and wandered in the unknown, in the Infinite of Art. I was once again a vagabond, a Bohemian, and I accepted the chaos. With delight I tore into the morsels the garbage offered up to my teeth. I tore away with all my heart and soul. Too long, I told myself, I had stayed among men for too long. Carried away by my newfound freedom, I crouched, I even lay right down in the stench, amid the flies' never-ending song. In the depths of the garbage I discovered a shoe with tantalizing leather, then a can stamped "Made in America," and finally a piece of cloth that smelled like the feast of the decade.

Far from my master's bar, at the bottom of the biggest garbage pile in Madagascar, I rediscovered life. I was hard at work losing myself in its convulsing belly when I heard the echo of children's voices coming from the window of the Party Headquarters. I perked up my ears and barked enthusiastically. Soon Soumi's face peered out through a windowpane, broke into a broad smile, and said to someone inside that it was me.

"Come!" he said from the door he'd hurried to open.

Were Soumi and I going to reconcile in the shadow of the garbage cans? Yes, it was the dawn of another era. Still, I trembled with fear. That far away from his father's house, I wasn't going let myself fall victim to his cruelty again. The kid Soumi was talking to was none other than that little Takou with the volcanic mother. It was his presence, and my curiosity about Docta and Rosalie's kid, that drew me back toward my little friend. I pretended to have a short memory. See, I'm not a bad dog. I didn't jump on Soumi and exact my long-standing revenge, but I stayed on my guard in order to avoid any new fury on his part. I barked out my surprise to see him there. He didn't answer me. My voice echoed in the emptiness of the Party Headquarters, like the cry of evil spirits. I saw Takou's face darken. "That's your dog?" he asked.

"Yes," said Soumi, suddenly my friend again, "don't you know him?"

"Keep making him bark and they'll find out we're here."

Surprisingly, it was Takou who looked at me suspiciously. My little master reassured him, saying that loud voices inside the Party Headquarters couldn't be heard at all outside. To show him, he let out a sort of animal cry that made me jump, and said, smiling, "Only you can hear me."

Soumi was showing Takou the paths to freedom the neighborhood had to offer. In a hush, he pulled a cigarette out of his bag and, trembling, lit it. "I hope you don't mind," he said to me, letting the smoke flow out of his nostrils.

Suddenly his eyes opened wide and he coughed violently.

"If you don't know how to smoke, give it to me."

That was Takou. With a confident hand, he took the cigarette. He took a long drag and blew circles over his head with the smoke. Suddenly he was an angel. With just one action, he'd established his ascendancy over my little master, who, for his part, was still holding onto his sides and coughing loudly. Then he heard his friend say, "Cigarettes aren't for everyone, you know."

Takou was smaller than Soumi, but he suddenly seemed older. I seemed to have turned up just as a battle for control was taking place, right when they were deciding who would be whose master. Children alone hold the secret of real surprises, that's for sure. I'm sure it was the unexpected nature of every-thing that took place that day in the Party Headquarters, events that were worlds away from my daily life in the courtyard of my master's bar, that gave me back my taste for taking walks far from The Customer Is King, trailing behind my master's son. Sometimes I just let myself wander along, but most of the time, as if by some innate reflex, I headed back to the garbage behind the Party Headquarters.

In fact, I was drawn much more to the chaos of that garbage than to a final reunion with my master's son and his sidekick. I hadn't really forgotten the cruelty that can brew beneath the candor of smart-aleck kids, and I didn't seek out their friend-ship on purpose. Besides, I soon discovered to my horror that it was Takou, egged on by his friend Soumi, who had called out "Etienne" when the commissioner was passing by and, without flinching, brought the thunder down on the backs of two men. To tell the truth, I was starting to get to know Docta's son. But, really, why should I be surprised? Takou was just a child, like Soumi. So later, when I saw him handing money to the ciga-rette vendor from time to time, I already knew he was up to no good.

"Who's it for?" the surprised cigarette vendor asked.

Docta's child had the naive look of a saint. He avoided look-ing at me, I think, so as not to lose his cool. In the end, he was already making his mark on this neighborhood, even though he was its most recent arrival. "It's for the man over there," he said, pointing at the street.

The cigarette vendor didn't ask for anything more specific. He didn't even look at the street corner Takou was pointing to, he just gave him the cigarettes he wanted.

11

On several other occasions I caught Takou smoking, hunkered back in the recess of a wall. It was always some local man who'd sent him, or so he told the cigarette vendor. And sometimes it was true. Then the kid would stop on his way back to try out the cigarettes he'd bought. Once he got carried away and finished a cigarette from the pack a deliveryman had asked him to fetch. When he brought them to the man, he said the vendor had made a mistake counting. That day the engineer's son's delinquency was almost exposed, because the man wanted to get things straight. He spent a long time arguing about it with the cigarette vendor, who wasn't going to admit to a mistake he knew he hadn't made. Takou put on his most naive face for the men and no one dared accuse him.

Only Panther, fuming in a corner of the courtyard of my master's bar, raised his voice and said: "*Jou me lou thùp mbe,** is that child gonna do his father one better? This is my son, this is my son! All he does is brag about it! And—am I right?—there goes his son, already ripping people off around here!"

"What's so surprising about that?" said my master. "Like father, like son."

So he forbade his son to play with Takou. Soumi acquiesced. I barked out my laughter, for I knew I'd catch him several more times, stubbornly sharing in little Takou's secret vices. Whenever I catch him, he'll shoo me away with some threatening gesture. So I'll steer clear of his secret, without asking for any reward, because I know full well what he's capable of. I'll just put one paw in front of the other, without ever giving too much thought to the direction I take.

On my walks, I usually followed my canine intuition. Or else I let myself be led by the wind. Or I followed the call of the sun running across the sky. On I walked, sniffing at the little things lying about on the ground. And on I walked, taking note of how dirty the quarter's streets were. The strays knew about my status as a bar dog and always looked at me enviously. I had made a vow never again to sink into their shit. I kept my distance from men, of course, but I wasn't a stray. None of the neighborhood dogs dared bother me with any of their stupid banter. Even the three-legged communist dog held his tongue when I passed by. Sometimes he grumbled something in which I'd catch only the words "capitalist dog." I'd perk up my ears and my tail; I didn't give a damn about his predictions of bad luck. He'd finally accepted that I was better than he. So on I walked, sometimes stopping beneath a tree and lifting my hind leg to douse it with urine. Then I'd keep on walking.

Going nowhere in particular, I wandered through Madagascar.

Once when I was out walking, I found myself in front of the gate of Mini Minor's *chantier*. Once again I froze in front of the big sign with the drawings of two dog heads that read: "Warning: dangerous dogs." Soon I heard their many, strident barks. I remembered their prior assault on my puny self and raised my voice to let them know I was there. To my great surprise, all I got in response was more of their insults. "Is that you again?" one of them asked.

"Dirty mutt," said another, "how dare you come back here?!"

They ordered me out of their fiefdom on the spot, to get out and take my stench with me. What's more, they called me a "stray." I wasn't going to put up with that. "Come and make me leave," I said, knowing the gate was closed.

The meanness of their remarks left me no choice but to respond. Scrambling with my paws, I pulled myself up on the wall surrounding this house of mystery and, ignoring all those written warnings, barked out my opinions to its canine inhabitants.

"You're worthless," I told them. "You're a cannibal's dogs!" And I added, "Just wait until your mistress eats you, huh, then you'll really have something to bark about!"

They replied that they'd rather end up in a plate of *ndole,* accompanied by ripe plantains and washed down with some Beaujolais, than to rot in the neighborhood's malodorous gutters. They said they'd never seen a dog that stank like I did, that I was the epitome of suffering, that they could see death in my eyes. I had to defend my dignity. But it was like I was barking at nothing. I couldn't catch a glimpse of their house over the *chantier*'s gates; I imagined a majestic palace, surrounded in lush green. So I answered the dogs without seeing them. Soon, though, I recognized Virginie's voice ordering them to be quiet, and then Mini Minor's, which said, "They're still sending their mutts here to soil my walls."

Too busy with the concert of my replies to the dogs, I didn't pay any attention to what was said. I heard a voice ordering them to calm down. "Only the Sanitation Department will be able to give us any peace in this quarter," said another. Then

Virginie's voice said, "I'm sure it's the dog of that Massa Yo again."

"You mean that dirty, mangy mutt that bit Etienne?"

"Yes, Auntie."

"And he dares to come back here? I'll show him."

I heard a furious tumult tear through the house. I didn't wait to find out for myself what she had in mind for me. Still, I came back to those walls from time to time. I wouldn't say I did it out of canine naïveté. Really, I came back to this closed-off *chantier* because I'd finally established some sort of line of communication with the many dogs living there. I'd come by and bark out my laughter over the gate to their fiefdom. I'd ask them what they got out of being prisoners all their life. "Are you tied up?" I'd ask. They said it was better to be a prisoner in a palace than to live in misery on an endless street. I told them it was a question of choice. They said they'd made their choice. Sometimes our discussion got a little heated, for each of us defended his lot in life. Our barks were loud, and from time to time I'd hear words demanding the dogs be kept quiet.

"It's that dog of Massa Yo's back again," said Virginie's voice. Mini Minor's exclaimed, "Again?"

"He's gonna get what's coming to him," said the first.

I didn't take these hints as threats. I didn't realize that by constantly barking at Mini Minor's gate, I was getting on her customers' nerves and putting my life in immediate danger. One day, right in the middle of my barked conversation, I was caught off guard by a rain of hot water thrown on me from the other side of the wall. Only my instinct for survival was able to save me from certain death. I howled and was surprised that the only response I got from the other side of the wall was a woman's cannibalistic laugh and the dogs' mocking barks. The dangerous dogs I'd been arguing with hadn't even deemed it necessary to warn me. I escaped from this adventure with the fur on my back all burned, and a much clearer sense of what the communist dog often referred to as "race consciousness." I ran to hide my pain in my master's bar. When Massa Yo found me racked with pain, the only thing he had to say was, "That'll teach you to go stealing fish from people."

I suffered in silence. Since the Mami Ndole affair, and since

the arrest of the cigarette vendor and the man in black, prudence kept all my master's clients from uttering Mini Minor's
name in anything louder than a whisper. No one knew just
how wide was the reach of her powers, and no one thought it
would be funny to find out. I knew that if Massa Yo found out
I'd been scalded at the home of that small-no-be-sick, he'd only
say, "You got what was coming to you."

Yes, I'd gone to the Chantier de la République against his
will. So now he didn't even glance at my painful coat. For weeks
on end I hunkered down in my suffering flesh. Sometimes in the
evening I'd go lie down on the grass growing by the side of the
road. I'd let the leaves' coolness penetrate deep into my body.
It did nothing to lessen my suffering. I hated all mankind, all
the dangerous dogs, and, of course, all their bourgeois masters.
Most of all, I detested Mini Minor, and I promised myself I'd
bite her calf, too, the next time she shook her behind and made
an appearance in front of my master's bar. Yes, I promised myself I'd give her the lesson I'd once given her lover. I promised
I'd show her that, just like her mutts, I had a fiefdom too.

So as to not miss the big day, I stayed around the house from
then on. But the misadventure of my boiling didn't just nail
me down again to the courtyard of The Customer Is King, it
also taught me to defend it like my own home. More than my
painful back, more than my master's threats, it was my vow
of revenge that turned me into a hard-boiled homebody. This
put an end to my wanderings for a while. But we dogs have a
very short memory. When I finally had a chance to punish Mini
Minor's calves, she managed to scare me off by revealing her
bizarre side once again. Sometime after my dousing, the little
woman stopped her car in front of my master's bar and asked
his customers to give her some help with one of her mysterious
boxes. I leaped up, stretching out my front paws and barking a slew of threats. Massa Yo threw his shoe at my head
and said threateningly, "Mboudjak, be quiet!" Then, falling all
over himself with politeness, he turned and reassured the little
woman, "Don't be afraid, ma'am, he doesn't bite."

As she followed the men carrying this other box, Mini Minor
snapped, with a shake of her hips, "You have to castrate dogs,
it makes them less stubborn."

That sentence shut me up. I pulled my tail back tight between my legs and ran to hide under my mistress's empty stand. I barked out my terror from afar. Suddenly the drama of the dangerous dogs from the Chantier de la République began to dance around in my head. What? Dangerous dogs, they were called? What do you mean, dangerous! Eunuchs chattering in the shelter of a witch's opulence, that's what they were.

Spread the word.

12

Then, without any warning, the Crow came back into our universe. One day I opened my eyes and there he was, sitting in plain sight right in front of my master's bar. I gave my head and body a good shake. I couldn't believe my eyes. I leaped up on my paws. Tossing aside all my scientific reserve, I ran to his feet and eagerly wagged my tail. I jumped up on him and loudly barked out my joy. He gave me a friendly pat on the back, lingering over my head and neck. His face beamed when he saw me. I have never felt such pleasure at being petted by a man's hand. I ran into my master's bar to tell him what he already seemed to know. Massa Yo's treacherous hand tried to hold me back. I sidestepped him and ran back to whip the philosopher's feet with my joyful tail once again. I barked to the street, calling it to come and witness the miracle. But as I soon realized, it turns out I was the only one happy about it. The whole street was paralyzed by the presence of the man whose fate had worried no one, and I mean no one.

The man in black spoke to me as if he were talking to those who hadn't rushed to welcome him back. "You're a very brave dog," he told me. "I thought a lot about you when I was in prison, you know."

I arched my back with pleasure. But then he grew indignant: "The flies are gonna destroy all your fur soon."

I grumbled out the real causes of my suffering to him and damned Mini Minor, whom I blamed for it all. I heard my master whistle for me to come. I pretended not to hear. I put my tail between my legs and let myself go with the Crow's caresses. Again he said to me, "A real hero, you are! This quarter's only hero!"

He was talking to me, but at the same time he was pouring out the lament of his aching soul. The betrayal of my master's customers had been harder on him than the weeks he'd spent in prison. Only the cigarette vendor came up to welcome him back. He offered the writer a cigarette, lit it, and then sat down on a crate next to him. I heard the two men exchange empty civilities, but silently pass over the one thing burning in their hearts; they refused to ask the one question that mattered: "Why?" I heard my master whistle for me again from behind his counter, and again I pretended not to hear. Then I saw him drag himself from the darkness of his hideaway and come put an open Guinness down in front of the Crow. Massa Yo came out of his lair several more times. From his stay in prison the man in black seemed to have inherited a bottomless pit in the hollow of his belly. Had his stay in prison turned him into just another common drunk, like those whose bare-assed failings I've already recounted? Several times, when the bottle was empty, the Crow lifted his elbow and signaled my master to bring him another. Filled with shame, Massa Yo kept busy. And me, I saw the eyes of the man in black get redder and redder after each bottle. He became someone else altogether. When he reached his limit, he got up and pulled out a roll of bills to pay his tab. I sighed. Still, I saw my master tremble. "It's on the house," he said, "leave it like that."

That's when I realized just how much disappointment the man in black had buried in his silences. First he paused and turned back as if to say "thanks," but then he leaned down to me and said, "Mboudjak, did you hear? Now your master's house is buying its own beer."

He petted my head and asked, "And you, do you think that's right?"

He was obviously refusing to speak directly to the men. Still, I didn't bark out my reply. And in fact, he didn't need any reply. He continued talking to me in the same monotonous tone. "Me, not at all."

He clucked his tongue several times and added, "Unless the house has lost its head, or else, hmmm, unless the house is feeling guilty for something!"

Turning back toward my master, he said in a calm voice, as if suddenly discovering the true face of his surprise, "My dear sir, I have always paid for the beers I drink, and this time won't be an exception. But I know shame is killing you. So above all, don't think you're going to wash your soul clean that easily, for the price of a few beers on the house!"

Then he addressed the courtyard of my master's bar. "For a few beers, you're not going to get off that easy, huh, you wicked men! You let your brother rot in prison, without saying or doing anything. Who could've believed it? Where's your courage? Where's your conscience? Where's your humanity? Are you trying to buy your humanity back for the price of a few beers? You think it's just that easy? Pathetic!"

Some people came closer, hoping to get a good look at the twists and turns of the drunken show put on by one of my master's customers. Those who knew the cause of the man in black's rage, however, kept their distance. I saw Docta, for example, disappear down the endless road. So the neighborhood's manufacturer of cowardice was tiptoeing his way out of there. Only the cigarette vendor moved closer to him, whispering a few words that only seemed to enrage him all the more. Then, as if bitten by some bug, the Crow flew off into the bar courtyard and repeatedly shoved his hand into his pants pocket, each time pulling out more bills. He held them out threateningly for the street to see. He waved them in the face of the misery all around, like they were a bouquet of flowers. The street froze. Even the women selling oranges, peanuts, and kola nuts left their goods and joined the growing crowd of curiosity seekers. I heard the cigarette vendor say to the angry philosopher, "My brother, let it be, that's the way things are in this quarter."

But who could bring the writer down from the high point of his anger? He had just come through an experience that had taught him what men really are: cowards. And now he was taking it out on the cigarette vendor. "You, too," he said, boiling with rage, "you got out of prison a while ago. What did you do?"

Nzui Manto intervened, forgetting that at that moment his words could only be superfluous. The Crow asked him the same question, "And you, what did you do?"

The little old man innocently raised his hands, saying, "Me? I wasn't there-o."

That only sent the other into even greater explosions of rage. He had begun to speak; he wasn't going to be silent anymore. "You weren't there either, huh. This guy didn't hear anything. That one saw nothing. This one's kid was sick. No one was there the day I got arrested, but all of you were there for your daily drink. You'll always be there for your date with the drug. That's the date I kept today, and I am gonna pay for my own dose of suicide, that's for sure!"

He showed the stacks of bills to the needy street. "I kept my date with your cowardice, oh yes. And this dear bartender tells me the house is buying my beers? Can the house buy a beer for everyone here? Can the house pick up the tab for the mass suicide it's orchestrating for this quarter? Why don't you answer, old friend? Are you afraid of going out of business, huh? But I'm going to pay you for your beers, I am! I have money, as you can see."

He stuck his hand into his bag and took out even more bills. As he spoke, he suddenly burst out laughing. His face lit up with madness. He was very clearly drunk. Bills fell at his feet and he didn't pick them up. He held his bouquet of bills out to passersby, just taunting them even more. Yes, he practically shoved his bills right down the street's throat. But when people got carried away by his giddy excitement, he suddenly grew angry and screamed, "All of you there, looking at me with your big eyes, how many times did you tell me about your suffering? Are you even ready to suffer for your brother? No, you all let me rot in prison, when it was defending you that sent me there. Where has the man in you gone? What have you become? Where's your head? Don't you even know how to demand justice anymore? Don't you know what your rights are? You're just a pile of rags! Incapable of reason, incapable of thought, incapable of courage! You're killing yourselves with alcohol, but you're bigger cowards than hyenas. How many have died in prison while you sat in bars getting drunk on indifference? Biya takes all your money and hides it in Switzerland; he lets you rot in the neighborhoods, and you spend all your time chattering, getting drunk, and fucking girls! Are you waiting for salvation to fall from the sky for you, huh?"

A passerby said simply, "He's a member of the opposition." The writer didn't flinch; everybody knew that already. He kept on talking, and white foam gathered in the corners of his mouth. I no longer recognized the man who had always kept quiet and listened to the neighborhood's complaints, and even less the man who'd gently petted my back just awhile ago. A volcano, that's what he'd become, a volcano spitting out his rage as he laughed in spasms. His eyes were ablaze. His gestures were jittery, and his body's momentum swept him along in his soul's fury. He wasn't just speaking to my master anymore, but to the street in front of the bar, to all of Madagascar, and, I'll even say, to the whole of Cameroon. No exaggeration, I'll say he was speaking to all the most unimaginable corners of the world! He gathered up all the muscles in his body as if he wanted, with one single gesture of rage, to shake up the haggard men around him and rouse the humanity buried within them. Suddenly I felt sorry for him. I was sorry for him most of all because, if the eyes of all those curiosity seekers around him had lit up, it was obviously just in response to the beckoning of that bouquet of bills he held over everyone's head like a promise of happiness.

"Beer, beer, beer!" he cried. "Now it's just *jobajo* that drives your greedy lives, am I right? You think you'll get by like that? But good God, where is the man in you? I'm asking each and every one of you: where has the man in you gone? Where is the man?"

Nobody answered him. Then a provocative voice threw out into the melee: "Stop that crazy man!"

The man in black just screamed all the louder, "Yes, I am crazy. I was crazy to have defended this cigarette vendor who didn't even come over to my cell to see how I was doing. I am crazy to have gone to prison for him, because he's just a coward. I am so crazy that after you all abandoned me in my prison, I came back here to offer everyone a round to celebrate! You want money, right? You have more respect for money than for life, right? Here's the money I brought you! It's the reward for your cowardice! Use it to buy the beer you love so much!" And then the man of silence threw his bouquet of francs up in the air.

13

A ripple swept through the crowd. The bills wafted as they fell, surrounding the Crow's body in a ballet of blue papers. The writer didn't wait for them to hit the ground. With a burst of laughter that defied comprehension, he threw himself into their dancing midst. His laughter shook the lampposts. His laughter made the bills dance all the more. Suddenly I saw the men who'd been turned into statues by his angry gestures come to, as if they'd shaken off the evil spell of that laugh and those bills. Silently, they opened up a path to let the furious and sinister iconoclast depart; then they moved even closer to the rain of money. Some voices whispered that it was Famla's money. Small disputes broke out. But soon a hand rose up to the sky and caught a flying bill. I saw a crafty foot come down delicately on a bill that had fallen too close to it. Then I saw a woman mechanically undo the top of her pagne and imprison several floating bills between her breasts.

I couldn't believe my eyes. So misery's power over men was that far beyond compare. Even after the disappointed Crow's insulting tirade, there were still hands that found the courage to take the money of their shame. And yet I should have known. What is that saying we have here in Madagascar? Insults only sully the mouth that utters them. Yes, when faced with money, men suddenly reveal their true selves: their rapaciousness. Some pretended to scratch their head and surreptitiously palmed one of the bills of temptation, silently stuffing it into their pocket. The words of the man in black had evaporated; the bills he'd used to expose mankind remained suspended in midair, like so many pointed questions. And even when those bills of shame were strewn about on the ground, for an instant they just lay there, right in the middle of the thousand undecided feet and hands. No one moved. Soon my master snapped out of it and shouted in the courtyard of his bar, "I don't want his money, I don't! Get the hell out of here and take this damned money! I don't want his money!"

"We've got to give him back his money," Panther's voice dared to say.

Perhaps it was this belated burst of dignity that set little Takou in motion. As if he wanted to commit suicide in the middle of those thousands of feet, the kid threw himself on the accursed bills, saying, "If you don't want it, let me stomp on 'em then!"

Ignoring the stony faces of the men paralyzed by the vision of temptation, Docta's son began hopping and skipping on the bills strewn about on the ground. And soon his hand was lowered.

"Takou," said the cigarette vendor's voice, "just leave that on the ground!"

"Why?" asked the child, picking up a thousand-franc note and purposefully crumpling it.

The cigarette vendor lunged at the kid and grabbed the bill from his hands. As if they'd been waiting for that signal, the men and women all around immediately threw themselves on the abandoned money. I watched their thousand rapacious hands wrestle on the ground, as their voices rose up in insults and cries:

"Leave that there, you motherfucker!"

"Your mama's a brood hen!"

"Leave it there for you to take?"

"I said, leave it there, you lazy do-nothing!"

"Is it your daddy's money?"

"Leave it, you dog, or I'll poke your eyes out!"

"Leave it, or you'll have to answer to me!"

"So do your worst!"

"Yeah, do your worst!"

"*Cougnafe!*"

Takou only barely managed to slip away from the suicidal chaos his tricks had unleashed. He ran for cover next to my master's bar. The cigarette vendor who'd tried to stop him was caught in the melee. I saw him, yes, I saw him lift his hands up to the sky like the others, while the child, faced with the spectacle of all those men gone crazy, said gleefully, "Woyo-o, things are serious today!"

Yes, Takou even tried to get back in the dance himself. I saw him jump up as high as he could and stretch out his little arms, too. Massa Yo smacked him good on the head, and I heard him cry as he ran off. In the chaos, I heard Panther's loud voice multiply its curses in Medumba. Faced with this generalized brawl, I sought cover under my mistress's empty fritter stand. I saw shirts torn open, exposing determined chests. I saw pants split. I saw scarves torn off. I saw pagnes come undone. Out of this brouhaha soon emerged the bare heads of scarfless women, and men with their heads covered in dust and their hair standing on end. They had a strange white gleam in their eyes and a fake smile on their lips for the tattered bills that were soon stripped from their hands. Sometimes a fist would rise up out of the dust actually clasping a crumpled blue bill. But then many hands would rise up after the momentarily victorious one and carry it back down into their churning waters. Men and women also stood up, their bodies covered in dust and their hands empty of those bills of sorrow, which had been so numerous there on the ground mere minutes before. The faces of these men and women were contorted in anger at the sight of their clothes torn and tattered for naught. Then they threw themselves back into the brawl with a vengeance. And how! Since they'd already sunk so low, they weren't going to come away empty-handed. For what it had already cost them, they were ready to sink lower still: they jumped back into the fight for money with a fury.

It was certainly one of those radicals reenacting humanity's fall who, with a thrust of his body, overturned the cigarette vendor's stand. Candies, matches, cookies, packs of cigarettes, were scattered on the ground. A few cans of food came rolling over to my feet. I tried in vain to sink my teeth into them and finally had to give up. The cigarette vendor came out of his stupor too late to protect his capital. With the contents of his stand added into the mix, those bill hunters who'd been left lying in the dust dove even deeper into it. Now they were after the candies and other treats rolling about. They were covered in dust, and they were not going to let this last chance to justify their actions slip out of their hands again. Even as he threw himself into the melee to save what he could of his livelihood, the cigarette vendor's voice rose up to the sky. "Thieves!" he screamed.

He flexed his muscles. Here he smacked a hard head and there a stubborn hand. He struck there, at a woman's round behind, and over here poked the screaming Panther in the eye. Here, too, he sawed away at an arm that rose up to grab what little he'd been able to salvage of his goods. There he stomped on a child's grasping hand. I watched him plunge into the unified, chaotic crowd and, like a boxer, strike killing blows, only to emerge soon with his own mouth bloodied. The curse of that evil money seemed to fall on the heads of all who had taken any of it, on all who, with their chattering silences, had previously given their stamp of approval to imprisonment of the man in black. He was clearly getting revenge by unleashing man against man. Yes, mankind had gone crazy. I barked out an appeal for help to the street, but only succeeded in drawing more men into the general brawl taking place in the courtyard of The Customer Is King. Here men took stock of their strength, while over there some of the onlookers ran off, their arms clenched tight around their bellies that bulged with the little packages they'd torn from the disorder. They protected their bits of booty, but couldn't hide their lacerated backs or their bare behinds.

If the men of Madagascar hadn't, in their insanity, made off with the bottles from The Customer Is King, it's because my master had immediately, reflexively, locked up his shutters. He'd put a crate in front of his bar's closed door and sat there, his arms defiantly crossed. Men and women had raised their evil-doing arms against him, but he'd beaten them back. Hands had grabbed his leg, and he'd stomped on their fingers. A thousand hands had tried to throw him down on the ground, to force him to abandon his sanctuary and allow his wealth to be pillaged. Massa Yo had put his life on the line. He emerged from this battle with the crazed crowd like everyone else, with his clothes torn and his face battered. His bar had been saved, at the cost of his blood. Only a few of his crates had been broken.

When peace returned to the bar courtyard, I was struck by his face, which looked like it was covered by the mask of a *njou njou Calaba*, and by his muscles, striped with lines of blood. Men were getting up and shaking the dust from their bodies. They opened their eyes wide and split the masks of dust and blood on their faces. I had succeeded in staying out of their reach. I watched Panther shake the dust off his white hair; another of my master's customers waved his arms around and cursed his neighbor's mother's ass. I saw the cigarette vendor scream at the sky and his own ruin, and I realized that the Crow was the true master of the speech that drives people crazy. I saw his lugubrious silhouette soaring ominously overhead, a birdlike portent of evil, watching from afar as man's fate played out in front of my master's bar. The Crow—that he most certainly was: a cackling crow.

Sometime after this mayhem, when those who had somehow managed to stash away some of that manna of money came back crying and announced that the writer's bills were really counterfeit francs, no one in front of my master's bar had the courage to scream their anger out loud or raise their fist in a curse. A silent shame enveloped the street. It was like the Crow's laughter had gotten even louder, and this time it shook everyone's soul down to the core.

Book II

THE TURBULENT STREET

Chapter One

Things returned to normal in the courtyard of The Customer
Is King. The Crow's shadow disappeared, but not his curse,
not the resonant echo of his laughter. The cigarette vendor still
came around, although he no longer had a stand. From my
master's point of view, he was becoming more and more just
another customer. Most evenings he headed home drunk. The
street's shame seemed to be eating away ever more ferociously
at his soul, and his alone. In fact, he was the only real victim
of the chaos. I watched him swerve and sway as he went on his
way, tripping and falling over his own feet. Men and women
spoke of possession. It's true, they blamed the man in black, but
I never heard anyone blame himself for the cigarette vendor's
decline. Some of my master's customers bought him beers, as if
they wanted to finish him off, and Massa Yo opened them with
a clear conscience, I'm sure. Several times I heard my master tell
his son never to pick money up off the ground, because "you
never know if it's Famla's money." And once again, Massa Yo
forbade Soumi from playing with little Takou, as if that smart-
aleck kid was the cause of the misfortune that had befallen his
bar. "He's a bad seed," my master said.

"No argument from me," a customer agreed.

Once, however, when Massa Yo tried to chase Docta's son
out of his bar's courtyard, the kid ran and hid behind the ludo
players who were becoming permanent fixtures around the
place. Then he stuck out his tongue at my master and laughed.
I saw my master rush at the kid, boiling mad and cursing all
the way. The ludo players protected Takou. I shook my head

in amusement, because I knew it was his own guilty conscience Massa Yo sought to silence by chasing away that kid.

One day I met a man picking empty bottles out of the garbage behind the Party Headquarters. With a thousand flies swarming around him, he seemed to be the heart and soul of the rubbish. I'd never seen him there before, yet it looked like he'd always been a part of that decaying universe. He plunged his hands deep into the shit, shook the trash, and from time to time pulled out a green, red, or yellow bottle. Each time he found something, his face lit up. A flame danced in his eyes. It was like he'd pulled a miracle from the muck. He'd delicately place his discovery in a large cart next to him, but only after carefully wiping it off with a grimy blue towel. His filthy body repulsed me.

When he turned around and spied me watching him, he smiled sweetly and went silently back to his work. "Are you the garbage genie?" I barked out to him.

The man looked at me again, his faced beamed with a broad smile. He didn't chase me away. I sat down on my behind, let my tongue hang down, and watched him work away. He didn't let my staring distract him, though I followed his every move. His belly was rather round and his eyes bugged out a bit. He mechanically swatted away the flies that were singing in his ears, and sometimes he let out a curse in his language. When his cart was full, he pulled a little bottle from his shirt pocket and took a swig. I saw his eyes catch fire. He wiped his mouth with the back of his hand, chased away the flies from his eyes, then bent down and picked up the handles of his cart. The squeaking of that contraption could have woken the whole neighborhood. Then suddenly he stopped and asked, "Aren't you coming?"

He looked at me in surprise, as if it were a foregone conclusion that I was coming with him. Without thinking I replied, "Of course I am!"

Why did I follow him without asking what was in it for me? It must have been because some of his quirks reminded me of the man in black. I had a feeling he could answer the thousand questions the Crow had left unanswered. Soon we arrived at a stream. A number of laundrymen were noisily beating their linens on the rocks and rinsing them out in red water. Together they filled the air with the syncopated rhythms of their songs and thuds. The man started washing his bottles. He filled them with bleach, then shook them around in front of his eyes and let the muddy mixture pour out at his feet. When we left the stream and started wandering through the alleyways of the quarter, I made sure not to shadow him too closely. I tailed him like a spy, keeping two or three meters between us. I'm sure he thought it was funny, but for me it was the mark of my distrust. Sometimes he'd turn around and smile when he saw me there. His song rang out in the neighborhood:

> *"One botrè, one botrè*
> *One botrè, oh, a one botrè"*

Suddenly a stone crashed down right next to me. The garbage picker turned around and, with a threatening wave of his arm, said to whoever had thrown it: "Leave him alone, huh, he's my friend."

I opened my muzzle to bark out my indignation but bit my tongue when I saw Takou—oh that bad kid!—standing in front of me with another big rock in his hand. Yeah, I thought, he is a bad kid! Takou wasn't alone, though. Soumi was standing at the other end of the path with a big rock in his hand too, one that if it didn't cripple me, would kill me for sure. With an evil glint in his eye, he kept tossing the rock up in the air and catching it mid-flight. He didn't recognize me. He thought I was just the garbage picker's dog. Doesn't every dog look like the man he follows? It didn't seem in the least to impress Massa Yo's son that I was the garbage genie's friend. It just seemed to make him even meaner. Soumi was waiting for the right moment to commit his umpteenth crime against my person. The genie understood his intentions and said right to him, "I swear, if you throw that stone at him, I'll make your *bangala* disappear just like that."

I saw the kid immediately shove his hand down his pants. Then I watched him rush to a wall and hurriedly piss. I barked out my laughter. I barked even more when I saw the two kids take off running, screaming they'd seen a sorcerer. Then I asked the garbage picker, "So you're the guy making men's *bangalas* disappear?"

He didn't answer. Still, I thought I'd better warn him. "You'd better not ever go into my quarter."

This man, who wandered up and down the streets of every quarter with his bottles, stared at me, his eyes open wide in disbelief. Then I said, "There are some guys there out to burn you alive."

2

Cursing the neighborhood's badly raised kids and following the bizarre bottle vendor, I had, without realizing it, entered the very heart of fear: into the belly of whispers, the arteries of fantasy, the intestines of the insanity that is Yaoundé. I followed the man of mystery, telling myself that just maybe he'd show me man's more humane face, a face I wasn't used to seeing. Maybe because Soumi's cruelty had turned me off for good, I started to follow in the man's shadow, without taking any precautions at all. I walked, hopeful a surprise was coming. If until then the courtyard of my master's bar had taught me only about man's misery, maybe, I told myself, the endless street would reveal its secrets to me. And so I explored the courtyards of houses along with the man of the multicolored bottles. A swarm of flies escorted us. At the squeaking of the pushcart's wheels, chickens stopped scratching. A lizard paused on a nearby wall, repeatedly lifting up its head before taking off again.

I was walking in my new master's shadow.

He pushed his loud machine, his veins bulging out. The squeaking song of his rusty metal cart enlivened the quarter's pathways. Men and women dragged themselves from their homes. They'd buy one or two bottles, then he'd bless them and continue on his way. Before heading up a hill, he'd pause, wipe off his brow, pull the little bottle from his shirt pocket, and, closing his eyes, take a swig. With the fire back in his eyes, he'd strain his muscles to push the cart on ahead.

Suddenly, the garbage picker stopped in his tracks and looked at me curiously, as if he'd never seen me before. Then he said, "Time to put those paws to work!"

I lowered my ears.

"You're just a dog," he said cruelly.

I cocked my head and barked out, "So what?"

And just what are you, I thought, a man? That's a laugh. I didn't bark out those thoughts.

"Instead of a dog," he added with glee, "what I need is a donkey." He thought for a minute then said, "Yeah, a donkey would be a lot more useful to me than you."

I didn't answer his insults. This guy really was a strange character. His noisy passage always brought out the kids. Many shouted insults at him. Many others imitated his cacophonous song, and still others ran alongside him for a while. There were some who tried to throw rocks at me. Sometimes dogs dragged themselves from their master's courtyard or from wherever they were headed and came to sniff my behind. Some threw themselves at me as if I'd stolen their shadow. I told them I was a bar dog, and just to prove I was better than them, I'd add that I was a scientist: "a researcher." They barked out their laughter and pointed to my mangy back. That scared me, because they were right. When I was tossed out onto the endless, bumpy street, I had changed classes, and my new master defended me only from the brazen kids. He left me on my own to settle scores with my fellows. Sometimes a kid or even an adult asked him, "So, *One botrè*, you've got a dog now-o?"

It was true, I was clearly the only wealth this garbage picker possessed. He answered with a smile as he pushed his loud cart and his song down the street. Sometimes he'd get angry at a comment made about the swarm of flies following him, or some other comment about his fat belly or how dirty he was. When people made fun of him, he'd answer back with a peppery insult, something along the lines of "If you think that's funny, some night I'll come eat your heart."

That would shut them up. Sometimes, though, the garbage picker grew violent. Once, when a kid making obscene gestures blocked our way, I was surprised my new master didn't just fan the thousand fears everyone had about him. On the contrary, he dropped his merchandise and took off down the pathways between the houses after the little devil. Soon he returned, with the kid in tears and walking on tiptoes. The garbage picker had him by the ear and was cursing him out: "Don't you know I can steal your shadow?"

The kid wailed.

"Do you know who I am?" the man asked.

When he finally let go of the poor kid's ear, he ran off between the houses, crying even harder. He's crying too much for the punishment he received, I thought. And sure enough, a woman's wrath exploded in the streets. Steps shook the houses and a whale of a woman appeared; full of herself, she got right in the bottle vendor's face. Her mouth was a volcano. Behind her, the kid my new master had roughed up was wiping his cheeks. "That's the guy who hit me," he said, pointing at the bottle vendor.

The woman began a tirade in her language. "Your son said that I screw my dog," the man interjected, bluntly. Innocently, he added, "Kids today are so badly behaved, huh?"

I watched an earth-shattering rage take hold of the woman. She wheeled around toward her kid and, with a loud, record-breaking slap, sent him flying right back into the passage between the houses he'd just come from. "Let him be, Ma'am," interrupted the garbage picker, "it's the city that makes them crazy. What can we do about it?"

"My child needs to respect adults," screamed the furious woman.

She apologized a thousand times. I heard her kid's tears fade off in the distance. Soon she shook her gigantic behind and headed back between the houses. The bottle vendor burst out laughing. He leaned down over me and said with a laugh, as if I were his new confidant, "That's the way it is."

You have to know how to be mean, he added, if you want to protect yourself from man's wickedness. Soon he pulled the little bottle back out of his shirt and gulped down a deadly swig. His eyes went blood red and I saw his soul dance in front of him. He practically turned into a satyr: "You can't drink, huh?" he asked.

Suddenly he became someone altogether different. The alcohol must have boiled his brain. A drunkard's face appeared. I lowered my ears. Flies sang over my head. "You don't need to get drunk, huh?" he went on.

I gave myself a good shake. The flies ceased their concert. Some of my flies went and landed on the rim of his bottle. The smell of alcohol was calling them. The garbage picker drank them down without realizing it, then wiped his lips and noted tersely: "Maybe dogs put up with life better, huh?"

He looked at me for a moment and asked, "Hey, what's your name anyway?"

"Mboudjak," I replied.

When he spoke, his spit splattered my face. Then he asked, "What kind of name is that, Mboudjak?"

To put an end to his questions and, more important, to escape from his sopping wet words, I said, "It's a dog's name."

When a kid called out to us, "Hey, *One botrè*, you talk to your dog now?" I finally realized that, in fact, we'd been talking all along, as if it were the normal thing to do. This garbage genie was the first man I could really talk with. It wasn't just that he understood what I was saying to him. No, he answered me too. I noticed that men passing by would stop and stare, as if we were some mysterious pair. They looked at the bottle vendor as if he were crazy. And maybe they were right. The man's voice grew louder and louder as he spoke to me. His gestures were out of proportion. Soon he reached out and grabbed me by the tail, like all the drunks did. Instinctively, I turned around and bared my fangs. Amused, he laughed. He tried again to grab me by the tail; he wanted to play. But his playfulness led him to blurt out a phrase I didn't stick around to hear twice: "You know, where I come from we eat dogs," he said, still amused.

I backed away from him without waiting to hear any more details. I barked out my indignation as I went. I knew all too well what sorts of instincts misery planted in man's belly. As I ran off, I heard him burst into a sinister laugh. He called me back, saying it was a joke. But I didn't go back.

3

I consoled myself for the loss of that brief friendship by repeating that maybe he was just a sorcerer after all, like Soumi had said. If not, I said, he was just a cannibal. I swore I'd never follow a stranger again. Had I lost the vigilance a dog needs to survive? Even for the good of Science, I told myself, I didn't have the right to put my life in danger and end up on somebody's barbecue: scalped, gutted, marinated, sprinkled with salt and pepper, served up and eaten! Escaping from that sinister fate, I decided to return to The Customer Is King. But then, as I tried to find my way across the city, I realized I was lost: I couldn't find the path that had led me away from my master's bar.

Yes, the garbage picker had led me too far away from my fiefdom, and he had always followed roads and paths that twisted and turned like a snake. Suddenly, all the houses looked alike. The neighborhood turned into an endless labyrinth. It was like the whole of Yaoundé had turned into one gigantic neighborhood. I found myself in unfamiliar courtyards. I found myself staring at open gutter pipes. I found myself where the sewers poured out their muck. Dogs chased me from their fiefdoms, threatening to poke my eyes out. Some made a show of coming up to sniff my behind, and then barking out their laughter. I fled their cannibalistic laugh. In my flight, I ran through living rooms and bedrooms. Doors slammed behind me and loud curses followed me. Faces appeared in the panes of the windows I had leaped through, promising to turn me into barbecue. I got even more lost. Stray dogs challenged me to fight. I didn't back down. I spent days and nights searching for the way back to my master's.

Once I met up with a black cat, whose fur immediately went up on his back. "Brother," I said to him, "I'm just looking for directions."

"I'm not your brother," he said drily.

"It doesn't matter," I admitted. "I need to get back to The Customer Is King."

I couldn't understand his mewed reply. Another, nicer cat told me to take two lefts, go down the first street after Death Square, then turn right, then continue on for about another twenty meters, and so forth. I followed his directions to the letter and found myself in front of a bar called Death-Be-Damned. I stopped believing what cats said. What didn't I run into? For example, a sparrow gave me directions straight over the rooftops, as if I weren't a dog. "Do you know Massa Yo?" I asked a hen.

"Massa Yo? What kind of dog is that?" the arrogant hen replied.

"It's not a dog," I said, "it's a man."

"Ah-ha," she said.

"He's my master."

The hen cackled with laughter. She called some other hens over and, shaking her head in amusement, pointed at me with her beak. "That dog just can't live without men-o!"

Flapping her wings and staring at me, she added, "Freedom sure is hard to take, huh?"

A less sarcastic rooster asked, "Which Massa Yo are you looking for?"

I told him, and then he told me there were thousands of Massa Yos in Yaoundé; he alone knew six. He started to give me the list, introducing them one by one: Massa Yo the taxi driver with the long mouth; Massa Yo the delivery man with arms like a chimpanzee; Massa Yo the tinker with the square head; Massa Yo with the bugged-out eyes who knew how to get by; Massa Yo the black marketeer, always dressed to the nines; Massa Yo the outhouse digger who was always covered in mud, also known as "Alcoholic Candy"—he digs graves, too, but they cost a little more. Cackling with laughter, the rooster started to tell me how Alcoholic Candy was such a good grave digger that no one would dare dig one for him when he died. I stopped listening and went on my way.

Maybe because I was so tired of looking without ever finding what I was after, I told myself I'd have to find out from men. They must know each other, after all. But how could I talk to them without making them angry? I knew all too well how a man reacts when a dog barks out a question. Yes, I always kept a safe distance when I watched men, with my paws ready to run. I perked up my ears to catch them in their cowardice, and I listened in on their conversations. Without meaning to, I kept up on the ins and outs of their daily life. Once, for example, as I worried a bone in front of a shop where domino players vied to see who was best and exchanged friendly insults, I heard one of them say with a laugh that members of the opposition returning to the country had been arrested right at the airport. The man telling the story stopped playing and exclaimed, "But it was Biya himself who'd asked them to come back-o!"

His adversary interrupted, shaking his head sadly, "If they believed him, they're the real idiots!"

A third man agreed, "Just the other day he had one of them stuffed in a box and sent back through the mail, so he could be 'brought to justice,' right?"

I'd already heard that story.

"Brother, if you are looking for trouble, you'll find it."

A man put an end to the conversation, saying curtly, "Cameroon is Cameroon."

Another day, when I was eyeing the lunch crowd gathered around a fritter seller's stand, I heard them talking about a taxi driver who'd been shot point-blank by a cop he'd refused to *tchoko*. Then I realized I hadn't seen a taxi come down the road all morning. The taxi drivers had all gone on strike to protest that glaring example of what I'll call man's endemic cruelty. Yet one guy shrugged his shoulders and said, "What do you expect? If they don't get paid . . ."

His neighbor was outraged. "Are they the only ones suffering in this country? We civil servants haven't been paid for six months," he said.

"Tell me about it. But 'Cameroon is doing just fine!'" another insisted.

Oh men! When you're hungry—and don't I know it—you're worse than rats. You don't just attack each other, no, you're ready to eat each other up. You're ready to eat everything sleeping within reach. When you're wallowing in your own misery, I have to disappear in the surrounding shadows to protect myself from your fury. Simply by observing the whispers of strangers, I realized that some of the truths I'd learned before in my master's house, things about men that his bar courtyard had taught me, or that my accursed life had led me to discover, were endlessly repeated all around, disguised only by a mask of difference. For example, how many times will I see men fighting, trying to strangle each other once and for all over a twenty-five franc coin? I'll see them scratch each other's face out over a chicken thigh. Each time I'll realize that an empty stomach is man's master. And I'll realize the extent to which misery eats up man's humanity.

"Instead of shooting an innocent taxi driver," said a dumbstruck man, staring at his fritter suspended in midair, "why didn't the cop take down the guys who aren't paying him, huh?"

"What do you expect, cops are all cowards!"

A man with a bald spot kilometers wide caught sight of me and said, "They're just like dogs: strong only in front of the weak."

That's someone who knows nothing about the courage of dogs, I thought. Repulsed by his stupidity, I thought I'd better be on my way. But happily the first man, the one who'd been so shocked, showed more intelligence as he continued, "If I were a cop who wasn't getting paid, while every day Biya and his men were off hiding our money in Switzerland, on May 20th I'd spend the national holiday up on the roof of the Main Post Office waiting for one of them to come by—a minister or whoever—and then, Pow! I'd sink a bullet right in his forehead!"

The man next to him said, "You've seen too many American movies, huh!"

But the first guy's anger wasn't going to fade so quickly. He got up, as if he were leaving, but then stopped: "You said it, but me, I know *they*'ll go a full two years without paying people's salaries because *they* know no one has ever shot a politician out in the open in this country! We just don't have a tradition of political assassination in Cameroon!"

Another man having lunch insisted, "Yeah, *they* do whatever *they* like because *they* know that when the good Cameroonian doesn't get paid at the end of the month, instead of threatening his boss, he just goes home and beats up on his wife and kids!"

The man stamped his feet, shook his head, and said, "*Those guys* sure understand psychology, don't they. That's why *they* manipulate us however they want."

He stressed "those guys" and "they" with uncontrolled disgust.

"But what can we do about it?" said another. "A starving belly can't think." Then he popped a fritter into his mouth.

"It's gonna stop soon," said the man who was standing. "Believe me, soon Cameroonians are going to hit their limits of suffering and misery."

I saw rage light up his eyes. He wasn't afraid to let his desire for blood explode in the street. He had the cold, fixed gaze of someone who will do whatever it takes to survive, even if it costs him his skin. That was the first time I'd glimpsed such frustration in the neighborhoods' idle conversations. The commentaries I heard in bars, shops, and fritter stands always gave me the impression that all the men I met suffered because they knew that they'd lived better days—a time when their humanity flourished which I, poor dog that I was, hadn't known and couldn't fully comprehend. Sometimes they'd conclude with a nostalgic "so what": *"Bia boya alors."* Every now and again I'd sense a rage lurking beneath those remarks, I'd see an arm tense up and a face suddenly turn terrifying.

Still, that man gave me my first glimpse of the volcanic rage churning beneath the surface of the neighborhood, extending beyond the confines of all the bars, and ready to explode at any minute. Suddenly I saw the flame of a strange insanity flicker above this very typical fritter stand.

"If just once someone takes down a politician, just once I say," the man went on, "by Allah! everything will change in this country."

As he said "Allah," he licked his finger and held it up to the sky.

4

At first I thought I was being choked by my own body's bad breath. Then I convinced myself that the haunting stench came from the neighborhood all around: from the thousand garbage piles, crumbling houses, busted-up streets, ammonia-filled bars, and leaky crap-ridden sewers, from the moldy restaurants, drugged-out cars, open-air outhouses, and wells dug into shit, from the streams battling with piles of garbage, from the filthy beds, and the living dead. I soon realized that behind me was a little stream, dammed up by a dead dog. My eyes opened wide when I saw the cadaver's three legs lifted up to the sky. My ears stood up straight with horror. Suddenly the far-off song of freedom sung by that communist dog from Madagascar began to ring in my ears. Terrified, I arched my back and took off down the road, wracked by nausea.

A moped almost ran me down.

"Damned dog!" said the driver, who'd lost his balance.

Yow! So that communist dog had been swallowed up by the street: run over and left like an offering in the sanctuary of the genie of the slums. His face was gone. His squashed body loudly proclaimed the fate our quarters reserve for idealism like his. Oh yes, I would have recognized that philosopher dog from my quarter anywhere among Yaoundé's millions of strays. Tossed away there, his cadaver only underscored his essence all the more. His muzzle was open, baring his fangs to the day. His eyes were open, too, open and unseeing. A whole mob of multicolored maggots was hard at work, moving in and out of them. A crowd of blue flies did a mourning dance, a *ben skin,* above his body. The dog's cadaver shunted the stream's water onto the street, soaking the foundations of all the nearby houses with his liquefied body. A few flies from his funeral procession peeled off and landed on my back. I felt the humid feet of one of them in my ear. It seemed its cannibal gluttony found my body to its liking. I shook myself. The fly circled my head, singing the anthem of my dubious canitude:

> "The dead are not dead
> They are in the flowing stream.
> They lie there on the streets' tar.
> Those who are dead are never gone. "

I snapped futilely at the fly; I couldn't make it be quiet. The quarter was indifferent to this cadaver of a dog. Men stepped over the stinking water that seemed to flow from the maggot-filled corpse before wending its way through the neighborhood's miasma. When I approached my fellow one last time to pay my final respects, I heard a noise behind me. *"Ye maleh!"* screamed a child's loud voice, "that dog is eating his brother!"

I jumped, overcome with nausea.

"Yuck!" said another voice, "dogs are savages!"

Right then a stone landed noisily next to me. It was time for me to get out of there. I stopped in front of a little shop. In the courtyard people were playing ludo. Their voices were loud. A woman was lighting a flame beneath her plate of plantains. Her baby was crawling next to the ludo players, who, captivated by their game, paid no attention to his movements. I saw the child pick up a millipede and stuff it in his mouth. I barked loudly. The mother looked up from what she was doing. With a panicked cry, she ran over to her kid and picked him up. She emptied out his mouth with her big fat hands. This roused the men next to her. A sense of responsibility swelled up and pushed them toward the baby, whom the mother was making vomit. The woman wouldn't let them touch her child. She insulted them, said they should all be ashamed. "Even just watching a kid is too much for you," she said.

"Watch him? Is he my kid?" asked one of the players.

Another asked, "So where's his father?"

This was a common scene.

At one intersection a woman was cursing all those who came in the night to devour her. She was waving her arms around like crazy and promising to go see Père Soufo,* the miracle-working prophet of La Carrière. Her voice grew terrifying: "You'll see," she said. "He'll squash you in my dreams!"

She promised even worse things to everyone who haunted her nights. Having them squashed by Père Soufo wasn't enough, no, she wanted them all thrown into the fire, then topped with hot pepper. She swore she'd eat them for breakfast. A passerby insulted her, saying she must be the real witch of the quarter. "You're the one who eats people, isn't that right?"

"I'll show them," the woman said.

But the passerby kept on talking, calling her an evil spirit. "Get out of here and leave us alone, will you, you *ndjum**!"

He pointed to some raw, bloody meat and said it dripped from the woman's teeth whenever she spoke. He said it was proof of her nocturnal orgies. The woman didn't reply but continued ranting, making even more threats. As one man passed near me, he shook his head and said to his friend, "It's between them."

His friend shouted, "This Nlongkak* of ours is a quarter full of sorcerers, huh!"

"Let me tell you," insisted his friend, "now they're eating each other up in broad daylight, no shame at all-o!"

"What do you expect?" said the first. "That's poverty for you!"

That's where I stopped listening, for at last I knew where I was: Nlongkak.

5

A blind man was sitting on the other side of the street. His head was tilted upward, his ear turned toward the street. He was wearing dark glasses with multicolored lenses; in front of him was an empty soup dish. His song shook the whole quarter, like the repetition of a curse. A kid walked up to him, but instead of placing an offering in the plate there for that purpose, he took a couple of coins from it. I saw the blind man start and, with the quick, accurate movement of someone who can see, grab the smart aleck's hand. Surprised by the blind man's unexpected precision, the scared kid backed up. The blind man opened his mouth and smiled, showing his big red teeth. Then, taking off his glasses, he said to the kid, "Get out of here, you little thief!"

Terrified, the kid scrambled away. As he fled, he bumped into a woman balancing a platter full of peanuts on her head. With a thrust of her hips, the woman managed to catch the falling platter, but her slap just missed the kid's neck. The kid's cries faded out in the distance. The blind man burst out laughing and the woman, frozen in her surprise, stared at him. The blind man automatically took his glasses off again and showed her his milky eyes. The woman was so scared she lost her balance, scattering the peanuts all over the ground. When she got her wits back, she bent over and grabbed the beggar by his rags. She insisted he reimburse her. "But I'm a beggar!" said the blind man.

His exposed face searched vainly for the sun. The woman wasn't having any of it. She cursed him in her language. A crowd quickly formed around this absurd quarrel, blocking my view of things. All I could do was listen to the quarreling voices growing louder in the street.

"Leave me alone," said the blind beggar's voice. "Don't you see I'm blind?"

"You can see!"

"Ma'am, just leave him alone," said a voice of reason. "Don't you see how his eyes turn back into his head?"

"Precisely! He did that just to frighten me."

"Be careful, ma'am, my glasses."

"Oh!"

"You've broken my glasses!"

"How did you see that?"

"You're going to pay for my glasses!"

"Did you pay for my peanuts?"

"Let's go to the police station!"

"Yes, let's go!"

The crowd parted and I was able to see the woman who held the blind man by his shirttail. He wasn't putting up a fight, but his white eyes were rolling around like crazy. Showing his wide-open, sightless eyes to the street, he poured out a thousand curses. He seemed to be dying right there where he stood, as if death were pounding on his back, sending epileptic waves through his body. He was speaking in a language no one understood. He spoke, but it was like he said nothing at all. The woman held his broken glasses in her hand. "Cut it out. Stop all these magic tricks," she said, "you're going to pay for my peanuts."

A man stepped up, "Ma'am, he's a beggar."

Voices rose up from the crowd: "Beggars are better off than civil servants, you know."

"That beggar's just a con artist."

"Aren't you ashamed to be harassing a blind man?"

"Who says he's blind?"

The quarrel wasn't about to end. When a policeman's blue uniform appeared across the street, the blind man tore himself free of the woman's hands and took off running through the crowd. The pack was hot on his heels, hooting with amusement. The woman raised her arms up to the sky, screaming, "Stop that blind man!"

The policeman whistled several times, pointing at the speeding blind man. That guy was running with such a fury that everyone jumped out of his way. He made it through the crowd without looking. He was almost hit by a taxi. Then he was lost in the neighborhood. The woman whose peanuts were scattered and smashed on the ground shook her head and cried. Her voice was drowned out by the street's laughter at the sight of that rushing blind man. "What kind of country is this!" she said, showing the blind man's multicolored glasses to the policeman. "Now even blind men leap over cars!"

"A hungry man," said a woman, "is an animal."

6

Commentaries were flying fast and furious in front of a shop. The men's voices shook the street. Everyone wanted to be right. Their hands rose up, as if trying to grab the clouds from the sky. Their eyes opened wide, as if trying to unleash their ability to reinvent the world. One guy was more agitated than the others. He was acting crazy; he leaped this way and that and gave a military salute. But when he smacked his neighbor in the eye, he fell over himself with apologies. He said that in Mokolo a policeman had died, standing on his own two feet with his cap right on his head, after drinking a whole bottle of *odontol*. To drive home the truth of his story even more, he acted out how the policeman was struck dead. None of his listeners believed him though, which just made him all the more theatrical. For a moment I thought the agitated talker was the Panther Nzui Manto. I'd soon learn, though, that the little old man who stood in front of my master's bar was just one of the many fabricators of reality found in front of almost every bar, in front of almost every shop. To convince his listeners he was telling the truth, this man would up and die, right there, standing up, just like the policeman with a cap he was talking about.

Each of those big talkers reminded me of the little old man. For example, the big-mouthed man I met in front of a *soya* vendor's raised stand, he too had Panther's hallucinatory imagination. Only he added a pinch of savagery to it. He was talking about a man with six testicles and was shocked that no one else knew the guy: "But he lives right there at Jean Vespa Square," he said.

According to him, with six testicles the guy could screw women like the singer Mongo Faya* did. He admitted he'd only seen four of the six testicles himself—"once, when he was taking a piss"—but he told any one who doubted him to go find out from a prostitute in the quarter named Prudence. He talked like a man possessed. Splaying his legs, he acted out the performances of his story's mythic hero for the lively street.

As I arrived in front of a shop one day, I met up with a smooth talker who was letting his anger split the street in two. He said they'd caught the wife of the finance minister at Orly airport with a big suitcase full of money. As he spoke he shook his head angrily, his eyes fluttering open and closed. His voice was cracking and bits of white foam gathered in the corners of his mouth. "That's how they're fucking this country up!" he said.

His neighbor asked if he was sure of what he was saying. The smooth talker replied arrogantly that he'd gotten his information from "a reliable source."

"Yeah, you just got back from Paris, right?" one guy interjected.

Everyone burst out laughing. That only made the smooth talker argue his point all the more. He lifted up his arm, revealing a dark circle underneath, and waved it over everyone's head as if to threaten the skeptics. He said he knew people in important places. He said he was in the inner circle, in the foyer of truth itself.

"You're Biya's close personal friend, right?" said one man.

Those listening burst out laughing. Carried away by this contagious laughter, I didn't hear a taxi screech to a halt next to me. The door opened and whacked me right in the butt. I howled. A woman got out of the taxi. The smooth talker fell silent, and immediately the men stopped laughing. Some whistled as they watched her walk by. They were drooling over her breasts. They devoured her behind. They called out to her. The woman's skin glowed, luminescent. She shimmied and slithered like a snake. She turned up her nose arrogantly, raising it high above the chaos.

"Whore!" said one man, the very one who'd ogled her the most greedily.

His eyes were bulging out. The woman turned around and stared him down, but said nothing. Then she disappeared into the quarter, leaving me in a cloud of her haunting perfume.

"Let our sisters get by as they can," someone interjected.

"What can we do, the country's in crisis."

That made me think of the regulars at The Customer Is King. Once again I saw my master whistle at girls who then stared him down, and I saw the cigarette vendor laugh at each of his failures. Most of all, I saw Docta. My heart ached with nostalgia. When you're far away, you even miss the deathly boredom of home. And when you're unable to get back home, the smells of your garbage from years past suddenly sparkle like diamonds. A duck wandered across the shop's courtyard, quacking softly. Its young waddled behind her, one after the other. Then a kid came running out of the shop. In his hand he had a bottle of beer, Top Rouge. Scared and trying to get out of his way, the ducklings broke ranks. With her bill low to the ground, the mother duck charged at the kid. The kid screamed and leaped to the side. Then he stopped, picked up a stone and threw it at the duck. Flapping her wings, she turned on the stone and pecked it to dust, before coming back to charge courageously at the kid again. The kid quickly decided this was a fun game. He faked left and right, and the duck chased him for quite a while. He laughed as he ran away, and then came right back at her. He didn't leave the duck alone until one of the big talkers told him to get out of there, "*Mouf*, get back home, cock-a-doodle-do!"

A red car appeared at the far end of the street, shaking the pavement with a devilishly funky beat. It seemed it would carry the whole quarter away with it in a dance to the death. When it pulled up in front of the shop, it put an end to the ongoing verbal explosion. The driver of the tricked-out car seemed lost. He said something no one could understand, given that he hadn't lowered the volume of his music. Kids came up to him. Instead of listening to what he said, their eyes opened wide as they stared hungrily at the car, an impossible dream right there in front of them. Their tongues hung down. A man tore himself from the group chattering in front of the shop and went up to the red car. He shooed away the dumbstruck kids and stuck his head into the car window. The kids regrouped not far from me. Each one gave free rein to his explosive dreams. One kid with a triangular head swore the car was his, thanks to some spell I'll never understand. Still, "his" car took off again, dancing down the street, leaving the kid surrounded by his friends in misery, but yet full of confidence. The guy who'd given the driver of the red car directions went back to his talkative friends and exclaimed, "A young guy like that, you tell me, did he just steal that money or what?"

I watched him with amusement. He shook his head and opened his eyes wide. He just couldn't find the words to describe what he'd seen inside that mysterious car.

"Hey, that's *them* for you, right?" was the only answer he got.

7

"Today is the day *they*'re gonna kill me!"

It was a woman's voice that ripped through the rumor of the street. Lured by her shouting, curious bystanders immediately came running. She was lying beneath a stopped bus. The driver had gotten out and was waving his hands, pleading with her. He tried everything to convince her. The voices of women and men rose up. Some were cursing while others burst out laughing. The growing crowd blocked my view of the woman and the events that had the quarter so excited. Some loafers asked the driver to get back in his bus and fulfill the wishes of that "sleaze, if dying is really what she's after." The bus driver was a debonair man, with a bit of a belly and sweat glistening on his brow. He clapped his hands and said, "It's just *ndoutou,** I tell you, bad luck. She wants to ruin my day."

Then I heard a loafer reply, "So give her what she wants, brother, then she won't bother you anymore."

"Give her what?" asked the bus driver.

Passengers in a hurry to be on their way got off the bus, grumbling. They cursed SOTUC, the bus company, swearing it would go under. A few stopped the first cab that passed and others demanded their money back. The chaos just kept on growing. Cars honked. Drivers shouted out insults. The bus driver was sweating profusely. He went from one side of the crowd to the other, waving his arms like a madman. He swore he was going to call the police. From under his bus, the woman's voice asked him to do just that. She wasn't taking him seriously. The driver backed up, out of the chaos, and scratched his head. He seemed to be dancing on a flimsy high wire. Overwhelmed by what was happening, he stepped back and looked at his bus from a distance. His passengers followed his retreat. Their voices were loud. They demanded a refund. They threatened violence. The bus driver said he couldn't do anything about it. He suggested they get the woman out from under the bus. "If you get that crazy woman out of there," he said, "I'll keep driving."

Some men bent down under the bus and started pulling the woman out. They screamed at her. She fought for all she was worth. The crowd surrounding her got even more excited. The woman wasn't going to be stopped from committing suicide. She hit one guy and bit someone else. "Today is the day *they*'re gonna kill me!" she said.

A old man passing by got involved in things. He said he knew the woman. People let him through. He bent down and dished up his litany of proverbs. He spoke of the ancestral founder of their tribe. It seems the woman just spit in his face. At least I saw him turn around and show his pale face to the gathered crowd, which burst into laughter. He faltered, like a devil losing his grip on the world. Then he walked away, without another word, shaking his head in shock. Just then a policeman came through the crowd, whistling and bringing his billy club down on the heads of the curious bystanders. The crowd tried to get out of his way and the driver walked back to his bus. Gesturing wildly, he explained his bad luck and pointed beneath the bus. The policeman's voice bellowed out: "Ma'am, get out from under there!"

"I'm not coming out!" screamed the determined woman.

The policeman, whose high-flying authority had just been trampled into the ground by that woman beneath the bus, told the driver to get back behind the wheel.

"If you don't get out from under there," the policeman told the woman, "I'll order him to drive over you."

"Then do it!"

So the policeman said to the driver, "Sir, get in your bus!"
The driver hesitated.

"Get in your bus, sir," the policeman bellowed, "or I'll arrest
you right now!"

I perked up my ears to see what was going to happen. The
driver got in his bus. The crowd froze in anticipation of what
would come.

"Start the bus!" screamed the policeman.

The sound of an engine kicked up a cloud of dust. Then I
watched the woman drag herself, coughing, from that hell. The
crowd burst into laughter. A voice said, "So now you're afraid
to die?"

The woman was a statue of mud. Yes, she was like a mummy.
Her eyes were two white holes. The bus's motor roared, pushing its big muzzle forward and scattering the many curious bystanders. They jumped aside, cursing and laughing, but didn't
clear the street. The spectacle of that mummified woman right
there in the street was just too enthralling.

"You should've stayed there, no?" said one woman.

Another roar of the engine and the crowd jumped again. The
bus brutally pushed its way through. Some riders threw themselves back into its belly, cursing the driver, who clearly wanted
to leave them and their curiosity right there. The driver hadn't
given any sign that he was leaving. I think he just didn't want
to wait for the woman with the suicidal urges to catch her second wind and throw herself back under the wheels of his bus.
Or maybe he just wanted to make up the time he'd lost? The
passengers who hadn't been able to jump back on the bus ran
screaming down the road after him. Then they stopped and
cursed the heavens. Some rushed toward taxis. With the bus
gone, traffic started moving again. The policeman handcuffed
the woman who'd caused all the trouble. He lectured her. Then,
bringing his billy club down on a few heads, he made his way
through the curious crowd, stopped traffic with an authoritative gesture, and took her across the street. Some loafers followed them, still shouting insults at the woman.

"*Mouf,*" one of them said to her, "why don't you just go
throw yourself in Central Lake, huh?"

Another asked, "What have you seen?"

"Oooooooh," screamed the crowd, "oooooooohh!"

The policeman scattered the crowd, threatening to send them all to prison. Those who were following backed off, but only to move right up again. Though stripped bare by their words, the woman didn't cower in shame. She responded to each and every one of the men mocking her with an awesome silence. I saw her head, now forever altered, rise up above the noisy crowd, although her mouth remained curiously silent. The policeman pushed her on in front of him.

Suddenly she stopped dead and burst into tears. The crowd hissed at her even more. The woman said she was sick of it: sick, sick, really sick of it. She said she hadn't been paid for the past ten months. Each time she went home, she found her kids starving but full of hope, though she had nothing to give them. Each time she went to the bank, they made her wait. Everyone was always asking her to wait, yes, to wait, and then wait some more. "Wait for how long?" she screamed. Then she added, courageously, "Until Jeanne-Irène has a kid?"

The poor woman didn't understand that no one, I mean no one in this country sympathized with her fate as a mother. She didn't understand that no one, and I mean no one cared about the worry eating away at her stomach, about the hunger sapping her strength: she who had always paid her taxes, she who had too many mouths to feed. Since the government didn't give a damn about her, since the government didn't even think she existed, she'd decided to end her life "and be done with it." She'd thrown herself in front of the "government's bus" so that the kleptomaniac government that couldn't even pay what it owed her—"the money I'd earned myself," she said—so that this swindler of a government could just finish her off, "once and for all." She was ranting like a crazy woman. As she spoke, she shook her dust-covered body. Her words made the lively crowd fall silent. The policemen, though, wasn't even listening to her.

"You can explain all that to the police commissioner himself," he said, giving her a shove.

He dragged her all the way to police headquarters. I thought about that woman for a long time afterward. I thought I recognized her in a crazy woman who was walking naked in the street, getting angry as she spoke to the sun. Soon, though, I realized I'd made a mistake. Was I just seeing that woman's hopeless earthen face everywhere? I gave myself a good shake to snap out of it.

8

The quarter of La Briqueterie opened up before me like a wound. The sun was high in the sky, and starvation was twisting my stomach into knots. Tossed into the middle of the neighborhoods' convulsions, I ambled on like a sleepwalker. My cold, observant eye had long since been ripped from my suffering body, and my spirit's calm was still disturbed by the thousands of flies that, let me tell you, were driving me totally mad. I shook my ears and they came right back and settled on them. I shook my body and they returned, singing the national anthem in my ears. Even in the deepest depths of my suffering, I had done my best to safeguard at least some of my ideals, my sworn objectivity first and foremost among them. "Mboudjak, you vowed always to uphold your reason, above and beyond the lies of chaos," I often reminded myself.

Yet when I saw right there in front of me on the road to the *Soya* Ministry an endless line of platters filled with sweet-smelling, dried meat, seasoned with reddish ground pepper, and carelessly lined up there along the side of the road, I resolved right then to put the last thing I had on the table: my reason. How was I going to do it? Life had turned me into an herbivore, or rather an omnivore, but it was the awakening of my body's own meat that sounded the funeral bells for my brain. Or maybe, I sincerely suggest, it was that incomparable smell of greasy *soya* that, in concert with the general dissolution of the neighborhood, took possession of me and, you might say, turned me into a real dog. My ancestral tastes, my primordial condition, my natural reflexes all came back to me in a rush. To put it plainly, my senses reacted to the meat. I was showering in my own drool. My angry heart cautioned me, "Think of science."

But I barked right back, "What do you mean, science? I'm a dog after all!"

"Think of the results of all your research," said my heart.

Even I was surprised to hear myself answer, "Results? Results? What do you mean results? Can I eat that?"

Yes, whatever I said, I ceased to be a thinking dog. There in the street, right in front of me, was a temptation too big to ignore. It called out to me: "Mboudjak, there isn't a stray dog alive who can see such juicy meat and do nothing about it." If I was a stray dog, then I'd better really become one and wear the uniform proudly. I saw those long white robes dancing in front of me—I supposed they were men. I heard iron hitting iron and opened wide my unseeing eyes. I shook my head, a last effort to tear my spirit from its sudden possession by the surroundings. And I saw a man sitting behind the row of *soya* platters, a man who was sharpening one of the biggest knives I had ever seen in all my life. He was running the death blade along his fingers, but, curiously, he didn't seem to be doing anything dangerous. He was singing a familiar song, keeping time with the screeching rhythm of the metal. His simple movements struck me as surprisingly familiar; they completely bewitched my will. I licked my chops and stared some more at the meat spread out in front of the man with the knife. Suddenly the endless platters were filled with raw meat, dripping with blood.

Terrified, I hurried on.

But I was held back by a voice from beyond that carved into my gut. "Mboudjak," the voice said, "you'll die seventeen thousand six hundred and fifteen deaths before you ever eat meat as juicy as that!"

Determined to kill that voice of temptation within me, I shook my head, practically tearing my ears from my body. It was no use! The voice's words were already in my head, already in my body, already in my paws; the voice had already taken full possession of my meatless soul. All of a sudden, I took on the hesitant, poor-old-uncle gait of a harmless dog, of a mutt turned herbivore, of a dog beaten by everyone, of a snot-nosed stray, one who considers himself happy to eat his ticks but who, from sunrise to sunset, from sunset to sunrise, keeps his eyes on the grand prize. Yes, I had the grand prize right there in front of me, and I thought if I disappeared behind a petty ruse, I'd avoid drawing the attention of the man in the long white robe, who was still singing and sharpening his knife. So when I saw the man chatting with a neighbor, I moved in on his meat. The decisive moment had arrived. I didn't even take the time to enjoy the smell. I opened wide and plunged my fangs into the feast of the century. Then I took off as fast and as far as I could, paws flying. That's when a furious voice screamed and swore right over my head: *"Kai wa lai!"**

I just barely caught a glimpse as a cutlass flashed, splitting the air and crashing down on the tar next to me: thwap! I dropped my hunk of meat and saved myself with a pirouette. A knife hit the tar next to me again—zing!—and cut the piece of meat in two. I didn't think about claiming my due. I took off down the endless road. There was only the screech of brakes and a loafer crying out "Get him!" to let me know that for the third time in just one second, I'd survived my own death. I heard a crash. The motorcyclist had fallen into a platter of *soya*. Hot pepper had gotten in his eyes. The street awoke to his multivocal cries, his crazy dance, and the thousand million curses flying at my back. All the knives of all the *soya* vendors in La Briqueterie were pointing at me. The chaos spoke with one voice: "Kill that dog!"

I threw myself down the first hole I saw. I didn't realize it would lead me straight into a butcher shop. A thick scent of blood finished off what was left of my senses. I slipped on the endless flow of blood washing over the floor. This time, when I saw an ax lifted up in front of me, I closed my eyes to say good-bye to life before it was too late. Although I'm not Catholic, I mumbled out an Ave Maria. The ax came down: kabong! I felt my brains leap in my skull. Then I heard the music of running water. I was startled by strange sounds right next to me. Something dripping on my back made me jump. I opened my eyes and was shocked to realize that although I was clearly covered with blood, I wasn't dead. The butcher was still right in front of me, using a knife to chop up the meat his ax hadn't cut through. He hadn't even seen me. I did an about-face, went back through the hole of my damnation, and set off again down the neighborhood's trails.

I ran like the sprinter Lekunze.* I ran on without realizing I was getting ever more lost in the neighborhood's labyrinth. I ran to escape my own liquidation. As I ran through the court-yards of houses, people turned around and grabbed their shoes to finish me off. I just ran all the faster. Dogs tried to catch me, but I even managed to lose my shadow. I slowed down only when I was sure I was far from the cutlass, from the knife and ax prepared for my sacrifice. I stopped cold in the shadow of a wall. I was panting like crazy. My tongue hung down to the ground. My nerves were raw, exposed. My paws were un-steady. Only one thing was clear: I had escaped from my own sacrifice. Right then I made a solemn vow to the Great and Merciful God, never again would I give in to the urges of my inner stray dog. I licked the blood from my coat, the blood from the butcher shop.

In my flight I'd also managed to lose all my flies. So some-where in the deepest recesses of La Briqueterie, I sidled over to the metal wall of a bathhouse and lifted my hind leg to urinate my relief. Suddenly I realized the metal was moving. I squeezed my kidneys tight and backed away before barking.

"Shhhhhuuuuushhhhhhh!" said a woman's voice, "some-one's there."

Everything went quiet. Soon the metal started dancing again. I barked out in surprise.

"Don't you hear that dog barking?" asked the woman's voice.

Then a man's voice boomed out: "Zambo," it said, loud enough for everyone in the world to hear, "just wait for me to come out and I'll teach you some manners!"

Then the man's head poked out from under the metal sheet-ing. His head was covered in soapy foam. His eyes wandered over the flat walls of the houses and his voice exclaimed: "Really, the kids today are just awful! What an idea, coming to peek at the grown-ups in the bath!"

So I went on my way. I knew the neighborhoods quickly turned threatening. I needed to get back out on the main road. Soon I came upon a huge pile of garbage that covered the pave-ment and even the houses alongside it. The flies welcomed me with a song. They seemed to recognize me. The blood on my coat awakened their vampirish appetite. Once again hunger began to sing its song of perdition in my belly. I knew garbage was always a sacred site among wandering animals. I defended my feast against agile and quarrelsome hens. Soon I found a bone and set to gnawing it, but I was interrupted by a metallic sound that split my soul. When I lifted up my head I saw a familiar silhouette pass in front of me, straining to pull an overloaded pushcart. The cigarette vendor's face was masked, crisscrossed by the furrows of his suffering, but I'd have recognized him anywhere, even in a crowd of ten thousand. He struggled on in front of his oversized load, sculpting his taut muscles. I leaped in front of him and barked out my joy at finding a familiar face there in my seemingly endless hell. First he shooed me away, because I was blocking his path. He had to make every bit of effort count. But I didn't budge. I didn't stop leaping and prancing in front of him until he put down his pushcart.

"Dirty mutt!" he said. He bent down and picked up a stone to finish me off, but stopped his heinous act when I made eyes at him. Slowly he knelt down, put his hand on his upper lip and said, surprised, "Mboudjak, I presume?"

I barked out my joy.

9

So, alongside the cigarette vendor turned pushcart man, I finally made it to the Mokolo market. The words of the man in black had ultimately condemned him to scaling Yaoundé's hills and mountains, straining in front of loads that were always too heavy. I was happy he'd been able to find some sort of work to keep himself afloat. He'd become someone who got by: a pushcart man. After he had set down his load in front of its owner's house and taken the money he'd earned, I saw his face open into a big smile. "Hop!" he said. "Now it's back to the Mokolo market!"

I'd never been there before. What's more, I'd never been to any market at all. How could I have? After selling her fritters in the morning, Mama Mado would usually tie her *kaba ngondo* around her hips and head off down the road to the market. I'd always watched her go, sure that one day I'd follow her and see for myself this place from which she always returned loaded down with food. I'd left my master's without fulfilling that wish and now, suddenly, after a long detour on the endless streets, I found myself well on the way to one of my dearest desires. Wagging my tail left and right, I walked behind the cigarette vendor—but from now on, let's call him the pushcart man. The happy pushcart man whistled as he pulled his cart, calling out as he looked for another job: "Push-push, push-push, I haul it all!"

To really get people's attention he added, "Yes, I even haul cadavers!"

The market was crowded with hefty women, pushing and shoving each other. They seemed to meld into each other. Some carried loads balanced on their heads. Their ample shapes made it hard for people to get by. This always annoyed the pushcart man, who needed to steer his cart between generous hips and slide his body past protruding breasts. Yes, sometimes he had to put a meandering behind blocking his way back in place with a never-welcome slap. "Who slapped my butt?" the woman would ask, grabbing the hand of the man closest to her.

As the market grew busy, the pushcart man continued on his way, lifting his call up to the sky. Me, I never had any trouble with the whales. I simply snuck between their widespread legs. Frightened, they'd jump. I didn't wait for their anger to explode. Behind me I'd hear men's laughter and women's threats: "If that dog comes by here again, I'll show him!"

I'd disappear in the teeming crowd. An *opep** made its way through the market, buried under piles of merchandise. The truck driver plowed straight into the men and women, like he was on the main road. Instead of hitting his horn, he revved his engine. The market crowd split in two to let him pass. Some women he'd really scared bent over and cursed the driver. He gave back as good as he got. Sometimes he spread his fingers wide and just swore, *"Ilang!"**

The truck had a whole pack of *bayamsalam** trailing behind it, running and holding their scarves. Various disproportionate parts of their bodies shook as they ran. Some of them ran with a baby tied to their back bouncing along, as if on horseback. Each woman focused on one spot on the back of the truck: at a bunch of plantains, a sack of tubers, or a bag of kola nuts.

The most zealous held on tight to their chosen goods, letting their feet drag behind them through the dirt. Their excited voices filled up the marketplace, drawing even more women. Some got up from their stands, holding their baby in just one arm. As they ran they'd deftly hoist him up onto their backs, and then they too would grab onto the goods piled up on the back of the roaring truck. Seeing these women in action was a real show. They spoke a thousand languages. Their many varied voices created chaos. I watched the life bubbling up within them, and I knew one thing for sure: I'd better always keep on guard if I didn't want to get squashed by the weight of their ever-distracted feet.

I scrambled between the piles of merchandise, got caught up in following the little gutters, and found myself facing the somber, wide-spread vulva of a woman right there in front of me, noisily watering fresh bunches of greens with her urine. Terrified by her destructive, animal-like action, I kept still. Next to her a kid with a belly swelled by kwashiorkor sucked on his finger as he watched his mother piss. A tearful pearl had left a line across his cheek as it dried. The woman turned around to spit on her urine and, frightened to see me, quickly covered herself with her pagne. She bent down and grabbed a plantain stalk that she brutally hurled at my nose. Speaking words I don't dare repeat, she picked up her kid; he clung to her back. As she leaned forward to tie the kid on with her pagne, she spoke in French, asking the men around to "stop their dog, huh." She pointed at me as I ran off in the distance, her eyes glaring red. I turned around and suddenly caught sight of the pushcart man's hand, rising above the human tide. I saw his mouth open, shouting the same phrase, over and over. Strangely, I thought I heard him cry, "Ripe mangoes! Ripe mangoes!"

But that was the duck-eyed boy next to me; he split the sky with the voice of someone dying a painful death. Then I saw the pushcart man stubbornly open his mouth again and scream: "*Mebala bidou!** Gets rid of mice!"

But I was wrong again. The crowd was making me dizzy. I felt trapped. The pushcart man's cry seemed to come from both near and far away at once. Only too late did I realize I was caught in life's tourniquet. This time I thought I'd actually made it to the center of the pulse. A young, heavyset man passed next to me, looking like he'd just escaped from hell. His black eyes seemed to express all the horror of his being. "I can even kill cockroaches!" he screamed.

A woman said to him, "Tell me you can kill a man and we'll be friends!"

The man looked around, measured the chattering silence of the thousand open faces around him, then smiled as he nodded, whispering to the woman, "Just don't ever tell anyone I sold you the stuff-o."

Stunned, I gaped at the man selling murder. In his hands he held metal traps, as well as a lot of little dark boxes. It was an assortment of poisons, each one surely capable of killing me ten times over. Terrified, I looked at him, and suddenly it was as if his eyes turned back into his head, as if his eyes had turned to milk, as if death had struck his soul with epileptic seizures. Yes, suddenly his face seemed familiar, like I'd already seen him somewhere in my wanderings. I barked out my suspicions to him. Caught red-handed in the noisy silence of this unseeing market, he jumped, and then started up again with his evil refrain as he hurried away. He was lost in the generalized confusion, taking his sinister cry with him. Only then did I realize it was the blind beggar with the glasses I'd run into before. I hurried on, sneaking between feet. But my blind murder vendor had disappeared in the mass of people. Or maybe his song had been swallowed up by the market's ever-deafening rumor, or maybe just by another, louder refrain, "Come and cheat me! Come and cheat me!"

That was the peanut vendor's refrain. I would have loved to ask that squinty-eyed man how many people he'd ripped off so far as he sang the praises of his own naïveté. His face was exploding here and there with pustulant pimples. His refrain went right through me. A woman nursing a kid I thought looked about ten years old stopped in front of him. The peanut vendor stopped professing his naïveté in song and asked her how many peanuts she wanted. The woman told him and he began to serve her. He filled his measuring cup with machine-like speed. The woman told him to slow down and asked to look inside his measuring cup. Shouting a curse from the south, the peanut vendor refused: "*Mi nal mi.*"* The woman brutally grabbed his hand in order to expose his tricks. The peanut vendor struck the poor woman's arm, saying she didn't have to teach him his job. She got angry and told the peanut vendor he was nothing but a crook. "And you, you're a card-carrying whore," the vendor retorted.

"Raving lunatic," said the woman, pulling her child from her breast the better to answer.

"Whore!" the vendor shouted again.

"Abracadabra!" said the woman.

"Whore!" the vendor insisted.

And then woman pulled out the word of the century: "Anti-constitutionally!"

The loafers all around burst out laughing. Their voices grew loud. The market got even livelier, the crowd more compact. The woman's oversized kid suddenly started to cry. He cried like a grown man. The peanut vendor scornfully dismissed the woman with a wave of his hand: "Ma'am, get out of here with your bad luck-o!"

And as the woman left, taking her kid's shocking tears with her and, yes, eliciting exclamations from the crowd behind her, the peanut vendor took everyone present as his witness: "A real witch that one is, I tell you!"

He got up on his tiptoes and, shouting over everyone's head, cursed the woman who'd dared to expose him in public. "*Youa mami pima!*"*

The woman didn't answer. She must have been out of range. Even her child's adult voice had already been eaten up by the ambience of the market. I scurried beneath some women's stand and took up position next to the naive vendor to observe him. I easily ascertained that his measuring cup was, in fact, stuffed with paper. I wanted to bark out my accusations when a voice above me spoke in my stead: "God alone is witness, God alone is witness to the cowardice of men!"

It was a Jehovah's Witness, a man with a beard like Jesus Christ and bulging eyes. He, too, had seen the trick of that man who sold his peanuts as if he were competing against the most naive man on earth, and who yelled at the customers who exposed his tricks. The man with the bulging eyes held up a big, black Bible with a big red cross on its cover. He spoke in the bright sunlight with the authority of a visionary.

"Go tell Him all about it then!" the peanut vendor retorted, brazenly pointing to the sky.

"Don't fool yourself, my friend," the Jehovah's Witness went on, shaking his Bible, "God's Great Eye is always turned toward Earth. His Great Eye sees all those little things you do down here."

The peanut vendor grew impatient. "Don't go chasing away my customers with that Great Eye of yours, huh!" he said, pushing aside the itinerant preacher.

The peanut vendor traced a circle in the dirt that the Witness was not to cross. His adversary accepted the distance imposed upon him, but only to cross it all the more insistently with his insatiable word.

"Yes, believe me," he said, "everything has a purpose here on this Earth! Even the most evil things you do in your own room, He sees them. The little thefts you commit and think are hidden, He sees them. The little tricks you play here at the market, He sees them. God's Great Eye watches over all of us and knows each of our sins. Why should we try to hide from Him that we are sinners when He has already seen all our sins?"

The curious crowd that had been drawn by the quarrel between the peanut vendor and the woman grew even bigger around this man who spoke over and against the market's insurmountable rumor. Inspired by his audience, the Witness pointed to Heaven and Earth. He pointed to the peanut vendor. He pointed to the face of somebody standing in front of him. He grabbed that person by the arm. The man resisted. "Repent, my brother," he insisted.

"I've already repented," the man said, trying to escape.

"It doesn't matter, repent again."

The man backed away. The Witness recited a biblical quote or two, citing chapter and verse at the end of each. Since his sermon was turning into just another boring, daily routine, I was getting ready to go when a woman's cries split the air, "Stop! Thief!"

The woman's shout was taken up by the throng. Those listening to the Witness roused themselves. They gathered around the woman, who appeared to have been struck on the head by that very One who sees All. I saw her pat her bosom, her stomach, her ass, stomp on the ground with her feet, hit herself on the head, search again in her bosom, and then search, re-search, and re-re-search once more in her bag. Her things fell all around her on the ground, but she didn't seem to notice. The Jehovah's Witness asked her to calm down. Waving his arms, he tried to calm the excited crowd. He threatened to bring his Bible down hard on somebody's head. The woman turned around, stared at the faces of all those gathered around, grabbed the hand of a young man standing behind her, and, showing him to the crowd, screamed, "It's him!"

The young man protested. He didn't seem to understand what was happening. The crowd squeezed tight around him. The woman kept accusing him. Voices were raised. Hands rose up over the young man's head. The woman said it was a plot. She said the young man had always been behind her. He'd followed her all over the market, she added. Yes, she'd noticed him. The young man protested. He lifted up his hands to show his innocence. He swore by God, by He who sees All, and even took Allah as his witness. But then, somebody hit him. It must have been the Jehovah's Witness, who asked him not to take the Lord's name in vain. The young man doubled over. A loafer hit him on the back. He fell down even further. A cowardly blow with a knee made him get back up again. He raised his torn and bloody lips. His voice became pleading. All I could hear amid the brouhaha of the crowd was his voice, crying. Yet his voice was too faint to calm the ever-mounting rage of the market around him. Some women next to me remembered thefts of which they'd been the victim, weeks, months, or even years before. Some *bayamsalam* came at him with plantain stalks. The young man managed to lift his bleeding mouth up above all the curses. He spat out his teeth and tried to protect his face with his hands. Each time, however, an assassin's hand uncovered his brow and struck at his eyes. The young man backed up. He backed up right into the corner where I was. He jumped on the counter under which I was hiding, leaped down on the other side, and took off running.

The crowd chased him, shouting "Thief!" The young man

took off across the noisy Mokolo market. Fists flailed behind him, trying to catch him, to grab his shadow. He ran as fast as he could, bumping into everyone as he did. The whole market chased after him, trying to smother him and stop his advance. He leaped over women's goods and just kept running even faster. I saw the young man disappear in the distance with a whole furious pack on his heels. He ran like a convict fleeing his death sentence. Sometimes someone would come out from behind a counter to strike him a mortal blow. Luckily the young man zigzagged as he ran. He sidestepped each and every arm that thought to deliver the fatal blow. He ran to save himself from the crazed market. He ran right to the Mokolo police station. I found the pack clinging to its fence. The men's and women's voices were still loud. Hands were calling for the man's head on a platter. They were clenched tight, whether forming a deadly fist or holding a plantain stalk. They shook the fence with all their might. The police commissioner poked out his peppery face. He held a walkie-talkie in his hand and screamed orders at the crowd. "Silence!" he told the gathered mob.

The pack wouldn't be quiet. It wanted the young man handed over so that it could punish him, show him what's what. I could still see that young man who'd managed to escape his lynching, spitting out his teeth. His shirt was covered with blood. He stood between two policemen, one big, the other small. From the signs he was making, he seemed to demand that they lock him up. I heard a voice next to me saying how he regretted not having taken part in the bloody feast.

"He got lucky, huh!" exclaimed one of the black marketeers.

"There are already too many thieves here in the market," said a loafer wearing dark gangster's glasses. "What do you expect, it's the crisis!"

The black marketeer looked at him and said menacingly, "They need to be taught a lesson!"

Just then, the woman who'd been robbed made her way through the crowd and ran, sobbing, to Mokolo's somber-eyed police commissioner. Her head was uncovered. Her ample form shook as she ran. The Jehovah's Witness was right behind her. When a policemen tried to stop him, he just said he was a wit-

ness. He showed them his huge Bible and threatened to bring
it down hard on a policeman's head. The officer stepped aside
and let him pass. Then the policeman took his revenge on the
anxious crowd, which wanted to follow in the steps of the last
witness. He shut the gates of the police station as if they were
the gates to Heaven. The crowd gathered, grumbling loudly
behind the locked fence. But I was able to squeeze through its
bars. I sidled along the wall and found myself right next to the
seat of the final judgment.

"Sir," the woman said, addressing the police commissioner,
"I'm so sorry."

I thought I hadn't heard right. "I was looking for my wallet
and just couldn't find it," she said.

I couldn't believe my ears. The young man went pale. And the
commissioner growled, baring his menacing teeth, "What?"

He stopped talking into his walkie-talkie. Opening his
blood-red eyes wider than you can imagine, he screamed at the
woman, "And now you've found it?"

"Yes, sir."

"This is impossible!"

Trembling, the woman pulled out her wallet, "You see, I'd
tucked it in my pagne!"

The volcanic commissioner tore it from her hands. Turning
to the two policemen, he said simply, "Officers, put *this* in the
cooler for me."

He put a deadly stress on the "this." And as the woman's
sobs began to fade in the darkness of a cell, the young man
she'd falsely accused was suddenly greeted like a hero by the
crowd clinging to the police station's gate, the very same crowd
that just moments before would have scalped him, no questions asked. With the back of his hand, the young man wiped
the blood off his face. The door of the police station opened
wide before him. Some loafers, all too happy at the surprising
turn of events, rushed to the police station's open doors to greet
him with an ambiguous joy. The police pushed them back to
the gate. Their voices joined together and rose up in one big
hoot, directed both at the woman too eager to accuse, whom
they could no longer see, and at the police who kept them from
giving full rein to their passions. A little while later, when only

the most stubborn of the curious onlookers were still posted at the police station gate, the Jehovah's Witness came out too. He must have tried to get the police commissioner to repent, because he no longer had his Bible with him, but had a big bump on his head instead.

The young man had stopped a second to piss out his relief against a wall. The Witness found him there and immediately launched into a sermon on the Greatness of God, "He who sees All." He apostrophized the marketplace, pointing out the miracle there urinating against the wall, saying he was living proof of God's omniscience. The young man stopped pissing to threaten him, saying he was the cause of it all. He screamed at him, but the Witness didn't respond. Tired of speaking for nothing in the crowded market, where everyone now stared at him like some sort of Lazarus, the young man hailed a passing candy vendor and ordered a Coke. He drank it, his eyes closed with pleasure. Then he stopped and violently spat out a mix of Coca-Cola and blood, again cursing the Witness who still hadn't shut up. But could the man who'd escaped from the clutches of the market silence his own legend? Commentaries were popping up all around him in an endless explosion. People said he was the first to ever escape alive from the wrath of Mokolo. And then I knew that the legend of this escapee from hell was sure to enrich the neighborhoods' unstoppable rumor. For the time being, though, the young man was going to disappear into the burning ambience all around, no doubt surprised to have escaped, safe and sound, from the fury of the *bayamsalam*.

"He was really lucky!" one of the black marketeers kept repeating, even after the young man had disappeared into the tightly packed crowd.

The black marketeer had his hand clasped over his mouth and kept shaking his head. His neighbor with the gangster glasses added, "If it were me, I'd go right home and screw my wife. I'm sure I'd give her twins!"

I shook my head. Oh! That's men for you, I said. Suddenly I realized how carried away I'd been by it all. Caught up in the rhythm of the market, I hadn't even noticed that I'd lost sight of the pushcart man since . . . well, a while ago. With great difficulty, I swallowed my new loneliness in the midst of the multitude. Suddenly, the thousand faces of the men and women and their indomitable voices said nothing to me. It was as if, with the pushcart man gone, I'd once again lost the way back to Madagascar, the way back to the craziness of my master's bar which was so familiar to me.

IO

A whole crowd of men were packed tightly around a woman with three big jugs of palm wine in front of her. Flies were dancing a ballet around her bottles. She chased them away with a clap of her hands. Her clients were noisy. Their devilish commentaries livened up the street. The men were talking in the chaos, and their voices created chaos. But still, in their brouhaha I picked out the voice of the pushcart man and ex–cigarette vendor. Yes, his voice was the loudest of all, and it shook the street with its passion. It was promising loud and clear to marry some woman. He must have been talking to the palm wine vendor because his voice also said she made the best wine in Cameroon, and then asked her to run a tab for him. The woman insulted the pushcart man, asking what he'd done with all the money he'd earned that day. The pushcart man's voice said that she, the palm wine vendor, had it all tucked between her breasts. He got up to see for himself and that's when I saw his already liquefied face. The woman covered her bosom. Her clients burst out laughing. The drunk pushcart man said, "I still want to marry her, in spite of her faults."

He danced as he spoke. My eyes met his illuminated gaze. "Leave somebody else's woman alone-o," a man said.

Soon the pushcart man came to urinate on a pile of garbage heaped up right behind the palm wine shack. He didn't even notice me next to him as he urinated, although I'd barked to let him know I was there. It seems he was already possessed by the vapors. He didn't even recognize me anymore. His eyes were shot red. He spat on his urine and, without zipping up his pants, went back to his seat by the woman, where he started up again with his line. I came and lay down at his feet. I had no choice, he was my only lifeline in the chaos of this market. He let me sit there and, happily, didn't pull my tail. The woman lifted her fly swatter. Since I'm no fly, I didn't move. She swore at me. The pushcart man came to my defense. "Let him be," he said, happy to realize I was there, "he's my dog. And don't go trying to change subjects on me. I've already told you, *ma din wa,** I love you. I know you only love money, but I still love you."

That got the men going. The words "I love you," tossed out in the middle of all the dissolution, caught their attention. Some applauded. Others guffawed. The pushcart man took a few coins from his pocket. He counted them several times, then handed them over to the palm wine vendor and said it was her dowry he was paying. The woman burst out laughing and poured him another serving of wine. "That'll only buy you this," she said.

"Pour a little more," begged the suddenly gluttonous push-cart man.

A man interrupted, "So it's not her dowry anymore?"

"That's family business," said the pushcart man.

Irritated, he turned back to the woman and shouted angrily, "Pour, will ya?"

"Pay first," replied the determined woman.

"Don't you know about the crisis?" said the pushcart man.

The woman poured out a few more drops. He sat down on an up-turned crate, poured a bit of wine next to my muzzle, and then shut his eyes before taking a drink. The men left him to his indecision. I watched him drink without shooing away the flies dancing around his glass. So that's what the cigarette vendor's become, I said to myself sadly, a drinker, yes, a *kwateur*. Around him the men's voices had quickly found another topic for their disputes and commentaries. I'm sure it's what they were talking about before the drunken pushcart man had launched into his routine: football. A man stood up. He had a bald spot too big for his head. His lips were peeling from all the red wine. He threw his big hands in the air, bitterly shaking his head, and noted that Cameroon was finished. "Yes," he said, "when you get beaten by Chad, I tell you!"

His neighbor spoke up, "Soooooooo trrrrrrrrue!" he said forcefully. He took a swig of his palm wine before giving his opinion. "We should just take away the citizenship of all those players!"

His eyes turned red. I can't say if it was the alcohol or his anger that made him explode.

"Which president was it who just sent his whole national team to prison, eh?" he asked.

"The president of Zaire," came the reply.

The man said that never, not ever had Cameroon been beaten by "a country like Chad," and six goals to none, to top it off. He shook his head again and said, "Lions like those deserve a lesson. They should be locked up for life for their affront to the national honor."

"What nation?" asked one man's voice.

Soon the man who'd spoken was on his feet. He had a head like a bulldog. He spoke of treason. He said none of the others understood anything, least of all the guy who was demanding they send the Lions to prison for life. "If we were beaten," he said, "it's because *that Biya of yours* made off with all the Lions' money, right? And you, you go on about national honor!"

He said "that Biya of yours" while pointing disdainfully at the road. But his voice was drowned out by the others' commentaries. Some seemed not to give a damn about either the nation or Biya himself. They preferred to talk about football, and nothing but football. They counted the errors made during the game. Others blamed the referee. They said he'd sold out. They shook their fists, letting their bodies be carried away by the force of their arguments. The palm wine seemed to make them even more vigorous. They became football players themselves. The Indomitable Lions. They struck at the air. They became the coach, Manga Onguene. They thought of a better lineup for the team. Sitting next to me, the pushcart man was silent. At times he turned back toward the woman selling palm wine and seemed to notice her for the first time. Then he'd try to whisper some sweet nothing in her ear. The woman shooed him away with her fly swatter. But he wasn't going anywhere. His eyes had turned to liquid, his gestures become slow, but he still wasn't a fly, no more than I was. He stammered incomprehensible sentences. I heard him say melodramatically, "Ma'am, I love you!"

Then he stood up and shouted again: "Yes, *ma din wa!*"

"But I don't love you," said the woman as bluntly as a *bayamsalam.*

The men weren't paying attention to those two anymore. The pushcart man seemed possessed. But a devil also seemed to have taken hold of the mind of the man with the bulldog head. Or rather, it was like he'd been bitten by some bug. He spoke and a spray of saliva flew out of his mouth. He spoke with grand gestures. Many of the drinkers in the shack were aligned against him. They all raised their voices to drown his out. That only made him argue all the more vehemently. He shook the shack with his free-flowing words.

"What do you mean, politics?" he said. "It's fear that's gonna kill you. Just what have they done to us, huh? *The Biyas* fuck over our national team, and we all blame the players. Think about it, brothers, just think! *They* eat up the players' money, and we say the players aren't worth anything anymore. And it gets worse: *they* empty the government's coffers, and we think the country is poor. Now we get beaten by any old team, and *they* make us believe we're not worth anything anymore. What's worse: they make us believe it's the referee's fault. When are we going to stop letting them manipulate us with their speeches? *They* tell us to leave politics to the politicians, and look how they fuck up our team! Look at how they fuck up our football! Yes, look how they fuck up our country! When are we going to get down to the real source of our problems, eh? You tell me, when are we going to get to the root of all our troubles?"

"I wasn't there, no-o," said one man as he left the group of drinkers.

One or two others left with him. Soon the palm wine vendor got up and told the man with the bulldog head she didn't want any politics in her shack. "You're chasing away all my customers with that big mouth of yours," she said.

That only got him all the more riled up. "Precisely," he said, "I don't want any more politics either! That's why I say we should arrest all the leaders instead, and put them in prison. If Cameroon gets back on track, you'll see, we'll finally have some good football! That's why our suffering, our misery, our decline, and even our defeat the other day are all about politics!"

The woman just couldn't calm him down. "Yeah, they're fucking over our country," he said. "They loot our wealth, they bleed our economy dry, they kill our football, they liquidate our well-being, they gut our future, they trample our will, they eat up our dreams, they knock off our grandeur, they squash our intelligence, they sell our kids into slavery, and each and every time they tell us to not get involved in politics. They distort our history and lie about our present. They put off anything good that might be coming our way. They say we're always to blame, and we believe it's our fault we're poor. They point out scapegoats among us, and we start tearing each other limb from limb. Dogs, they're all nothing but dogs! And you go on about national honor! They starve us, they sell us out, they steal our lives and turn our bodies to stone. They eat our shadows, and we say it's just fate, or that it's Famla. That it's because of the crisis, or colonization. That it's because of the whites or because of a bad exchange rate. That it's just bad luck, or the curse of Ham! But really it's those imbeciles, yes, it's *they and they alone* who're responsible for our decline!"

He insisted on the "they and they alone," still pointing at the street. The space around him had cleared out. His ideas about dogs didn't exactly endear him to me, either, so I stepped away too. The men who stayed were whispering things I couldn't quite get. A couple of times I caught just the words "opposition" and "crazy." There was no way to shut the man up. Even the palm wine vendor had finally left this bottomless pit of words to himself. Cursing him all the while, she picked up her jugs of wine and put them in the nearest pushcart. The pushcart man smiled, because it was his cart. The woman knew whose it was, but she had no choice. A stubborn suitor is better than a member of the opposition who just won't shut up. As she left her shack she said to the hurrying pushcart man, "If you break my bottles, you'll pay for them, huh!"

I ran to catch up to the mismatched couple. Just then the voice of the man with the insatiable anger rose up above the frenetic drumming ambience of the Mokolo market: "It's the Biyas who should lose their Cameroonian citizenship!"

"Who says he's Cameroonian?" another voice asked.

There was a dry laugh, "Yeah, Biya is French!"

The palm wine vendor ordered the pushcart man to hurry up. She set herself up far away from those subversive words. Some of her customers followed her, plugging their ears and leaving the talking man of Mokolo alone in the clearing emptied by his uncontrollable logorrhea. As for the pushcart man, once he'd emptied his cart, he stumbled off down the road. I followed him. He wasn't in love anymore, but he was still thirsty. He stopped in front of a bar. Its door read, "Credit Died Yesterday—Bar." When I tried to follow him in, the curt barks of another dog told me to get out and go calmly on my way "if I didn't want any problems." It was a minuscule, starving mutt.

"There's no place here for stray dogs," he said.

I didn't have the strength to respond. Suddenly a wild nostalgia for my master's bar enveloped my soul.

I I

After many twists and turns, when the pushcart man finally stopped in front of Massa Yo's bar, I could hardly recognize the mustachioed man slunk down behind the cash box as my master. Yet neither the courtyard of The Customer Is King nor my master had changed. Only the cigarette vendor's stand was missing, and with good reason. Yes, with good reason. Ludo players were noisily wasting their day, sitting around Mama Mado's stand, otherwise empty at that hour. The Panther Nzui Manto was with them. He, too, was arguing loudly. He clapped his hands and hit himself on the head in disappointment. As he spoke, his words shook the sheet metal that made up the little stand. His word was impassioned, like always. A cackling hen scurried in front of me. She thought she'd seen a canine ghost. I reassured her and watched her lift her crest and repeat her surprised cry: "cluck cluck cluck!" My master lifted his head and saw the pushcart man leaning his cart against the wall of the bar. "So now you have a dog-o," he said, surprised.

So the cigarette vendor turned pushcart man meant that little to him after all. "It's *your* dog," he replied with a laugh.

"What?"

"Don't you see? It's Mboudjak!"

My master tore himself from his torpor. Yes, it was really me. After an eternity, I'd come back. I saw Massa Yo debate what sort of punishment he could inflict on me. I saw him hesitate, not knowing if he should punish me or just tell me to get out, to "take my bad luck and go." Later he'd ask Soumi to wash me and tie me up, "so I wouldn't start again. Enough is enough!"

Later he'll say my relapse was unforgivable, but this time he just didn't have it in him to take it out on my behind. I had simply gone too far. "Four months," he kept on repeating. "Four months, I tell you!"

Me, I was worried about other things. The season of my wandering had quickly come to an end here in this courtyard, where I'd returned on my own four feet. Now my freedom of movement was suddenly cut down to the length of a chain tied around a post. Should I be happy about this? The hens that had recognized me when I'd arrived came over to hear the stories of my explorations. Seeing me tied up, they lifted their beaks in surprise: who can prefer chains to wandering? They didn't believe me when I said I'd come back because I missed my master's bar. How so?! They believed me even less when I said that life on the road is no life at all, and that in order to survive, you have to give up your intelligence. They repeatedly raised their voices: "Freedom has no price."

I said that for me, freedom of the *mind* was dearer still. I stressed the word "mind." They burst out laughing but didn't get mean about it. Yes, the hens tried to understand, they did. Other animals just made fun of me outright. For example, a lizard ran across the wall of the bar and cocked his head several times. *"Aschouka ngangali,"* he teased, "who asked you to come back?"

I lay down and covered my eyes with my ears, so as to block out his insults. I stayed that way all evening. I got up and barked angrily only when one of the local strays came to lord my plight over me by strutting proudly in front of my master's bar. Then I leaped up and bared my threatening fangs. The chain held me back, hurting my neck. I promised I'd tan his behind when the time was right. He barked out his laughter. "Come and get me then," he said, waving his behind at me, albeit from a safe distance.

It was my master who chased him off by flinging a shoe at his head. Even as he went on his way, he kept right on making fun of me. His barks were strident and split my soul in two. I opted to cover my head with my paws so as not to hear him anymore. I stayed like that a good while, cut off from the wide world, with my head covered by my ears and my paws. I was ripped from my seclusion by Panther's lively voice, which had suddenly taken over the whole of my master's courtyard. The little old man was talking about a lack of respect. He said kids today had no respect for their elders. He spoke of the dog days, taking as his own the title of the book by the man in black. It was because little Takou had told him he talked too much. Dumbfounded, Panther wanted to punish the cheeky little kid, but he'd sought protection behind the ludo players. One of them immediately came to the kid's defense. "Come on, you know it's true, Panther," he said, "so why are you getting mad, huh?"

His partner added that the little old man should be careful, since a crazy, loudmouthed fool had been arrested in Mokolo. He went on to stress that in a country like this where even the crazy were arrested, you had to know how to keep your mouth shut if you wanted to stay out of trouble. "Cameroon is Cameroon." Panther took that moralizing lesson poorly and got even angrier. He left the troublemaking kid and his ludo-playing defenders there and ran to my master for support. Massa Yo just said, referring to little Takou, "Don't you always stick up for him?"

It was clear what was going on. Panther had come up to my master when he was serving a customer. Massa Yo just didn't want to get involved in the argument. Shunned on both sides, then, Nzui Manto vented his disappointment to the street and the quarter. He went on about a loss of values. He called Madagascar a "quarter full of bad seed." He went on about how morals lost their meaning in the city, how white hair was nothing more than cotton, and added, "*Ba tchùn boun makoup**— idiotic city folk!"

The ludo players who'd gotten him riled up wouldn't keep quiet.

"Chief," one of them said, "nowadays, in case you don't know, we have a tradition of silence, huh."

I didn't bark. I was learning again how to stand up to little Takou's trickery and the daily routine of Madagascar. In the end, I told myself, Docta's son was just a kid like all the others.

A beggar passed by. His face was twisted around toward his back, like he was singing his sinister song to his shadow. It was the world's worst tune. A kid held his arm to keep him from falling. My master's customers plugged their ears and closed their eyes. They were obviously horrified by the beggar's infirmity and by his song—but since I knew them well, I'll say here that it was simply because they were misers. The beggar just kept on singing even louder. He sang loud enough to crack the tar on the street. He sang to drive you crazy, shaking his backward body. His kid stopped in front of The Customer Is King. He looked at my master with his sad eyes and showed him an empty plate. Massa Yo tossed in a coin and shooed him away. The kid didn't move. He looked at my master's customers and, after emptying the plate, held it out to them. Behind him, his father kept singing his hellish melody even louder. "That's enough already," said my master, unable to take it anymore, "get out of here!"

The kid ran to his father for protection, but the beggar didn't move. On the contrary, in a stumbling French he grumbled out his shock at the dryness of men's hearts. He pointed inside my master's bar as he spoke. He said men were wicked by nature, that they plugged their ears as soon as their bellies were full.

"You think you're going to make people give you something like that?" asked Massa Yo, clearly irritated by the continued presence of the beggar in his bar courtyard.

He turned back toward his customers, "He's gonna bring me bad luck, I tell you!"

"And you, brother," a customer said to him, "don't be so stingy. Give him a little something more. It's not gonna ruin you!"

"So why don't you give him something yourself?" replied my master.

"Do I have any money?" the man said. "We're the ones in crisis, right?"

As if in response to the customer's words, the beggar's voice turned prophetic. It spoke of the end of the world, of Signs, of tens of thousands dead, of the Apocalypse. Freed from the grip of Yaoundé's noisy, violent streets, I suddenly understood the truth of these words. I barked out my sympathy to the beggar. My master didn't believe a word of it. He stubbornly tried to put a stop to it. Then he headed back inside his bar, abandoning his courtyard to the beggar's evil visions. Just then Mama Mado crossed the courtyard on her way back from the market. She had a platter balanced on her head. Soumi ran to help her and she put the platter on his head. I saw the kid turn into an ugly midget just like that. I barked out my welcome to my mistress. But I was also barking to let her know I was back. She saw me, gave a start, and immediately made a face. She walked by the beggar as if there were nothing strange about it. As she passed, she put a little something in his son's plate, asked him to leave, and went into her husband's bar. My mistress's voice was drowned out by the melodies of the beggar, who still wasn't leaving. I thought I heard Mama Mado arguing with her husband in the bar. Soon she came back out and went on into the house. "But I'd asked him not to bring another dog here!"

Clearly she thought I was some other dog. I was a little let down and grumbled as she passed. When the beggar's kid gave his father my mistress's offering, he immediately ceased his curses. He thanked his benefactress profusely, covering her whole family with blessings. Then he raised his voice and said, pointing to my master's bar, "Do not be cheap like that man there-o!"

He immediately started in again with his supplicating melody:

> "Those who don't take care of their neighbor
> When their own belly is full
> Will soon have their last laugh-o!
> The end of the world is near
> For those who exploit their brothers-o!
> Help a poor blind man, cut down by life-o!"

On he sang without budging. My master came out of his bar wielding an empty crate to chase him away once and for all. Massa Yo's eyes said he was ready to commit a crime. The beggar tripped as he fled backwards, but he didn't fall. I saw him hurrying away behind his kid, although it looked like he was coming back into the courtyard of The Customer Is King. My master screamed that he was lucky he was a cripple or else he would've "shown him what's what." When my master turned back to his bar, he met the amused faces of all his customers. One of them said, shaking his head, "The world is really something, let's get on with life!"

"Con artists," said Massa Yo, putting down his crate. "You help them and they just curse at you."

As he went back into the bar, he looked at me and shrugged. In the distance, the dissonant revelations of the beggar with the kid started up again.

12

Even though I was tied to a stake, I rediscovered Madagascar's daily routines. Or rather, I rediscovered my master. If I had looked at him once before my wanderings, now I looked at him nonstop. My movements were limited, and of course I couldn't see when he was hidden behind his counter, but all the same, yes, all the same: what could be going on there that I didn't already know? To tell the truth, with the passage of time each of Massa Yo's gestures had lost its triviality. My master hadn't changed in the least, and strangely he was someone else altogether for me. The way he stared out down the long street to draw in as many customers as possible. The way he answered the passersby who greeted him with the arrogance of someone whose only friend is money. And of course the way he looked at, no, devoured the behind of every passing girl. Suddenly it all seemed quite remarkable to me. I was a little sad he hadn't changed the least bit, and yet, hadn't I come back to him, looking for the familiar routine I had missed so much when I was wandering down the city's endless streets and the neighborhoods' alleyways? I looked at my Massa Yo of a master standing in front of the door to his bar, and in his repetition of the same old time-worn gestures, I tried to discern the symphony of the wholly new.

Night fell.

The courtyard of The Customer Is King had emptied out, and suddenly I saw the man in my master come to life. He was making eyes at a skinny woman, one last customer who wasn't really one, but who was still there, sitting on an upturned crate. She was an *associée*, a hooker. He was chatting with her casually. I even had the impression he held his stomach in and pumped out his chest, trying to look younger. Yes, much to my amusement I realized he had actually started to wobble, walking bowlegged like a gorilla. Suddenly he was laughing a lot more than usual. And when he laughed, he showed all his teeth. He told some pointless story and laughed at it himself. The woman wasn't listening to him. She wiggled her foot nervously and occasionally rolled her eyes, as if to say "*A bo dze-a!* What's he up to?" Growing impatient, she soon said: "*Asso*, aren't you even gonna give me a little something?"

She didn't have time to waste. I saw my master jump. It was like the crucial element missing in his pursuit of the girls had been revealed, suddenly hitting him smack in the face.

"Just for your eyes, ma'am," he said, gallantly. Then he bowed. "It's on the house."

Now the woman was smiling. I looked at my master. Suddenly I realized what had changed. While before he'd looked just at the girls in the street, the young talent straight out of high school and middle school, now he wasn't so picky. There's always some guy who's the butt of everyone's jokes, and that's him. Massa Yo was rushing headlong to make up for lost years. For the first time he seemed old to me. His gestures were awkward. You could see the nervousness in his steps. Like a stork who still hadn't caught anything at the end of the day, he was pecking at everything that moved. He seemed to be playing a role, but it was himself.

"If that's how it is," said the woman, and she paused, "then I'm only drinking imported beer."

Scratching her nails as she thought for a moment more, she said, "An *nsansanboy*, ice-cold."

As she ordered, she shook her shoulders and shut her eyes. My master answered with an innocent smile, "No problem."

Massa Yo disappeared into his bar and came right back out with a bottle. "Here," he said, as he opened it and set it in front of the woman. She didn't even say thank you. She put the bottle to her lips a few times. Her eyes closed with pleasure.

Still standing in the entrance to the bar, my master watched her drink. I watched his Adam's apple move as his appetite grew. He went quickly into the bar, as if he'd forgotten something, then came right back to the door and crossed his empty hands over his belly. His eyes were fixed on the woman. His Adam's apple danced again. He looked up and down the empty street in front of him, as if a curious spirit were passing by, spying on all his business. Soon the woman got up and said, quite sure of herself, "So off we go?"

My master looked at the street again as if she had told him to get lost! "Where are we going?" he asked.

"Your place, right, *asso*?"

My master interrupted, "What do you mean, 'my place'?"

I saw the woman's eyes laugh: "Hee-hee," she giggled, "are we gonna do it *here*?"

She waved dismissively at the interior of my master's bar, at that ridiculous "here" with the little bed hidden behind the bar, that "here" that groveled on all fours, eager to show the amused woman its smelly horror. My master courageously admitted, "Yes."

He had to cut through the *associée*'s surprise to get out his humiliating "yes." I saw her close her eyes ever so slightly. I saw her turn up her nose in a gesture of disdain. I saw her lips freeze in a sneer. I saw her hands clap together, as if she were ready to let loose with one of those laughs only the women of our neighborhoods can make: "Hee-hee-hee!" The light inside the bar lit up her face as she stood there in the courtyard, looking in. She stared down the bar crates, undressed the counter, spit on the displays, and exposed that dirty little cot I was sure my master always had on hand in the "here" of his bar. You could read the discomfort on Massa Yo's face. His hands were shaking and his gestures were even more awkward than ever. His Adam's apple was dancing a *makossa*. I watched his metamorphosis: he was the spider dying of shame before the multicolored butterfly caught in his dirty web. Yet the woman didn't burst out laughing. She just shook her head and said, "So what are we going to do!"

She went into my master's bar. It seemed she'd seen worse, "especially in these times of crisis." Before closing the door on his prey, Massa Yo looked up and down the street like a thief. I shook my head and again covered my eyes with my ears. In all the time I'd been watching him whistle after the girls, this was the very first time my master closed the door of his bar behind one. And I, Mboudjak, could already see him beating the drum the next day, letting the whole neighborhood know he'd discovered his humanity that night, yes, that very night when he'd expected it the least. Although it's not what'll be told in the neighborhood later, I actually heard him say, as he shut the door of his bar on his late-coming long-awaited victory, *"Today na today."*

13

"Woyo-o!" screamed my master's voice inside the bar. "Woyo-o!" The bar door opened with a crash and he appeared in the rectangle of light. He was wearing only a pair of red nylon underwear. His stomach stuck out, topped by a big outie of a belly button. The suffering of his soul made his flesh quake. His repeated cry split the night. You could read the distress on his face. Massa Yo opened his mouth wide and wailed, like a man in mourning. I barked out my surprise. He didn't answer me. He ran into the bar courtyard. He ran left and looked. Then he ran to the right, to be sure. He backtracked, completely unsure of what to do. He started to run again. He disappeared into the heart of darkness, but soon came back into the light streaming from his bar. He knelt down in the middle of the street, repeating his unchanging cry of suffering in the night, "Woyo-o!"

The windows and doors lit up in houses all around. Men and women came running out to the bartender who'd lost his mind in the night. Some came with flashlights. Others had a sheet wrapped around their hips. Some had only a small pair of shorts covering their nakedness. All their faces were creased by sleep, but their eyes were wide-open and they stared inquisitively at their neighbor's suffering. A few came out with a sledgehammer in hand. Among those gathered, I easily picked out Panther's agitated silhouette. All the men were trying to calm my master's crazed gestures. They each tried to bring him back to reason. Dozens of flashlights and lamps were held in front of his face, which only made the mask of his suffering all the more visible. Imprisoned in my corner, I couldn't stop barking. The local dogs lifted up their distant voices. They asked me what happened. But who had any idea what caused my master's possession? I could only speculate. I remembered the woman who'd followed my master behind his counter the previous evening. I saw the bar door shut behind her again. I didn't know any more than that.

The courtyard of The Customer Is King was filled with a thousand voices. The men's speculations formed a thick coat that only my master's cries managed to pierce. "Woyo-o!" he cried.

In anxious voices, the crowd begged him to name the source of his suffering. "What is it Massa Yo, tell us?"

"Woyo-o!" replied my master's voice.

"Tell us what happened to you!"

"Woyo-o!" replied Massa Yo with his unchanging cry.

But soon he added in Pidgin, his dialect of disaster, *"She don kill am!"*

I felt a wave move through the crowd: "She who?" a hundred voices asked.

"Dan sapack," * said my master, "that whore."

At once everything fell silent. Each of the men and women who'd come out began to suspect what had happened. The men looked at each other. Some smiled in the darkness. Others, closer to me, laughed outright. There were some who just went back home, shaking their heads. The yellow light of their lamps went off with them, as if they were spirits walking in the night. "To drag us out of bed because of a hooker," a man said as he passed by me.

The voice walked on, shaking its flashlight. It kept shining the flashlight right in my eyes, blinding me.

"She stole your *bangala*?" another man's voice wanted to know.

"No!" said my master's voice.

"You know her name?"

"No-o."

"Was it a Mami Wata?"

"Woyo-o!"

"So what did she do to you?"

Then my master's voice took the lively street's breath away. *She don take ma million!*

"Million?" screamed everyone in surprise.

"You said 'million'?"

"Really, a million?"

And my master's voice simply replied: *"She don kill am!"* There was no way to calm Massa Yo down. The word "million" drew the thinning crowd back around him. Just then Mama Mado appeared. The shouts in the street had woken her too, or maybe her husband's voice had dragged her from her bed. I recognized her nervous gait by the dancing circle her flashlight made on the ground. The crowd let her through. I saw people rubbing their hands. There'd be a battle, wouldn't there? It's true, there was nothing left to hide now. Soon my mistress's anger made the moon hide half its face, while the chattering of the crowd's shadowy faces grew louder. I heard laughter here and there. I saw Mama Mado head back to the house, her light's circle dancing even more nervously on the ground. She spit with disgust as she passed near me. Her voice cursed Massa Yo, and all men with him. She said her husband had got what he deserved. "It's God who punished you," she said.

In the distance I heard her tell those following her, "What are you looking at? You don't deserve any better, huh! Jerks! You're all a bunch of cheaters! You're no better than him! Zeros, that's what you are, totally worthless!"

No one contradicted her. Her indignation blanketed the whole road, rousing even more of the neighborhood. This would stir up the *kongossa,* really give people something to talk about. Her voice soon disappeared into the family home. My master didn't follow her. He seemed to have sunk too low in his defeat, or maybe he knew that all excuses were useless given the seriousness of his sin. He was *bole,** that's all there was to it. He wasn't just burned, he'd been burned alive. "My million!" he cried, stubbornly.

Next to me a man holding a dimly burning lamp said, "These people are really something. Pretending to be poor when he had a million hidden in his bar!"

"Me, if I was the whore, I'd have taught him!" swore another whose shadow alone was moving.

"Still, you gotta say, women are really something," said the voice of a third man. "She lays him good, sends him to seventh heaven, and when he starts to snore, bam! She takes all his money and is gone!"

"What was he looking for outside-o?" asked a woman's voice.

"His own wife wasn't enough for him?"

"He wanted to be like all the others, and that's what did him in."

"So now he has a 'second office,' right?"

"Yeah, if he only knew where it was!"

"A million!"

"I tell you."

"So the man who can never give me a beer on credit is a millionaire?"

"Shhiiit!" exclaimed a shadow. "A millionaire living in a poor neighborhood, tell me about it!"

"That's the Camers for you."

"I tell you, Cameroon is Cameroon!"

"This'll teach him!"

"If he couldn't spend his money fast enough, that *mbok** was going to help him, isn't that right?"

"A hundred thousand, two hundred thousand, three hundred thousand, four hundred thousand . . . a million, da-addy!"

I soon noticed that the voices that condemned my master the most vehemently were the very same ones who spent their days in the courtyard of his bar. I easily recognized Panther's voice, then the pushcart man's, and most of all Docta's. Yes, the engineer, he didn't brush his teeth before he spoke. While this shadowy crowd multiplied its many expressions of surprise, my master's voice suddenly boomed out above the rumor, as if somewhere in the depths of his suffering, he'd found the solution to his problem. "Mboudjaaaaaakkk!" he screamed.

Just then I saw his demented eyes right in front of me. A thousand lamps shone down on my puny self. Without really knowing why, I was suddenly cast into the footlights. Massa Yo hurriedly undid my chain. He spoke to me as if I were a man:

"Mboudjak," he said, opening his eyes wide, "you're my last hope. I'm sure you saw which way that whore went."

Although he freed me, I didn't budge. The thousand eyes of the local men and their hundred and fifty thousand lamps cut through the obscurity of my prison only to nail me down even tighter to the ground. The stifling presence of everyone crowded all around made me dizzy. My master's strained breathing swept across my face. The rumbling rumor coming from his many neighbors curdled my blood. Massa Yo was an animal, and I just couldn't bark anymore. Honestly, I was a little afraid. Yes, I was shaking with fear. My tail was pulled tight between my legs and I was ready to run and hide. Only there were a million feet in my way. I plastered myself to the wall of the bar and tried to find a way out. My master's hand held me back. His other hand pointed at the street. I struggled. He shoved me. I backed up. He pulled me by the ears. I pulled my head back. He knelt down in front of me, showing me his tearful face. I bared my fangs. "If you are my dog," he said, trying to sound friendly, "save me!"

In fact, I couldn't say which way the woman had gone. I barked that to him, but he didn't understand. Maybe she'd left during one of my moments of distraction. To hide my shame at being chained up, I had covered my eyes with my paws on the one day I ought to have had them open to watch what was going on. The only day when I ought to have observed, I'd shut my eyes to the night's mysteries. Yes, the only day when my scientific method might have been useful, oh yes, the day when I could have lifted the song of my proud canitude up over the walls of my master's bar, I'd fallen asleep. I cowered, but my master's arm lifted me back up on my feet. He bent down to my level. He got down on all fours so he could look me right in the face. He hit the ground with the palm of his hand to rouse me from my torpor and pointed at the street. *"Katcham!"** he said.

Still, I didn't budge. Massa Yo got up on his knees and looked down on me with surprise. Dumbstruck, he stared at me. He stared, ready to kill me. He stared and raised his hand. A man—thank you, my savior!—told him to leave me alone. The man said it wasn't worth the trouble, that I wasn't going anywhere. "Dogs are like that," he said.

My master paid no attention to him. He calmed himself down and, undeterred, leaned over to me and said in a thousand different tones:

"Mboudjak, *a say: katcham*!

Mboudjak, I tell you, *katcham*!

Mboudjak, *katcham*!

Katcham, Mboudjak!

Kaaaatcham!

Katchaaaaam!"

My eyes grew ever more fearful as I watched at him. My tail was pulled in so tight it had practically retreated up my anus. Then suddenly my master stood up, turned back toward his neighbors, and found his tearful voice again. "Good God!" he said, pointing at me on the ground. "What good is a dog who can't even catch a thief-eh?"

Lying flat there in front of him, I could already see the fatal blow falling on my back, punishment for a crime that was his fault, and his alone. Happily, another man—one of those who were still chattering on about my master's mourning for his million and laughing in the darkness at his suffering—sidled up to my master and whispered in the middle of his volcanic eruption. "*Mola*," he said, "my brother, I know where she went."

Immediately, my master got up and shoved his face, pale with hope, under the man's raised lamp shade. "What?" he said.

I didn't wait for him to remember I was sitting there in the dark. I took off, as far as I could. In fact, Massa Yo didn't have time to think about me again. From my hiding spot beneath his wife's empty stand, I soon saw him run into his bar. He came back out, shaking all over. He was dressed. With a loud clanging of keys, he shut the bar door. The man who'd given him hope was waiting there, lamp in hand. My master rushed off with him toward La Cité Verte, followed by some of the curious and by dozens of luminous lamps. As he walked, he cursed all the women in the world. Just as his raging voice faded out in the distance, I saw Mama Mado cross the bar courtyard. She was dragging two suitcases behind her. The light from her flashlight was dancing wildly on the ground. She was also dragging Soumi along; he let himself be led away into the night, rubbing his eyes. My mistress's fury seemed to put wings on her feet. She stopped a taxi and got in with her kid, without telling the driver where to go. When the car took off, all I heard her say as she stared at The Customer Is King was, "A cockroach like that, I tell you!"

Soon only the barking of the quarter's dogs filled the dark sky. When my master came back in the morning, he had lost his fury. The night mist had left pearls of water in his hair. His eyes were popping out of his skull. His head was sunk low into the bed of his shoulders. He must have spent the whole night wandering. He hadn't found his million. How could it be any different? Me, I knew that someone with a million stashed in his bag doesn't snore the night away in bed. At ten o'clock Massa Yo noticed his wife hadn't yet set up her fritter stand, but he said nothing. He didn't go knock on the door of the house. He just sat down on a crate in front of the door to his bar and watched the sun rise in the sky. It was another day.

14

The quarter's words killed my master. For an eternity he just stood behind his counter like he was nailed down, avoiding the sun's rays and the street's eyes, avoiding the shadow of any word, even whispered. I stayed on guard, suspecting that one day or another he'd get the idea to take the loss of his million out on me: me, the dog who hadn't been able to tell him which way the thief had gone. From then on, I lowered my behind and pulled my tail up between my legs when I passed in front of The Customer Is King. My steps were always hurried, and I hid beneath Mama Mado's stand as soon as possible. Even though he'd left my collar around my neck, Massa Yo didn't tie me up anymore. But I pitied him too much to leave him in the time of his tragic retreat from the street's words. That's because I, Mboudjak, am not mean.

The neighborhood nicknamed him "Massa Million," "Massa Mill" for short. Some, like Docta, took perverse pleasure each day in remembering the night he'd lost his million. With his never-ending teasing of my master, it was like the engineer was getting back for his own humiliation, which I, for one, had not forgotten: the humiliation still evoked by his own nickname, Totor, short for "ass wipe." At least one thing was certain, he got his revenge. He, too, had found his *mbout,* someone more cowardly than himself. He said everyone would get their turn, only for some people, their turn was something for the record books. And wasn't he right?

The story of the million stayed alive in the neighborhood's memory. The Customer Is King became famous. People passing by on the street would point to my master's bar, whispering and sniggering. I think that from then on people taking a taxi to The Customer Is King just said, "To the Millionaire's," or, to be even quicker, "To the Mill's." The myth of the million hidden under misery's bed, the myth of the million that disappeared between the hot thighs of an *associée* added to the rivers of words flooding out of all of Yaoundé's neighborhoods.

"*Me tchùp mbe ke?*"* said Panther, with a newfound ambiguity. "What did I tell you? It's the banks in this country that are really to blame for this. If the banks worked, no one would keep money under their bed! Massa Yo is right. The Mbiyas have emptied all the money out of the banks! Go put your money there so they can use it! Massa Yo, I say you were right to keep your money in your bar."

My master didn't flinch. He knew the little old man only took that political detour so that he too could make fun of him safely. Like Panther, the whole quarter laughed from then on when they saw Massa Yo standing in the door of his bar. My master grew irritable. He was angrier in the mornings when, out of pure spite, people asked where the woman who sold fritters in front of his bar was (yes, "*the* woman," as if they didn't know she was *his* wife!). I'd see Massa Yo go back into his bar, cursing everyone who just wouldn't stop sticking their nose into things that didn't concern them. I'd hear his insults shake the counter of the bar. Even when he retreated all the way to the back of his house, he couldn't escape the neighborhood's laughter, the laugh that ricocheted off his bottles of beer, the laugh that took detours just to come back and hit him when he least expected it. Once, for example, little Takou came into his bar. He slapped a coin down on the bar, like an adult would have, and said in a haughty voice that wasn't his own, "A *jobajo,* ice-cold!"

My master leaned over the puny little kid. "So who told you children come into bars now?"

Takou didn't say a thing.

"Who sent you?" my master asked.

In response to that question, the kid simply picked up his money as if he were leaving. My master grabbed his arm and threatened him in a fatherly way. Takou got away easily, but he stopped in the bar courtyard and said, "You can afford to chase away customers, no? You're the millionaire of the quarter, right?"

I watched my master rush out of his bar and run after the kid with the shameful words. He bent down, picked up a clump of dirt, and threw it after the kid's shadow. Takou sidestepped it and then, once he was a good distance away, over there, behind the ludo players, he stuck out his tongue. Massa Yo cursed him a thousand times, promising him a record-breaking punishment. As he went back in his bar, I heard him say, "You're just repeating what your father says, right?"

My master thought it was Docta ("That do-nothing Docta, yes, that worthless jerk") who'd put his own slanderous words in his son's mouth. He said a kid like Takou didn't come up with stuff like that on his own. He said *kongossa* would kill everyone in Madagascar. He said the scheming engineer was too caught up in "things that were beyond him" and had abandoned his kid to the streets. That's what had happened. And it was true, too, for in the meantime, Takou had set himself up as the mouthpiece of the neighborhood's whispers. The ludo players had clearly taken him on as the errand boy of their laziness. He was the mailman of their cowardice. He delivered their stuttering words. For example, once, a little while after the scene with the million, I saw a man put a couple of coins in the palm of the kid's hand and whisper something in his ear, while pointing his little finger at a woman sitting selling oranges on the other side of the road. Takou ran to deliver the lover's rhymes. He stood in front of the whole street and said this, which was supposed to be an ode to an orange vendor: "Ma'am, the man there says he loves you."

The woman jumped. Her neighbors burst out laughing and clapped their hands. "Hey-hey-hey, hoo!"

"I tell you, that kid's not afraid of anything, huh!" one of them said.

"What man?" the orange vendor asked the child.

He answered, "That one playing ludo over there."

The woman turned around and saw a man sitting behind a ludo board give her a friendly wave, a plastic smile on his lips. "Doesn't he have his own mouth?" she asked the kid, haughtily.

She stared down the man from a distance and continued setting up her oranges. But when the kid started to leave, she stopped him, whispered something in his ear, and gave him a few little coins too. Takou went running back across the courtyard of my master's bar to lay out the good news for the impatient lover. The other ludo players guffawed. Soon I heard the message sender complain about the rudeness of the neighborhood women: "Those bare-assed whores!" I soon learned that the orange vendor had sent the kid to ask her cowardly suitor the only question that meant anything to her in these lively streets of ours: "Where's the man?" And Takou had asked it out loud, though as usual he lowered his eyes.

Yes, that's what had become of Takou in the meantime. My master wasn't so wrong to blame his father Docta for what the kid said. That very day I heard the Panther Nzui Manto complain as well about everyone sending the engineer's son on errands. *"Bi fang men ngo kou'-o!"** he'd said. "Let somebody else's child grow up!"

I barked out my laughter, because Panther was speaking from his own experience.

In truth, Massa Yo was never able to put an end to the circulation of the myth of the million under his mattress, for if the neighborhood's words are sure to have a beginning, they never end. The best he could do was deafen his own ears to the chattering of his bar courtyard by buying a Grundig stereo and pointing its two big black speakers right out toward the street. Just like that, the courtyard of The Customer Is King turned into an *essamba*, a disco. He must have told himself that from then on, it was the music of his bar, and nothing but the music of his bar, that would shake up the neighborhood.

Chapter Two

I

That's about how it was on that evening in May; things had
started heating up around the neighborhood, and then the pushcart man returned and stood in front of my master's bar with
a piece of news so serious he'd reveal it to the street only in a
whisper. He sat down at the door of The Customer Is King with
the dignity of a visitor from afar, and between little sips of his
beer, he told his story. He spoke with a conspiratorial air, glanc-
ing around fearfully. As he spoke, *that thing* he'd torn from the
realm of his drunken hallucinations seemed to multiply and
grow all around him, and yet strangely he wasn't drunk. I saw
his listeners open their eyes wide and, like him, look left and
right down the road. Their surprised faces scanned the quarter
around them, and they all covered their mouths, as if to stop
themselves from screaming. My master left his counter to listen
in on this story that seemed on a wholly different scale than
all the other rumors he'd heard before in front of his bar. And
this time it wasn't about him. The pushcart man said that the
opposition had come out of the shadows. I perked up my ears
and heard him underscore the irrefutable evidence of his Revelation: "If you want proof," he said, "right now, as we speak,
students are protesting across town, in Obili.*"

The next day Docta told everyone that the students were demanding their scholarships be paid. So the pushcart man wasn't
just telling stories! "People," he said, "just aren't gonna take it
any longer!"

I perked up my ears even more. What? The starving masses
were starting to shake their bodies! The engineer added that

they'd gotten support from some civil servants who hadn't been paid in months. I shook my body. At last, after a long, drunken binge, Man was waking up in our neighborhoods!

"I think Biya's days are numbered," Docta said.

A few days after this intrusion by the unnamed thing, the Panther Nzui Manto took over the whole courtyard of the bar with the same conspiratorial air previously assumed by the pushcart man. He spoke of far-off places and said names I'd never heard before. No one believed him either. "But I'm telling you, people were killed," he said.

"Where?" asked one of my master's customers, wholly unconvinced, "at Ntarikon or at the university?"

"Ntarikon, where's that, eh?" my master asked.

"In Bamenda, stupid."

"Don't insult me, huh!" threatened Massa Yo.

"Nzui Manto," said an amused customer, "why don't you tell us you're just back from Bamenda."

"Yeah, tell us you've got wings," said my master.

"Lie to us, just tell us lies."

"You fly at night, isn't that right?"

Panther wasn't laughing. I think he'd never been so serious. His eyes were wholly possessed by History and saw nothing but the bloody reversals he described.

"It was just like Douala in the fifties," he said, with the authoritative tone of a chief.

Plunged back into the darkness of that violent past, he shook his head. Curiosity and surprise burst through on the faces around him. I saw my master go quietly back into his bar. I knew he'd be the hardest to convince. The loafers who'd been speculating around the ludo table drew closer. They were taking in the news, too, and I was struck by the seriousness of their eyes.

"Twenty dead?" screamed a man. "It was a massacre!"

His neighbor said, in disbelief, "All of that, just because of a protest march?"

Another concluded, "And you keep saying Biya's not a dictator!"

A few times I heard voices pronounce the word "dictatorship." I also heard the words "march" and "demands," and then "freedom." A loafer who swore his version of History was a lot closer to the truth than Panther's said, "Well, I heard there were a hundred dead."

He looked like someone just back from the morgue. Yes, he looked like someone who'd counted each of the cadavers himself, one by one. He stared intently into the faces of each of his listeners, as if to fill them with his rumor. And just like that, I saw the little old man become his disciple. Panther cocked his head, took in the eighty additional dead, and shocked himself as he wove them into his own story. Look, there's someone else who knows what happened, he seemed to say. The group in front of my master's bar kept growing. Sometimes a wave of indignation swept over the whispers: "Dead, just because they marched!" In a gesture of rage, a man exclaimed, "They're the first to die for democracy!"

The word "democracy" seemed to rouse the old cowardice lurking in my master's belly. He seemed to suspect evil spirits were present, that the sinister specters of ancient crows had awoken, and he rushed from behind his counter to chase the somber big mouths away from his door. He was boiling mad.

"Get away from the front of my bar!" he said.

He was waving his arms all around. His eyes were threatening. He said categorically, "I don't want any politics in my bar!"

Grumbling, the men who'd gathered to comment on the day's events stepped aside. Some threw insults at him and called him a coward. A few asked if Biya had helped him find his million. That only made my master even more furious. Roaring like a wild animal, he chased everyone away. I looked at him but just didn't recognize him anymore. He was shaking his hands, he was shaking his body, and he would have moved everything up and down the path. With a piece of white chalk he drew a clear line of demarcation in front of his bar and said only his real customers were allowed to cross it ("real customers," he insisted with a snarl, staring at the Panther Nzui Manto). As he went back into his bar I heard him grumble, "All they can do is talk, buying just one beer is too much for them!"

2

As the men moved away from my master's bar, History too went on its way. I learned later that before it shook up the stoop of my master's bar, the news of those who had died because they had marched, as the little old man put it, had already crossed a good many kilometers, maybe even buzzing over the length and breadth of Cameroon on its way. I admit that I'm just a dog, yes, a dog whose wanderings have never taken his paws beyond the borders of Yaoundé's neighborhoods. And yes, I concede that for my canine intelligence, Yaoundé's city limits are those of Cameroon, and Cameroon itself is the center of the world. When the men were speaking, Ntarikon always seemed like it was right next to Madagascar. In fact, I had no idea about the geography behind the rumors that my master's apolitical anger had momentarily silenced in front of the courtyard of The Customer Is King. That is, not until the next day when I heard Panther say the government had refuted the death toll "invented by the hallucinating, power-hungry opposition."

"*They* say there were only six dead," said the little old man, frustrated at the sudden loss of ninety-four deaths from his History. Indignant, he insisted on the "they." Panther had stopped beneath an electric pole, over there, next to a woman selling oranges and at a safe distance from Massa Yo's anger. He shook his head in disbelief and waved his arms about. Men quickly gathered around him. I perked up my ears to hear better, but a noise I couldn't quite make out sent me scurrying under Mama Mado's empty stand. It was little Takou, filling up the quarter's empty spaces with his games. When he saw me, he immediately started to bark. He barked and shook his head. He barked for all he was worth, but wasn't saying a thing. I'm sure he wanted to provoke me, to make me chase him across the neighborhood. With Soumi gone, he'd lost a partner for his adventures. I barked out that I was sorry he was bored, but I didn't want to play. I'm sure he didn't understand because he ran to hide behind some crates of beer. His happy laugh filled up the place. Poking his head out from behind the barricade of crates, he barked again. Massa Yo's voice called me back into the bar. Takou was waving at me. When I again barked out my situation to him, my master came out of the bar, boiling mad. He chased the kid away from his crates, insulting him as he went. Takou ran across the road, stopped on the other side, and stuck out his tongue.

"Don't let me see you here again!" screamed Massa Yo.

He grumbled that the kid was a subversive element and went back behind his counter. I didn't follow him. I lay down in the courtyard. Flies danced around my head. Beneath the electric pole, the big talkers gathered around Panther hadn't yet lowered their voices. They were talking and waving their arms about. It was like they were putting their lives on the line with each of their words.

"No no no," swore the little old man. He licked his finger and lifted it up to the sky. I turned my ears to listen more carefully to that unnamed thing that was making him so serious. Then it happened: suddenly a man's face lit up. The man exclaimed, "But you just don't get it, Chief! If *they* already admit there were six dead, then they confirm they shot at the protesters! So *they* officially admit *they*'re killers!"

The little old man still didn't believe it. "*Menmà,*" he said, still indignant, "my son, didn't you see the television last night? *They* said the soldiers only charged at the protesters because they were singing the Nigerian national anthem. *They* said it was just a bunch of Biafrans.*"

"Biafrans?"

"Good God!"

"*They* say the soldiers didn't shoot at anybody. *They* say those Biafrans just died, that they trampled each other."

"Biya is really something!" exclaimed Docta.

"Soon," a customer said, "he's gonna say the dead shot themselves in the head, I swear."

"Cameroon is Cameroon," said another meaningfully.

And I know, yes, I know it was only to stop that rumor of ninety-four censored deaths from circulating so close to his bar that my master turned on his stereo full blast. The street, oh yes, the whole street started dancing to the dissonant music of silence. It was a devilishly raucous *bikutsi: essamba essamba,* go go, faster faster!

3

Even so, echoes of what was happening in Ntarikon spread rapidly. Soon everybody knew that the "six Biafrans" in question were actually Cameroonians who'd gotten mad—and who'd done so without asking anyone's permission. Some, like Panther, could reel off their names, their *ndap,** and even their family tree; others were a little more humble, claiming only to know one of the victim's cousins by sight. With the scent of this human flesh brutally turned into sausage meat, Yaoundé suddenly grew turbulent. The silenced demands of the six men who died because they had marched brought a lot of people out into the city's streets. Before, it had been the students and some civil servants. Now the black marketeers got into the dance. They refused to keep being eaten alive by the municipality.

Then the taxi drivers again refused to work, to protest the legal shakedowns by the police. The day they went on strike, all of Yaoundé's streets were empty. From time to time a helicopter crossed the sky, like a fat, threatening mosquito. That got the hens going; panicked, they cackled and ran to hide. I ran barking across the bar courtyard too. Men hid in shops, shopkeepers closed their doors. They said the helicopter carried tear gas. Some said it was napalm, others toxic waste. They shouted that Biya had decided "to kill us all," that the day of the Apocalypse had come. Hysteria seized the quarter each time the helicopter flew overhead.

Once again, everyone in the neighborhood was shaken up by the big, bold headline of a newspaper Docta held up:

OPPOSITION MARCH
LED BY A FOOL

All the regulars of the place bent curiously over the newspaper's open pages. Even my master had been drawn in by the strangeness of this bit of news. I snuck underneath this newspaper that captivated the street's many eyes. On the first page there was a big photo, showing a little man with a bulldog head leading a united crowd. He was covered with mud and seemed to have come straight out of an asylum. He was naked. His hands were spread out and his mouth was frozen in a cry that the newspaper didn't translate. At the sight of his face, which seemed strangely familiar, I opened my eyes wide. I easily recognized the unstoppable big talker from Mokolo, and a shiver ran through my body. So he hadn't stopped talking! Maybe he'd changed his opinion on dogs? I barked out to the men that I knew that History-making man. I barked and leaped about. The newspaper was lifted up and soon I felt the men's hundred faces fixed on me. Panther's evil foot was raised but, just then, I heard my master's voice say, "Don't touch my dog-o!"

The little old man's foot froze right there. With my tail pulled back between my legs, I snuck out between the men's thousand feet and joined Massa Yo in the loud music of his bar.

4

I was lying down in the courtyard of my master's bar, surrounded by a concert of buzzing flies. Every minute or so I furiously shook my head. From time to time I gnawed on my back. Occasionally I got up and gave my whole body a good shake. Some hens pecking at the dirt next to me scurried away each time I shook myself off. They'd stop at a good distance and raise their voices in surprise. There were still no taxis on the road.

When I wanted to shut my ears and protect myself once and for all from the flies' hymn, singing voices suddenly filled the quarter. The surprised hens squawked even more. The closer the commotion came, the higher they lifted their heads. I lifted up my head, too, and saw four silhouettes coming our way. Mini Minor, the police commissioner, Virginie, and Docta were walking right down the middle of the road. Cars honked and swerved to avoid them. All four were dressed in white. It was as if I were watching the biggest wedding parade of the century. When the marchers reached my master's bar, I heard what they were chanting:

"Paul Biya—Paul Biya, Paul Biya—Paul Biya
Our President—our President—oh
Father of the Nation,
Paul Biya, our guy's hot . . ."

Then I said to myself: so Docta finally got what he was after, the world's most strategic scam—and a place in the system. Mini Minor, his godmother, cocked her head as she sang. She cut through the air in front of her, marching in time. Cradled in her arms was one of her dogs, who started barking insults when the parade of marchers reached The Customer Is King. That dog brought me rushing to the roadside. I wanted to chase him from my fiefdom. Next to the little woman, the police commissioner sang, keeping time in military style. Docta, he was marking each beat with a step, which meant he was walking a lot faster than the others. He realized this and slowed down. As for Virginie, she stayed in her aunt's agitated shadow, singing almost silently. The little woman's strong voice drowned hers out anyway. The marchers shook up the street. Each time they finished a couplet, the little woman clapped her hands four times and lifted her voice in the same refrain, "Hot-hot! Hot-hot!"

My master's customers also gathered along the side of the road to see the singers they knew pass by. Mini Minor waved at them to join in the song. When she called out to one man in particular, though, he grimaced in disgust. He closed his eyes, said "Yuck!" and emphatically spat on the ground. Some women openly turned away, or else covered their eyes with a corner of their pagne. Some loafers burst out laughing. They laughed and pointed at the tar behind the marchers. "*Ye maleh!*" they shouted. "Look!"

They were shouting so loudly that those who'd stayed sitting on their crates got up and ran to the road to see what was happening. A big, fat roach was scurrying on the ground in the little woman's shadow. The hens jumped up when they saw the roach. The fastest among them made it through the wall of curious men and struck the tar once with its beak. The roach was gone. Then, as if possessed by some maniacal force, I rushed at the hen, broke her wings, grabbed her neck between my teeth, and bit down hard. She struggled like crazy and almost scratched my eyes out with her hard, bony feet. I soon felt her body go limp and die between my teeth. I didn't even have the chance to eat a leg. A woman, who must have owned the hen I'd killed, burst through the crowd watching the marching singers. Screaming curses, she started to chase me. She chased me across all the paths of the quarter. She had a knife in her hand and fire in her eyes. She swore she'd catch me, cook me up with *ndole* sauce, and eat me with fried plantains.

Soon I realized it was Mini Minor. Her overly perfumed scent filled up my spirit and overcame me. I coughed furiously and roused myself from my hallucinations. I shook myself good. I hurried into my master's dark bar, seeking protection from the street, which had fallen under the cannibalistic spell of the crazy little woman's hymn. My flies followed me, dancing in front of my eyes. Massa Yo was standing behind the counter. He was whispering and counting his receipts for the day. A soft melody shook his crates and bottles. Now and again, he'd stare blindly out at the courtyard of the bar, but then he'd bury his eyes right back in his money box. He seemed to want to ignore the drama unfolding outside in the street. I knew it wasn't wise to bark out my fears to him in his moments of deep concentration. I already knew what his problem was: he had to recuperate a million francs, one way or another, whatever the cost.

5

Although I did my best to avoid falling victim once again to the inebriation of the real, and although I was able to guarantee my own survival only at the cost of a thousand sleepless nights, for their part, all of Madagascar's inhabitants had chatted their way to an acceptance of the nightmarish reality of their daily lives. Endlessly chattering on about how History was dragging them from their beds, they were eager for any and all information about History's various ups and downs. They'd plunged into the dramas of their famished existence, and more and more I suspected that on their own they were incapable of formulating any dreams worth the trouble. They were surprised by life's waves, by the thousand crazy little stories the street threw down at their feet, but they saw them as nothing more than hot pepper to spice up their daily life, useful only to kill time. Once, when the Panther Nzui Manto came to tell them that the man in black they knew so well, yes, the Crow, yes, the writer of the city's dregs—you remember, don't you?—that he'd been arrested, their only reaction was "Again?"

Some of them said the little old man had made up the story to remind them of the curse the sinister man had once cast on the quarter. "He had a bad sense of humor, that guy did," one of them said, "so bad he once dared to give counterfeit francs to his unhappy brothers." Yes, the men of Madagascar refused to remember how humiliated they'd been, but they didn't condemn him outright. Shame was still eating away at their souls, that's for sure. Docta simply said that one day the man in black would find what he was looking for. And when Panther added, "He was arrested because he wrote to the President of the Republic," each of the men around him just shrugged. They all seemed to have found once again the undeniable proof of his bizarreness. Really, the cowardice of Madagascar's inhabitants seemed incorrigible. The little old man said the letter from the man in black had been printed in the opposition newspapers and they'd all been seized. He said that the man in black had given a firsthand description of daily life in the poor neighborhoods, that he'd expressed the fears, hopes, and frustrations of the people of Madagascar, among others. At that point, some of the men seemed comforted by the fact that their voice had carried so far, that their life was at last inscribed on the pages of a newspaper so important it had been seized by the government. Others were a little disappointed by the seizure of the newspapers that talked about them—no one would ever be able to read about their dramas. For many others, however, there was nothing interesting for the President to learn about in the neighborhoods, nothing except the shameful, leprous face of their misery. What's more, the very idea of a letter written and sent to the President of the Republic struck them as strange. Really, who other than a fool could write to the President of the Republic "just like that," they wondered.

"Why not write to him?" countered the now irritated little old man.

"Nzui Manto," a man interrupted, "if you know Biya's address, just tell us."

"You're going too far, huh," said another.

For once the engineer came to the little old man's defense:

"Don't you think Biya's address should be public information?"

"You're the one with the long pencil, right?" one of my master's customers said. "If you know the President's address, why don't you write to him? Maybe you could ask him to find you a job."

All the men laughed. "I'll tell you one thing," one of them said to the engineer, "if you want to find work in this country, you have to write directly to his wife, to Jeanne-Irène herself. She's the one who takes care of the sick, the orphans, and the unemployed."

"You could write her a love letter, just to get things going."

"You never know."

"Keep on wasting your time chasing Mini Minor and her Virginie," added the little old man, "in the meantime, others write to the President of the Republic to complain in your place."

"If it's just going to get you arrested . . . hmm."

"Leave us alone, Chief," a man interjected. "You're gonna write to Biya and tell him what, eh? You're gonna write him about the idiocies you spend your time spreading around this quarter? At least the Crow is a writer. But you, what do you have to say?"

Panther was getting irritated. "Do you even know what the Crow asked the President? He just asked him to come take a walk through a neighborhood, if he had the courage. He gave him an invitation, you know. Like a gentleman. That's all. And that's why he was arrested."

"You'll be, too. If he invites the President, does that make them friends?"

"What would the President come here for?"

"And where would he sit?"

"What would he offer him to drink?"

"Precisely. He invited him so he'd see how we live here in the neighborhoods. *A yi la*—how things are here. So he'd see how we're bored to death here. So he'd see how we gnaw on our fingers all day long. So he'd see how we're dying of hunger. So he'd see something of the face of the country he's running."

"You're trying to tell us," said a man, "the Crow was arrested because he invited the President to come see everything here . . ."

Then he stamped his feet and added, "Just keep on lying."

The little old man looked at him knowingly. "Don't you know," he said in a conspiratorial tone, "Mbiya is more afraid of Yaoundé's neighborhoods than of General Semengue himself? No no no. Isn't that just what the Crow said? He was right, *à me ben tchùp,* that's what I say. Have you ever seen Biya step on the brakes when he's driving through La Briqueterie? *Bi lode mebwo,** take a look around. When he drives through La Briqueterie, his windows are always up, and he's going a hundred kilometers an hour. Yet he walks next to the army generals without trembling. Only he knows what it is here that frightens him. That's what I say, only he knows."

Nobody believed Panther's pumped-up proofs. Even for me it sounded too much like the chattering silence of the courtyard of The Customer Is King, which I had finally gotten used to. It sounded too much like the insanity and delusions of grandeur that thrive on the misery of wasted lives. It sounded like the hallucinations born when death is too close at hand.

Now what!

I watched the little old man shake his wrinkled muscles and hurl the neighborhoods' regicidal power at the sky, and I couldn't help thinking of that day when Docta appeared in front of my master's bar, his mouth smashed and his eyes dilated. He looked like he'd escaped from night's cold tomb; he was vomiting blood and shit. His feet trembled. He fell down in front of The Customer Is King, cursing under his breath. Takou, who was playing over by the ludo players, rushed over to him, crying: he thought his father was dead. The little old man himself put his hands on his head and intoned a syncopated Nkoua song. Initially struck silent with unasked questions, the street had soon relaxed. Everyone smiled in amusement when they learned what had happened. It was the cop, the *mange-mille* who was going out with Virginie, yes, the very one who was "dressed by the State right down to his underwear." Having gotten wind of how the engineer was stubbornly circling around his girl, he'd caught him and given him a good beating, to show him that when it came to strategic scams, sometimes an elementary school certificate is worth more than any engineering diploma.

"I'll show him," the engineer promised, spitting his teeth on the ground. Hatred's flame danced in his eyes. "What can you do about it?" asked my skeptical master. "Cameroon is Cameroon, huh!"

Really, what I mean to say with this sad bit of reminiscence is that on that day, the engineer made a lot of noise, but ultimately he shut up. No one in the quarter sought vengeance on his behalf, each one said he'd been looking for trouble: "When somebody is bigger than you, brother, just carry his bag-o." Yes, I remember this story as if it had happened yesterday. And now the little old man was talking about the power of the neighborhoods! "Nzui Manto," I barked out to him, "you're all talk. *Web-web* is your forte, right? If you had listened to me, you'd be talking about cowardice instead!" But Panther paid no attention to my barking.

6

It's so true! Commentaries on daily life are the drug that day after day helps Madagascar's inhabitants drown their stubborn misery in megalomania. In fact, the neighborhoods' ambience is matched only by their impotence. The day that Panther, dancing with joy, tossed out in the street the news that the opposition had decided to march on Etoudi Palace, where the President lives, I understood that the vertiginous depth of the neighborhoods' misery produced the wildest hallucinations. I saw the little old man get excited and I knew he was drunk: a fool. Yes, I tell you, he was possessed by the intoxication of starvation. I shook my head, wholly convinced that the breadth of the streets' insanity is matched only by the empty pit in men's bellies. Isn't the endless chattering the only measure of the depth of the streets' suffering? Yes, yes, yes, and yes, I know: behind the laughter lies the tears. Still, the awakening of Madagascar's inhabitants came with a bang. A shot split the noon sky over the neighborhood, sending the hens in front of my master's bar scurrying. The panicked voice of an orange vendor screamed, "Woyo-o! *They've* killed him!"

I had jumped when I heard the gun shot. I barked out a jumble of words. The hens repeated their surprised cries, lifting their heads up high. As for the road in front of my master's bar, it was struck silent. It was devoured by terror. There was only the woman's voice, repeating "Woyo-o!"

And that's when I saw that the police commissioner was the only man still standing. It seemed he had also gone mad, or else was overcome by panic. His head spun around on his shoulders, like a sentinel on high alert. He was walking backwards, pointing the barrel of his little black gun at the quarter. He seemed to be expecting some word, some action. Emptiness and silence were the only responses he heard. He got into his car, gunned it, and took off. Then I saw the men and women who'd thrown themselves down on the ground get back up. They ran to the body of a child lying there on the sidewalk. It was a kid. It looked like he was sleeping on a dark, purple stain. His head was turned back against the tar, his arms and legs spread wide. He looked like a bird with its big wings splayed on the ground. With trembling hands a man picked him up. The kid gave in to the elasticity of his little body and there, exposed to the street's terrified eyes, was Takou's face, with a big hole right between his teeth. When they saw the kid's face, the women lifted their pain up to the sun and let loose their mourning cries.

"Woyo-o, *they* killed him-o!" they wailed. Saying *they*, the women pointed at the endless street. "Woudidididididi," they cried, with their hands on their mouths. There was a chorus of women, cursing death in the street.

"Woyo-o!" they said. "The commissioner killed Takou!"

There's no way to describe the chaos surrounding the child struck down by death. Men and women came pouring out of paths, trails, houses, and beds to see what had happened. The thousand feet of the hurried curious riled up the whole quarter. It was like a troop of elephants suddenly started to move. This rumor of Madagascar's awakening shook the tar. The crowd pressed tight around the cadaver of the quarter's silenced child. Struck down mid-flight by death, Takou was now without fault. He turned into an angel: the angel of the neighborhoods. I saw women put their hands on their heads and start a dance of suffering. There were men, too, who raised their voices full of rage, filling the whole road with their curses. They raised their threatening fists to the heavens. Their anger tore the clouds from the sky and threw them down on the ground.

"The coward!" said a man, burning with rage. "Killing a child!"

"Why?" a woman asked.

"They killed him-o!" cried the peanut vendor as she raised her hands to the sky. "Why this?"

Emptiness was visible in everyone's eyes. No one had an answer for this banal act of savagery. In the midst of all the chaos, I saw Panther get to work. Along with some other men, he was trying for all he was worth to save what remained of Docta's kid's life. He shook the kid in desperation, covering himself with his blood. He struck the kid's chest and called out to him as loud as he could. "*Wo men ngo-o!*"* he kept repeating. "Oh! Somebody else's child!"

He called on the Medumba ancestors for help and threw all the proverbs in his library up to the sky. Takou still didn't move. Powerless before death, the little old man's voice cried out, splitting the street with his wail, "*Wo, bou zui men ngo!*"* They've killed somebody else's child!"

"Assassins!"

"Where's that police commissioner?"

"He took off!"

"The coward!"

"Killing a child!"

"*They* killed him-o!"

"It can't be!"

"A child!"

"Just a baby!"

Everyone's shock and tears soon parted to let the strategist engineer, little Takou's father, pass through. It seemed that the events in the street had caught Docta right in the middle of some scam. His eyes were altered. I didn't recognize him. It was, yes, it was—how can I put it?—it was as if the path of his anger had led him straight to paternity itself: a vision of manhood. The drama on the street had been driven home and hard: it was Takou, his son, his flesh and blood, who was dead. You could see, really see, that this crime had short-circuited him, blinded him to the awful truth. He walked into the crowd's cries and wails with the silence of someone who wants to see for himself before he believes. Suddenly I saw the engineer rush back through the crowd, running like a fool right into the courtyard of my master's bar. He seemed to have lost his mind. He seemed possessed. He was looking around frantically, at the ground and the walls of the houses, along the endless road he knew so well and that had eaten up his kid's life. In the blast of voices from all over the quarter, he kept on repeating, "That's not my child!"

As if suddenly struck by his own responsibility, he also said, "They are going to give me back my child!"

Docta ran toward my master's bar and came rushing back with the former cigarette vendor's pushcart, which had been leaning there. His face was a mess and his gestures mechanical. He kept repeating the same jarring words over and over. He picked up his child's cadaver and put it in the iron cart. I watched him run off down the road, with the whole quarter following behind him in a crowd. Cars swerved around him, honking their horns. The regulars from The Customer Is King, the women who sold oranges or peanuts, the *soya* vendors, the ludo players, and the street's nonstop commentators joined his angry march. I joined him in his dash, too, and went up the road from Madagascar to Mokolo along with the pack.

"Where are you going with that child?" asked some of the curious.

"We're going to the Mokolo police station!" one man said.

"Yes, the killer ran to hide in the police station!"

"The coward!"

"Killing a child!"

"We'll show him!"

Docta's voice was insistent, "They are going to give me back my child."

With the death of that kid he'd previously abandoned, he'd suddenly become a father. At the sight of his kid laid out on the asphalt, he'd become a father. Clothed in his angry paternity, clothed in his painful paternity, he walked down the street behind his kid's body. As he pushed Takou on before him, the veins on his brow were ready to burst. Next to him marched the Panther Nzui Manto, whose heart too had been struck by the sight of the cadaver of that smart-aleck kid who just didn't deserve this. Trailing behind them was all of Madagascar, marching. The rumor set off by the quarter in motion shook the walls of the houses. Women wailed, men grumbled, vengeance was decided upon, power was cursed, children cried out in surprise, hens jumped, cats howled, lizards cocked their heads, and dogs barked too.

Yes, a whole colony of my fellows jumped and barked at the head of the dead child's convoy. The dogs formed the march's avant-garde. This time, yes, this time *they* had gone too far.

7

Our march didn't get very far, however. The repression was horrifying. The police didn't just use their noisy helicopter to disperse us. They also kept showering us with bouquets of smoke that made us cough and tore the soles off our feet. What they wanted most, it seems, was to prevent our march from taking over the Mokolo market, and from there spreading across the whole city. That would have been like letting the fuse light the powder keg. It would have let Madagascar's anger reach the very heart of Yaoundé. It would have cut off Yaoundé's breath. The police also came with a blue truck that scattered the crowd with a burst of salt water spit from its long, elephantine trunk. They got out and ran after the men, women, and children, chasing them into the depths of their beds, billy clubs raised high.

They raped women and came out laughing, triumphantly pushing their husbands along ahead of them with their rifles. With dark space helmets on their heads, they all looked like devils. I noticed some still had their pants unzipped. For hours the rumor of death and rape hovered over Madagascar, stopping from time to time to plant more tears. The quarter's inhabitants didn't just roll over, though. Even after being pushed back down into the dissolute depths of their lives, they rose up again and rushed down the road with even more rage. They attacked cars parked along the roadside. They flipped them over, pissed on them, poured gas on them, and set them on fire. They threw rocks at the police. Sometimes they threw wads of burning cloth. Only the repeated salvos of gunfire silenced them. Sometimes I heard a man's voice cry out, "You're going to give us back our child!"

And it wasn't only Docta's voice. Sometimes too it was the voice of a man who'd been shot: the cry of a dying man. The whole quarter had come together in a fury to mourn the engineer's son. So Takou had been able to graft his delinquent soul into each person's belly. Each of the men who'd used the kid as the messenger of their cowardice felt, I'm sure, a little responsible for his death. Yes, it wasn't just the very real horror of the police commissioner's act that led to such revolt.

That evening, all along Madagascar's pavement, the police lined up groups of loafers, their heads and feet bare, covered with mud and ashes. With their hands on their heads, they looked like condemned prisoners awaiting execution. I recognized the cigarette vendor turned pushcart man. His eyes were drunk with defeat, but in them I also saw the illumination of a determined man. I barked out my sympathy and jumped up on him. A policeman pointed the barrel of his rifle at my muzzle. I don't know why, but that time I ran and hid. I heard the policeman burst out laughing.

When I emerged from my hiding place, I saw the police putting the little old man into one of their "no-fare taxis," along with all the others arrested. The police remained in the quarter for a long time. With their weapons drawn, they stopped and checked the papers of everyone who went by. Some were arrested and made to sit down in the mud. Sometimes they were stripped, had their heads shaved with a shard of broken glass, and were told to disappear. When night fell, I decided to go back to my master's. Here and there, scattered along the way, were the remains of burned-out tires. I ran into small groups of policemen, talking together in the shadows. The street responded with a precarious silence. A strong smell surrounded the police, announcing their presence. At first I thought it was the acrid smell of death, but later I heard people from the quarter saying the police were lurking in the shadows, getting high on *mbanga.**

Yes, later it will be said that . . . Oh, what won't be said about this later? People will even say Takou wasn't killed. They'll say that at the first gunshots, the smart aleck got up from his push-cart and set off running. He took off so fast he lost death in the labyrinth paths of the neighborhood he knew so well. Later I'll learn that the police commissioner shot him because when they crossed paths, just as our official was going to take his lover in his arms in the Chantier de la République, Docta's overly talkative kid had stamped his feet, shaken his head, and said, loud enough for the whole street to hear, "Really, Cameroon is Cameroon, huh!"

They were someone else's words, heard often enough on the street and, what's more, they were spoken by a child. But the police commissioner had taken it too personally. He had simply pulled out his weapon and shot at the powerful opposition fig-ure. The child fell silently. Maybe that's why some wicked gos-sips—and yes, there were some of those!—said Takou had been looking for his death. My master was the first to spread this idea around, and from the door to his bar he added that he'd always seen bad luck following the kid. And besides, Massa Yo continued, he had always known the kid's mouth would kill him one day. My master didn't go on too loudly, though, be-cause later everyone would learn that he hadn't marched along with the turbulent street. Happily, no one got the idea to say that Massa Yo, yes, Massa Yo had sold Takou to Famla to get his million back. The street's words are capable of anything, you know! The crime that had befallen the kid was too brutal, and had happened right in front of everyone's eyes. Besides, do you always have to believe what people whisper when they're crouched in the shadows of their Philistine chattering, slunk into the talkative stench of their cowardice?

The whole quarter cried out its indignation!

And that was enough.

Yet, I admit, even today the image of Docta's son rising up from his pushcart to flee his own death comes back to me per-sistently, filling my whole body with illusions. In it I see the cry of those desperate men and women in the face of the police commissioner's unspeakable barbarity. Suddenly, even I miss the kid's naive words, yes, his shameless words. Yes, I even discover deep inside me the desire to run with him across the quarter and disappear, even in Mbankolo forest. In order to enjoy his delinquency again, I silence my canine suspicion and, foolishly carried away, I even forget that Takou was really just a kid like any other.

8

Oh, I, Mboudjak, am only a dog. It's true the tear gas prevented me from seeing the path ahead, from living with my eyes wide open as events unfolded, from marching to the very end of Madagascar's endless road, to that damned police station in Mokolo where the murderous cop had hidden, from seizing the police commissioner with the turbulent streets' thousand tentacles and crushing his ribs. The gas also dragged me into an uncontrollable place where the world was intoxicated and where, as if I'd chugged bottles and bottles and bottles of a cocktail of *jobajo, odontol,* and palm wine, I suddenly heard the world around me singing. Yes, I saw it dancing around me, dancing under my paws, dancing dancing dancing dancing dancing, dancing and singing all at once:

> "Liberty, eh, eh
> Liberty, eh, eh, eh, eh
> All-powerful God, ah, ah
> Soon we'll be free!"

Today, with a little bit of distance, I can no longer believe the rumor on the street, the *kongossa* announcing Takou's resurrection, because I stayed right with the pushcart carrying the kid, right until I lost consciousness. I lived through it all, or almost. And besides, even if I didn't live through it all, what don't people say in the neighborhoods? The Panther Nzui Manto didn't even give his tongue time to rest (yes, people even said that to get away from the long arm of the police, he'd told them just one of his stories and they'd gone stiff with shock). He just kept shaking his many wrinkles and riling up the street with his devilishly raucous words. He said Docta had actually made it to the Mokolo police station, despite the police barring the way. He said the engineer had been shot through and through, but that his will to get revenge for his child had taken his feet right through the walls of repression and up to the office of the police commissioner. He added that he himself wouldn't have believed it if someone had told him that story, if someone had said that "that *nkaknin* of a Docta, that imbecile, had been capable of such a thing." He went on to say that at the door to the police commissioner's office, a policeman had dropped his weapon, opened wide his bloodshot eyes, and asked him where he was going. With all the calm his voice could muster, Docta had replied, "I'm bringing a cadaver to the commissioner."

Trembling with fear, the policeman supposedly then asked, "Which one?"

What surprised me most was that this incredible story amused the little old man. He stammered with laughter as he spoke, but was it really laughter? He told his stupid story, acting out the gestures of the dumbstruck engineer who pointed at the body of his child stretched out in the pushcart in front of him and knocked at the door of Mokolo's criminal police commissioner. He told his unbelievable story, changing his voice to imitate Docta's exact words—those of a man who'd become a father too late. Drunk with words, Panther kept talking, then suddenly he said, as if possessed, "Somebody else's child, I tell you!"

9

And yet Madagascar's anger was only the first wave, the little finger announcing a much larger fist of rage. Takou wasn't the only one who'd been killed like that, silenced in the middle of the street because he'd said too much. I learned that students had been shot, black marketeers had been crushed, and many protesters shouting out their rage in the streets had fallen, the banners of their demands turned into shrouds. Like a sinister host, death hovered over the quarters, over the city, over the whole country. More and more courageous people rose up, demanding the freedom to speak out about the heinous *Fochements,** daring to utter the wicked name of *his* right-hand assassin—even if it cost them their lives! Yes, death's ugly face was everywhere, and Yaoundé breathed in the obsessive odor of hundreds of dead. The opposition had started with a transportation strike, "operation dead foot," then came "operation dead house," then "operation dead city," and finally "operation dead country." They wanted to force Biya to listen to the voice of the poor neighborhoods, to hear the convulsive word of the streets and, if he was really deaf to the howling of those brutally murdered, to get him to resign because of a chronic physical disability, or even just because his senility was all too apparent.

The doors of The Customer Is King stayed closed for weeks and months. Each morning Massa Yo sat in front of his bar, looking sadly at the street which brought him only the cadavers of those cut down in the full bloom of life. How was he going to get by? The circle he had once traced to stop the neighborhood's crazy words from getting into his courtyard was still stubbornly there, but now his courtyard had been abandoned to chattering hens and to ducks who weren't afraid to shit wherever they wanted and then dash off. My master learned at his own expense that in Yaoundé there is no real bar customer who isn't also a smooth talker–football coach–sorcerer–fortune teller and, of course, potential politician. Sometimes I wandered around by myself, me, his dog. Sometimes a brown-headed lizard crossing the deserted courtyard of The Customer Is King would stop and look, first at my master and then at me, at my master and at me, again at my master and then, full of reproach, at me. "Just what have you seen?" he seemed to say.

Raising his brutal hand, my master shooed him away. I watched the lizard disappear along the walls of the bar, leaving his unanswered question behind in his frightened hurry. Massa Yo's inactivity had made him more irritable than ever. So I, too, fled before his shadow and sidestepped his company. I knew what he was capable of when the humanity was dying in his belly, or in his customerless courtyard: I knew he was a killer lying in wait. To avoid being his chosen victim once again, I dug in beneath Mama Mado's empty fritter stand. There in my peaceful retreat, I opened my ears to the street's regicidal rumors. Yes, I kept my spirit open to the fever of change that had suddenly taken over Madagascar and run away with Yaoundé, carrying the whole of Cameroon along with it in the rush that seemed to be shaking up all of Africa. I saw faces pinched tight, I caught glimpses of raised fists, I heard curses, I felt a flow of lava make the heart of the streets tremble, sending terrible cracks along their surface. I saw the air get dense, I felt the future suddenly challenge the present, and repeatedly one exact same sentence exploded in the doorways: "Red Card to Paul Biya!" A sentence repeated a thousand, ten thousand, a million times, yes, repeated twelve million times. A sentence that wouldn't back down before death's creeping assault, a phrase hammered out in English in the noisy streets:

BIYA MUST GO!

A sentence that, for sure, could only be barked out. The rumor of the turbulent country, the rumor of turbulent Yaoundé set all of Madagascar into motion: it trembled with the continuous barking of that one sentence. Everyone was listening carefully to its uncontrollable spread. What am I saying, listening carefully? Everyone helped its subversive spread: *kongossa,* sidewalk radio—those voices spreading news up and down the streets—the independent presses of the *Le Messager* and other such publications, even Radio CRTV and its news from the countryside. But mostly it was the foreign radio and, especially, Boh Herbert on Africa Number One, along with the international broadcasts of CNN. And yes, it was also something that talked as much and was as much of a smooth talker as Panther, but more serious, more nervous, more engaged, more convincing, and younger too. Something that said it suspected words would soon turn into concrete action, that said it could see a cure on the horizon, and that gathered around it ten, a hundred, a thousand, a hundred thousand loafers. Yes, more than anything else, the street was on the move again!

I stood in front of The Customer Is King's empty courtyard, leaning forward on my front paws, panting, with my ears perked up high, my tongue hanging down, my eyes opened wide. Suddenly, right there in the street in front of me, amid starvation's rumor, amid the angry rumor of mortified Madagascar, Man was reborn. I couldn't believe my eyes. Yes, the tar exploded, yes, there was a cyclone in the streets, and yes again, I say, the neighborhoods were in motion: Man had begun to march once more. I tore myself from my seclusion and marched along with him, ran on ahead of him. United we were, Man and me, in the spasmodic rush of our language: our barks. We marched, not only to bring somebody else's child back to life, but above all and foremost to chase out the crazed lion. We marched, hunters in the urban jungle.

We marched and yet, why not admit it here? Despite the indomitable birth in our neighborhoods of that unconditional pedestrian, despite the uncontrollable rage of his words, and beyond all the city's speculations, I was still waiting for the arrival of Rosalie-Sylvie-Yvette Menzui, Rosalie, for short—or as I alone called her, Rosa Rosa Rose, little Takou's mother. And I said to myself—please convince me it won't be just an illusion—when she comes, it will surely be the last march of all: the march for the demands of the mother brutally weaned from her child. Each time I passed by the place where Takou died, I sniffed, re-sniffed, re-re-sniffed, and I re-re-re-sniffed the tar that, more than anyone, had witnessed the abrupt silencing of his infantile words. Yes, you can believe me, dear readers, the scent of his blood was still hot.

Offenbach, December 1996
—Hausen, February 1999

Glossary

Unless otherwise noted, all glosses are from notes by Patrice Nganang included in the original French edition of the novel; some of the original notes, mostly translations of phrases in Pidgin English, were not included here.

A bo dze-a!: "What's he gonna do?" An interjection from southern Cameroon.

A fit buy am tout ton plateau: "I can buy your whole tray full."

À me ben tchùp: "I'm telling you myself."

acops: a prominent point at the back of one's head

AIDS: acronym for "almost an income, difficult to secure"; starvation wages due to the economic crisis. [In the original, Nganang uses the French acronym for AIDS, SIDA: "salaire insuffisant, difficilement acquis."—Trans.]

Anti-Zamba ouam!: an interjection, curse. [The word *Zamba* is often translated as "God."—Trans.]

Aschouka ngangali: a phrase children use to tease

associée (asso, for short): prostitute

Ba tchùn boun makoup: "These city folk have lost their minds."

baisedrom: someplace to screw (Trans.)

Bak a yùn: "We'll see."

Bamileke (pejoratively shortened to Bami): a Bantu ethnic group from the Grassfields in western Cameroon. [The Bamileke make up about one-quarter of Cameroon's population. After independence, when the government crushed the rebel UPC, many Bamileke were killed or displaced. *Dog Days* takes place in Madagascar, one of Yaoundé's largely Bamileke neighborhoods.—Trans.]

bangala: penis, dick (Trans.)

bayamsalam: market woman/women

Bèbèlè: a curse

Bi fang men ngo kou'-o!: "Let somebody else's child grow up."

Bi fang nda-a!: "Let it be!" (Trans.)

Bi lode mebwo: "Take a good look."

Bia boya: "What can ya do?" (Cameroonian-style translation)

Biafrans: pejorative term for Nigerians

bifaga: a dried fish

bikutsi: a type of Cameroonian music

bobolo: stick of dried cassava root (manioc)

bole: wiped out, exhausted

chantiers: private homes turned into cheap restaurants, also called *circuits*

Chômecam: Cameroonian unemployment service

choua: efforts to find or obtain something (particularly friendship)

compressé: fired, sacked; lost one's job

craning: bravura, bragging

Dan sapack: "That whore."

Dan sapack i day for kan kan-o!: "These whores are so moody!"

Dan tendaison for dan woman na big big, huh?: "That woman's butt sure is big, huh?"

Etienne: a pun on the name "Etienne" and the congugation of the verb *tenir* (to hold), il/elle *tient* (Trans.)

Famla: a Bamileke secret society

Fochements: reference to Jean Fochivé, head of the Intelligence Services under Ahmadou Ahidjo and head of Internal Security under Paul Biya

Ilang!: "Asshole!" (Trans.)

jobajo: beer

Jou me lou thùp mbe: "Didn't I say it . . ." (Trans.)

kaba ngondo: a large, loose-fitting woman's garment

Kai wa lai!: an interjection

Katcham!: "Catch her!"

koki: dish made of beans

kongossa: gossip

kwassa kwassa: Congolese rhythm

Lekunze: a runner from Cameroon

longo longo fil de fer: tall, thin person. [Also, a snake.—Trans.]

ludo: a dice game (Trans.)

Ma din wa: "I love you."

Ma woman no fit chasser me for ma long, dis donc! Après tout, ma long na ma long!: "My woman can't throw me out of my house, I tell you! After all, my house is my house!"

Madagascar: a largely Bamileke neighborhood in Yaoundé, home to

Massa Yo and Mboudjak; not to be confused with the country of which the poet Jacques Rabemananjara sang

Maguida: an ethnic group from northern Cameroon

makossa: Cameroonian dance music

Mami Wata: female water spirits who, from time to time, come to torment men. Mboudjak is the first dog in whom they have taken an interest.

mange-mille: the lowest ranking member of the police force, unbeatable when it comes to extorting taxi drivers on the streets of Yaoundé. [Literally, "eat-a-thousand."—Trans.]

mbanga: marijuana

Mbankolo: one of Yaoundé's quarters

Mbe ke di?: What are you saying?

mbok: prostitute

mbout: coward, cowardly

Me tchùp mbe ke?: "What did I tell you?"

Mebala bidou: an interjection

Medumba: a Bantu language, one of those spoken by the Bamileke

Menmà, you tcho fia?: "Son/child of your mother, are you at peace?" [Traditional Medumba greeting.—Trans.]

Mi nal mi: a curse from southern Cameroon

Mokolo: one of Yaoundé's quarters, famous for its market

mola: friend (Trans.)

mon vieux: an unfortunate loss of hair, resulting from the furiously tight braids worn by African women

Mongo Faya: a popular Cameroonian singer

Na jeune talent, non?: "Those are just young girls, right?"

nangaboko: homeless; without a permanent address

nchoun'am: my friend

ndap: praise name, matrilineal

ndjum: an evil spirit

ndoutou: bad luck

njo: for free

njou njou Calaba: a masked figure from the west of Cameroon and Nigeria (the Calabar); by extension, an evil spirit

nkaknin: imbecile/s

Nkoua: people from southern Cameroon, either Beti or Ewondo

Nlongkak: one of Yaoundé's quarters

nsansanboy: term for a brand of German beer (Satzenbrau)

Nsong am nù: "Tell me something I don't know."

nyamangolo: literally, "snail"; by extension, both a nonchalant person and trivial affairs

"O Cameroun, berceau de nos ancêtres": "Oh Cameroon, cradle of our ancestors," the start of the Cameroonian national anthem (Trans.)

Obili: one of Yaoundé's quarters

odontol: a highly alcoholic Cameroonian beverage

opep: delivery truck

Melen: one of Yaoundé's quarters

Père Soufo: a prophet from the hills above La Carrière, a miracle worker

Put oya soté, for jazz must do sous-marin: "Put enough oil in so the beans are like submarines."

rumta: minor, young girl

sans payer: Cameroonian police van. [Literally, "without paying" or "no fare."—Trans.]

second office: mistress

siscia: a threat or to threaten

Sitabac: Société de Fabrication de Tabac, or Tabacco Manufacturing Company, and, by extension, its owner

small-no-be-sick: a sort of Chinese balm that, apparently, cures everything. The term also refers to a woman of small stature. [In English in the original.—Trans.]

somebody else's sweet hubby: a liqueur-flavored candy. [In the original *un mari d'autrui est sucré.*—Trans.]

soya: grilled meat (Trans.)

tara: brother, father, fellow; friendly form of address

tchoko: tip, bribe

tchotchoro: tiny, little, insignificant thing

web-web: talk, chatter (Trans.)

Wo, bou zui men ngo!: "Oh! They killed somebody else's child."

Wo men ngo-o!: "Oh! Somebody else's child!"

Ye maleh!: an interjection

Youa mami pima!: a curse

Afterword

Reading around Nganang's Yaoundé

AMY BARAM REID

If context is everything, in what context should we read Patrice Nganang's *Dog Days*? As a Cameroonian novel? An African novel? A francophone novel? Yes on all counts, but the novel also has its place in the fields of French, German, and American literature. It is a political novel, an urban novel, and, as its own subtitle proclaims, "an animal chronicle." *Dog Days* is unarguably a novel written by a francophone Cameroonian about one particular neighborhood in Yaoundé, but it locates that neighborhood on a global map. The meanderings of the novel's canine narrator allow the author to explore Yaoundé's urban landscape with a perspective that combines both familiarity and distance. As he pursues his "scientific" quest for the truth that would explain man's behavior, Mboudjak is equally attentive to the commonplace and the extraordinary, to long-standing traditions and the rapid transformations of global consumer capitalism, to intimate dramas and the emergence of political protests in the streets. Although it is written in French, one of Cameroon's two official languages, the novel's interweaving of utterances in Pidgin English and an array of Cameroon's national languages, as well as in the urban slang known as "Camfranglais," emphasizes that Yaoundé is not just the capital of a bilingual nation but a truly multilingual city. And while *Dog Days* was first published by a French press as part of their French fiction collection, Nganang was living in Germany when he wrote the novel and had already moved to the United States by the time it appeared. Thus, in 2001 *Dog Days* received the Prix Marguerite Yourcenar, which recognizes novels written in French by authors residing in the United States, and in 2002 it was awarded the Grand Prix de la Litté-rature de l'Afrique Noire, a prize given in Paris for works from francophone Africa.

So where should we situate *Dog Days?* Each of the aforemen-tioned categories is germane to Nganang's work and speaks to its richness. Each places Nganang's canine narrator in a differ-ent pack, so to speak, by invoking a different set of intertexts, from the fables and folktales with animal protagonists that are common to both African and European traditions, to Kafka's "Forschungen eines Hundes" ("Investigations of a Dog"). To-gether they invite us to consider the various references and concerns different readers might bring to their reading of *Dog Days,* and, at the same time, they foil any attempt to pigeon-hole the novel. While the novel makes explicit reference to a number of works—paraphrasing several verses from "Souffles" by the Senegalese poet Birago Diop, for example—it also in-vites readers to make their own connections (Diop's poem is again instructive: some will recognize it as the song "Breaths" sung by Sweet Honey in the Rock). Mboudjak's adventures and insights will remind some readers of the novel *O Caõ e os caluandas* (*A Dog in Luanda*), by the Angolan writer Pepetela, others will think of Paul Auster's *Timbuktu.* As a professor of German literature, Nganang foregrounds the novel's Germanic sources: its subtitle, "animal chronicle" (*"chronique animale"* in French), is his translation of the German *Tierdichtung.* When he discusses the novel, however, his literary references range from Boccaccio to the political cartoons so popular in the Cam-eroonian press; he even acknowledges that Mboudjak's family tree includes not only other dogs but literary cats as well, from E. T. A. Hoffmann's Kater Murr to the unnamed "author" of Natsume Soseki's *I Am a Cat.*[1] In the end, however, despite and perhaps because of the novel's myriad connections to literature from around the world, *Dog Days* is decidedly a novel of Cam-eroon. It is the product of Nganang's will to put Cameroon's past and present down on paper: "As for my writing, and its deep roots in the soil of our homeland, it results from my con-viction that we—me, you, all Cameroonians—are obligated to tell our history, in our own words, from our own perspective, unashamedly, as a matter of course, because if we don't, we will have to endure the words and perspectives of others."[2] Nganang's vivid and original depiction of life in Yaoundé's poor neighborhoods has led one Cameroonian critic, André Ntonfo, to position the novel as a watershed in Cameroonian literature.[3]

That said, the field of "Cameroonian literature" remains a challenging construct. For some scholars, such as Richard Bjornson, in *The African Quest for Freedom and Identity,* Cameroonian literature provides a case study for the emergence of national literatures in Africa; others, like Claire Dehon, in *Le Roman camerounais d'expression française,* opt to situate Cameroonian literature relative to French literature. Still, many scholars, including Dehon and Eloise Brière, also recognize that, owing to the geographic and cultural disparities between different parts of the country, what passes for Cameroonian literature might better be termed a regional literature representative of the south and its urban centers.[4] Thus as recently as 1991 Ambroise Kom could state that "no one has yet sought to show what might set Cameroonian literature apart from other works of literature from the region or even the continent: from the Congo, Gabon, Ivory Coast, Senegal and, why not, Nigeria."[5] For Kom, as for Dehon, Bjornson, and Brière, a meaningful definition of Cameroonian literature would not rely on arbitrary national borders but rather would find in its geography, history, and traditions, and in the ongoing dialogue among political institutions and writers of different political orientations, the factors that nourish literary production in Cameroon. At the same time, Kom has also identified various forces that have inhibited the growth of Cameroonian literature, including (self-imposed and semiofficial) censorship, governmental support for works that serve its political agenda, regardless of literary merit, and the continued reliance on Paris as the arbiter of literary quality.[6] If, however, following Ntonfo, we are to view *Dog Days* as a sort of literary watershed, it is because of the ways in which Nganang seems to take up Kom's challenge.

In *Dog Days,* Nganang explores some of the major issues confronting Cameroon: the legacy of colonization and the struggle for power postindependence, the corruption of the political regime, and the profound social consequences of the country's economic crisis. In his efforts to represent the flow of rumors, stories, and languages in Yaoundé, Nganang also speaks to the difficulty of constructing Cameroonian identity independent of ethnicity, given the persistent influence of tribal affiliations. He points out the dangers that writers face if they criticize the regime, but refuses to idealize the figure of the author or to imply that words alone are capable of bringing about real change in the country. Seeing the world through Mboudjak's eyes allows Nganang to strike a balance between a micro- and a macroview of Yaoundé. The author's desire to look unflinchingly at the challenges Cameroonians face, on both a personal and a collective level, is reflected in his decision to situate the novel in real and recognizable locations in and around Yaoundé—in places like Madagascar, Mokolo, or La Briqueterie—and to anchor the novel's plot in a precise historical moment. At the same time, however, Mboudjak's uncertainty about Yaoundé's layout allows Nganang to unsettle any reading that would use the novel's specifically Cameroonian context to marginalize it and the political issues it raises: "I admit that I'm just a dog, yes, a dog whose wanderings have never taken his paws beyond the borders of Yaoundé's neighborhoods. And yes, I concede that for my canine intelligence, Yaoundé's city limits are those of Cameroon, and Cameroon itself is the center of the world" (186). Thus, although *Dog Days* depicts both a specific moment in Cameroonian history and familiar places in Yaoundé, the question Mboudjak insistently poses, which is echoed by various other characters over the course of the novel, "Where is Man?" speaks to the universality of Mboudjak's concerns.

Dog Days unfolds in a period of transition leading up to the official reinstatement of multiparty politics in 1991. Nganang is clear that his intent in the novel was to "describe what it meant to be Cameroonian between 1989 and 1990, when people found their voices in a phenomenal way, a moment I witnessed and which now in Cameroon seems so long ago!"[7] As we follow Mboudjak's trail, we hear the voices and rumors of Yaoundé's poor neighborhoods, or *sous-quartiers,* voices that cheer, jeer, gossip, and protest in French, Pidgin English, and an assortment of Cameroon's national languages. For readers familiar with Yaoundé, Nganang vividly depicts scenes of daily life: children jostling around Mama Mado's fritter stand; men arguing about football and politics over glasses of palm wine; market women, or *bayamsalam,* clamoring after a rickety truck laden with produce. Whether designated by name (Massa Yo, Mini Minor), nickname (Docta, Panther, the Crow), or role (the cigarette vendor, the police commissioner), the novel's characters are intended to be familiar caricatures. Nganang's talent, however, resides in his ability to move beyond the caricature and to allow us an intimate glimpse of the individuals that lie beneath, with all their quirks and pathos.[8] And this is what draws readers in, whether they are familiar with the serpentine paths that lead from Madagascar to Mokolo or not.

The novel is divided into two books, "First Barks" and "The Turbulent Street," each of which comprises two chapters with numbered subsections. On one level, it traces the maturation of the narrator, Mboudjak, from a naive overconfidence in his own abilities to a hopeful skepticism grounded in the experience of collective action. Although his pride sometimes clouds his judgment, Mboudjak proves to be a keen observer of human nature. As a watch dog, this would-be social scientist is able to observe his owner Massa Yo, his family, and his associates in their unguarded moments, and to see how patterns of injustice are repeated. In the first chapter, Massa Yo loses both his government job and his status as a civil servant. Forced to make ends meet, like so many others in Yaoundé, he opens a bar, The Customer Is King. As Massa Yo and his clients take out their frustrations on those around them, Massa Yo's son, Soumi, vents his on the family dog. When Mboudjak decides to try his luck on the street, however, he finds little comfort in the company of other stray dogs. Despite the lip service some give to the ideals of solidarity and "canitude," the strays are as violent and self-serving as the men they disdain.[9] So Mboudjak returns to Massa Yo, having realized that knowing his enemy is his best defense.

The second chapter broadens the focus to encompass not only Massa Yo's regulars but others whose political connections link them to the world beyond the neighborhood of Madagascar: the police commissioner, his mistress Mini Minor, and the Crow, who has written a book about Yaoundé's poor neighborhoods entitled, of course, *Dog Days*. When the men gathered around Massa Yo's bar stand idly by as the police commissioner arbitrarily arrests the Crow and another regular, Mboudjak alone bares his fangs and shows his courage. After the Crow's release from prison, he confronts the bar's patrons with "the price of their cowardice," causing a riot when he throws handfuls of counterfeit bills into the air.

In book 2, "The Turbulent Street," Mboudjak's disillusionment with his master's cohort sends him off on misadventures across the city. As he wanders from the garbage pile behind Party Headquarters to the makeshift stands where men drink glass upon glass of palm wine, he struggles with the often blurry distinction between reality and hallucination, between rumors of fact and rumors of fiction. When he finally he makes it back to The Customer Is King, Mboudjak is ready to compromise his freedom for some sense of security, which he calls his "freedom of spirit." As tensions rise in the bar and around the city, the end of book 1 is echoed when Massa Yo is robbed of his "million." Money, or its illusion, is what makes the city go 'round or, as the characters repeatedly say, echoing President Paul Biya, it is why "Cameroon is Cameroon."

The novel's final chapter shows Madagascar overwhelmed by political events in the larger city. In The Customer Is King, rumors of arrests and protests replace the daily banter. Despite Massa Yo's efforts to stay out of it all, the bar's music is drowned out by crowds calling for the president to step down, chanting that "Biya must go!" When police brutality claims a familiar victim, even the determined drinkers of The Customer Is King take to the streets. Although the police response is brutal, Mboudjak still sees reason for hope: the persistent smell of spilled blood becomes for him a sign that patterns can be broken, that mothers bereft of their children will bring about a change. The novel's concluding line, in which Mboudjak addresses his "dear readers," closes the frame opened earlier with the discussion of the Crow's book: even in these "dog days," sacrifice will not be forgotten.

From the very start of the novel, Nganang makes it clear that the politics of language are a central concern. Mboudjak's introduction calls attention to the power of naming and to language's ability to shape consciousness:

> I am a dog. Who else but me could admit it with such humility? Since I see no reproach in this confession, "dog" becomes nothing more than a word, a noun: the noun men use to refer to me. But there you have it; in the end, I've gotten used to it. I've assumed the destiny it places on my shoulders. From here on out, "dog" is part of my universe, since I've made men's words my own. I've digested the structures of their sentences and the intonations of their speech. I've learned their language and I flirt with their ways of thinking. (7)

Mboudjak's musings on the consequences of adopting another's language signal both the linguistic legacy of colonialism and the ongoing debates over language use in Cameroon.

Geography, history, and contemporary politics all inform discussions about language in the country.[10] The linguistic makeup of Cameroon is exceptionally diverse, with some 250 national languages.[11] While in some parts of Africa the process of colonization left behind an educational system and a language that could help unify the country, Cameroon still struggles to overcome the divisions set in place by its complicated colonial past.[12] Following the establishment of European settlements in the mid-nineteenth century, Germany laid claim to the region, which it ruled as a protectorate from 1884 until World War I. In 1916, under the auspices of the League of Nations, German Kamerun was divided into French and English sections. The British administered the two western provinces under their control as part of neighboring Nigeria. The bulk of the country was governed by France, and gained independence in 1960 as the Republic of Cameroon. Following a plebiscite in 1961, one of the British-controlled provinces, known then as Southern Cameroons, voted to join the Republic; together they formed the Federal Republic of Cameroon. Since independence, the country has been ruled by two autocratic leaders: Ahmadou Ahidjo, who was in power from 1960 to 1982, and the current president, Paul Biya, who had served as Ahidjo's prime minister. Although the federal system was abandoned in

1972, when President Ahidjo declared a unitary state, Cameroon remains an anomaly in Africa: a country with two official European languages, French and English.

Although "bilingualism may be described as the bedrock of the Cameroon nation,"[13] and despite governmental policies aimed at encouraging bilingualism, relatively few Cameroonians are fully conversant in the two official languages.[14] Moreover, in both population and political sway, the French-speaking regions have dominated the country since reunification. Eight of Cameroon's ten provinces are officially francophone and two are anglophone; in terms of population, French-speakers outnumber English-speakers five to one.[15] To focus on the opposition between French and English, however, is to gloss over the real complexity of language use in Cameroon, where for most citizens the official languages are second or third languages.[16]

In addition, urban communities tend to reflect the linguistic fragmentation of the country, with neighborhoods forming along ethnic lines. In "Unilingual Past, Multilingual Present, Uncertain Future: The Case of Yaoundé," Gisèle Tchoungui highlights the paradox of language use in the capital, where patterns of immigration have led to the creation of a patchwork of monolingual quarters. While she ultimately concludes that for most residents of Yaoundé "learning French is a matter of survival," Tchoungui also notes that in the city's self-contained Bamileke and Hausa neighborhoods, one "could spend weeks without speaking French or English."[17]

Dog Days is set in the principally Bamileke neighborhood of Madagascar. Bamileke is an umbrella term referring to various Bantu peoples originating in the Grassfields in western Cameroon; it is estimated that they currently make up about one-fourth of the country's population.[18] Their position in Cameroonian society has been marked both by the colonial division of the country and by the struggle for power postindependence. During the colonial partition of the country, the Bamileke found themselves on opposite sides of the Franco-British border.[19] In the years surrounding independence, from 1958 through the early 1970s, Cameroon was wracked by a civil war, often referred to as the "Bamileke rebellion," in which the Union des Populations Camerounaises (UPC) battled government forces.

The government's suppression of the UPC was brutal; many Bamileke fled or were forced to leave their homes for other parts of the country.[20] Lingering tensions related to this period—amplified by concerns about how ethnicity, or "tribalism," threatens to fracture Cameroonian society—surface in *Dog Days* when a stranger to Madagascar unwittingly uses the term "Bami" as an epithet: "He had clearly forgotten he was in a Bamileke neighborhood. Immediately, a man stood up and let go with a verbal Molotov cocktail. He was talking about tribalism. His noisy arguments were seconded by all the others, who immediately turned on the man they had just been defending against my master" (65).

In conversations among the regulars at The Customer Is King, phrases and exclamations in Medumba, one of the Bamileke languages, are frequent.[21] One character in particular is singled out for his enthusiastic use of Medumba: the doubly named Panther Nzui Manto (*nzui manto* is the Medumba word for panther). Panther, who represents an older generation of Bamileke immigrants to Yaoundé, is depicted in part by his accent; when he pronounces the name of the current president, for example, he says "Mbiya" instead of "Biya." And while Panther frequently regales the bar crowd with his outrageous stories of hermaphrodites and cannibals, he also revels in his use of Medumba instead of French: "His Medumba rolls off his lips with shameless delight. When he speaks, his eyes close a little and his eyelids flutter. Most of the time, he takes it for granted that everyone in the streets of Madagascar understands his language, which he clearly doesn't consider foreign but an authentic part of Yaoundé culture" (62).

Here and throughout the novel, Nganang carefully draws the reader's attention to differences in speech patterns and language choices, differences that reflect not only a character's ethnicity but also age and social position. For example, in stressful situations Massa Yo often falls into Pidgin English, revealing his roots in the western part of the country. And while Mini Minor's alternation between formal and informal phrases in French reflects her disdain for and manipulation of her neighbors, the efforts of other characters to show their mastery of French vocabulary produce a comic effect, such as when

Mboudjak pompously declares that he has "a thesis, an antithesis, a synthesis, and a prosthesis" to explain human behavior (23). In other instances, Nganang's playful deconstruction of language also carries a more serious message. For example, when Massa Yo's adolescent son Soumi lets loose with a slew of insults, he shouts "Guinea pig! Fornicator! Ruminant! Individual!" (16). In a parallel scene, in response to the taunts of a dishonest peanut vendor, a woman shouts "Raving lunatic!" and "Abracadabra!" before coming up with "the word of the century: 'Anticonstitutionally!'" (154). While the primary impact of these scenes may be comic, the eruption of words like "individual" and "anticonstitutionally" reflects Nganang's attention to the underlying political concerns of the country.

At the other end of the linguistic spectrum, Nganang also peppers his writing, both dialogue and narration, with a plethora of expressions in the urban slang Camfranglais. As its name suggests, Camfranglais is a linguistic hybrid, comprising elements taken from Cameroon's national languages, French, and Pidgin English. While Labatut and Marie Mbah Onana note that Camfranglais has become a sort of anthem for Cameroonian youth, Edmond Biloa suggests that it developed not only among students but also among "the unemployed, the workers, the black-marketeers"—in other words, among people like the regulars at Massa Yo's bar.[22]

Biloa provides a detailed list of terms used in Camfranglais in order to illustrate the varied sources for its vocabulary, but his real interest lies in how speakers switch between the various languages at their command, inserting terms from one language into a sentence governed by the grammar of another in order to create a code impenetrable to the noninitiated.[23] A look at the glossary included here will give some idea of the numerous Camfranglais expressions and phrases Nganang uses. Some words, such as *njo*, meaning "for free," or *siscia*, "to threaten," are borrowed from Cameroonian languages, like Duala or Basaa, while others are hybrid terms, like *craning*, meaning "bravura," formed by adding the English "-ing" to the root of the French verb *crâner* (to show off).[24] Take for example: "Ma woman no fit chasser me for ma long, dis donc! Après tout, ma long na ma long!" Here we see both the mixing of English and French terms (as in "ma woman"), and the ways in which Camfranglais redefines some of the words it borrows (the English word "long" means "home"). For Nganang, Camfranglais is both a means of representing the vitality he sees and hears on the streets of Madagascar and an invitation to his own wordplay.

Nganang's efforts to render the patterns of speech of Yaoundé's poor neighborhoods suggest useful parallels to the works of authors such as Michel Tremblay and, especially, Patrick Chamoiseau.[25] Like Tremblay's portrayal of Montreal's Plateau Mont-Royal and Chamoiseau's depiction of the disappearing oral histories of Fort-de-France, Nganang's representation of Yaoundé's *sous-quartiers* redefines the parameters of French. It demands that the reader bend to the Cameroonian context and attempt to hear the dissonant harmony produced by the novel's multiple linguistic lines.

A more revealing intertext for *Dog Days*, however, is found in the political cartoons of the Cameroonian press; the novel shares with the work of the country's best-known cartoonists both a historical frame and a political stance critical of Biya's regime. Political cartooning took off in Cameroon in the early 1990s, in the wake of the protests described in *Dog Days* and as a response to censorship of the press.[26] While independent papers were being shut down for their criticism of the government, political cartoons were usually ignored by the censors, a move that, according to Célestin Monga, overlooked the broad appeal of the form: "Indeed, the influence of cartoons was highly underestimated. Since they were easy to understand and unusually funny, they attracted readers in both rural and urban areas, increasing the readership of the private press, even among illiterate groups of the population. Their success was so fast that the number of newspaper buyers in 1991 was almost four times as great as in 1990."[27] Several papers devoted to political cartoons appeared, and political cartoonists, most notably Nyemb Popoli, became important public figures.[28] Nganang has acknowledged the impact that political cartoons, particularly Popoli's, had on his writing of both *Dog Days* and his third novel, *La Joie de vivre*.[29] While the protests of the early 1990s provide an obvious link between Cameroonian political cartoons and Nganang's novel, the influence of the cartoons can be seen in other aspects of the novel as well. Nganang shares with cartoonists such as Popoli, Jean-Pierre Kenne, and Tex Kana both an approach to the representation of the man on the street and a recognition of the power of the spoken word. Where they differ, however, is in how they articulate their criticism of Biya and his political regime.

Although cartooning is primarily a visual art, Achille Mbembe and Francis Nyamnjoh both pay significant attention to the language developed by the cartoonists, a language that, like Nganang's writing, amplifies the voices and rumors of the streets. Nyamnjoh suggests that the blending of languages in the cartoons is integral to their ability to reflect the thoughts and experiences of Cameroonians excluded from the power structure: "These cartoonists draw extensively from Pidgin English which they blend with French and some of the popular national languages, to give a new language rich in innuendo, irony, and sarcasm, and which expresses the predicament of the common man in ways unmatched by the English and French of the power elite."[30] While Mbembe contrasts the "banality" of the cartoons' text to the richness of the drawings, his argument hinges on the ways in which their drawings "speak."[31] The cartoons exist in and are the products of "a culture that had preserved its oral character"; and in the struggle against the repressive regime, the cartoons' weapons are those of the people: words and rumors, which Mbembe calls the "poor man's bomb."[32]

For Nganang as well, rumor is the force behind history's unfolding. The climax of *Dog Days* comes with the explosion of rumor's verbal bomb, with the power that is unleashed when the people speak not as one but with many voices:

> There in my peaceful retreat, I opened my ears to the street's regicidal rumors. Yes, I kept my spirit open to the fever of change that had suddenly taken over Madagascar and run away with Yaoundé, carrying the whole of Cameroon along with it in the rush that seemed to be shaking up all of Africa. [. . .] The rumor of the turbulent country, the rumor of turbulent Yaoundé set all of Madagascar into

motion: it trembled with the continuous barking of that one sentence. Everyone was listening carefully to its uncontrollable spread. What am I saying, listening carefully? Everyone helped its subversive spread [. . . .] Yes, more than anything else, the street was on the move again! (205)

Despite the clear popularity of political cartoons in Cameroon, and despite the optimism that glows at the end of *Dog Days*, it is not clear that the cartoonists' criticism of the government has had any significant political impact. While Nyamnjoh suggests that the cartoons fulfill a cathartic function, Monga concludes that although they are a "very powerful means of communication," they actually undermine the forces of social change by presenting a "demobilizing conception of politics."[33] Mbembe goes further in his elaboration of this paradox. He argues that by proliferating and circulating images of the country's ruler, however mocking they may be, political cartoons effectively and perversely magnify his presence and his power. What results, according to Mbembe, is a sort of hallucination: an omnipresent and omnipotent autocrat.[34] It would seem that Nganang has sought to avoid falling into this trap. In fact, Nganang's repeated references to the unnamed "thing" (*la chose-là*) in the novel's final chapter resonate clearly with Mbembe's argument. Moreover, Nganang's description of Mboudjak's misadventures consistently underscores the dangers inherent in the street's hallucinations, whether they result from alcohol, hunger, or rumor's sleight of hand. Keenly aware of how words can cut both ways, Nganang does not just circulate rumors and reiterate popular criticism of Biya's regime; rather, he carefully constructs the ruler as absence.

Although Biya's name appears sporadically throughout the novel, and more frequently in the final chapter, the context is designed to limit, not magnify, his presence. This is one effect of Panther's mispronunciation of his name, "Mbiya," for example. Rumors of Biya's corruption fly, but recognition of his authority is limited to a discussion of his responsibility for the humiliating defeat of the national football team, the Indomitable Lions. The one authority figure who does appear in the novel is ultimately less powerful than cowardly; after shooting a child who has dared to address him, the police commissioner cowers and flees the scene. The significance of authority's absence is lost on no one. As Panther explains:

> "Don't you know," he said in a conspiratorial tone, "Mbiya is more afraid of Yaoundé's neighborhoods than of General Semengue himself? No no no. Isn't that just what the Crow said? He was right, *à me ben tchùp*, that's what I say. Have you ever seen Biya step on the brakes when he's driving through La Briqueterie? *Bi lode mebwo*, take a look around. When he drives through La Briqueterie, his windows are always up, and he's going a hundred kilometers an hour. Yet he walks next to the army generals without trembling. Only he knows what it is here that frightens him. That's what I say, only he knows." (194)

Biya's absence from *Dog Days* is neither accident nor hallucination; it is the reflection of Biya's fear, a reminder of the unharnessed power of the street, and an antidote to the dictatorship's hallucinatory hold on the country. Regardless of the literary context in which one reads *Dog Days*, the full meaning of the novel is revealed by this political backdrop, by Biya's construction as absence. And in this specific Cameroonian context, there is only one satisfactory response to Mboudjak's universal question, "Where is Man?": "Biya must go!"

About the Author

Nganang's writing is firmly anchored in the day-to-day of his native Yaoundé, but, as for many of his compatriots, his studies and his career have led him far from home. Born in Yaoundé in 1970, Nganang left Cameroon in 1992, in the wake of the protests described in the novel, to pursue his studies in Frankfurt and Berlin. After completing his doctorate in Germany, he joined the faculty of Shippensburg University, in Pennsylvania, where he teaches German and French language and literature. He is already proving to be a prolific and well-received author. In addition to scholarly essays (his book on Brecht and Soyinka, *Interculturalität und Bearbeitung: Untersuchung zu*

Soyinka und Brecht, was published in German in 1998), Nganang has to date published a collection of poetry, *Elobi* (1995),
·three novels, and several short stories and novellas. In 1987 he
received the CREPLA (Centre de Recherches et de Promotion
de la Littérature en Afrique) Prize for the story "Histoire d'un
Enfant Quatr'Zeux." My translation of another of his short
stories, "Our Neighborhood Fool," appears in the anthology
From Africa: New Francophone Stories, edited by Adele King.
"Our Neighborhood Fool" intersects with *Dog Days,* recounting an episode from the demonstrations that erupt in the novel's concluding section. As mentioned above, *Dog Days* has
received two prestigious international awards, the Yourcenar
Prize in 2001 and the Grand Prix de la Littérature de l'Afrique
Noire in 2002.

Dog Days is Nganang's second novel. His first, *La Promesse
des fleurs,* was published in 1997, and his third, *Joie de vivre,*
in 2003. While each of these novels stands alone, together they
form a triptych about contemporary Cameroon. They differ
markedly in narrative tone and perspective, but they share a
great attention to the sights and sounds of Yaoundé's urban
landscape, and to the lives of the city's underclass. *La Promesse*
is in some sense the most narrowly focused; it follows a group
of youths as they face the challenges of coming of age in a
desperate Yaoundé. *Joie de vivre,* on the other hand, is almost
epic in scope. Recounting the lives of twins born just after independence, it moves from the Grassfields to Douala and, finally,
Yaoundé; from the bloody suppression of the UPC in the 1950s
and 1960s to the unchecked violence of the city today. The
novel's title is ironic: the picture it paints of Cameroon is bleak,
the internecine rivalry between Mambo and Mboma standing
in for the country's linguistic and ethnic fissures. Unlike *Dog
Days,* which concludes with Mboudjak's hopes for change, *Joie
de vivre* hammers home an image of youthful hopefulness undone by the violent reality of postindependence Cameroon.

Since completing this initial cycle of novels, Nganang has
switched gears and genres, publishing both a series of stories
and a pair of essays. *L'Invention du beau regard* (2004) is made
up of two *contes citadins* or "urban tales." It shares *Joie de
vivre*'s pessimism, although this is somewhat muted by the ge-

neric conventions Nganang invokes. In "L'Invention du beau regard," Nganang uses a storytelling frame to buffer the reader from the series of tragedies that befall Taba and his family, while in "Les derniers jours de service du commissaire D. Eloundou," he spins an ironic variation on the hard-boiled detective story, told from the perspective of a corrupt police investigator on the eve of his retirement. A third urban tale, "La Chanson du joggeur" was published serially in the Cameroonian newspaper *Le Messager* from July to early September 2005. *Le Principe dissident* (2005), which contains the texts of two speeches Nganang gave in Cameroon in March 2005, offers insights into the political and philosophical ideas that shape his work. In "Le Principe dissident," he condemns the silence in Cameroon that seems to condone the policies of Biya's government, and asserts his vision of the writer as a sort of town crier who express "our eternal anger at the status quo of our present, and who thereby invents peace in our future."[35] "La République invisible" is Nganang's eloquent response to a question he feels is asked too often of African writers: For whom do you write? What these essays make abundantly clear is the pressing need Nganang feels to write, as an individual, as a Cameroonian, and as a citizen of the world's "invisible republic."

Notes

1. Nganang refers to Boccaccio in an interview, noting that, like *The Decameron, Dog Days* incorporates stories from a variety of oral sources (Tervonen, "L'Ecrivain à l'école de la rue," 9). In various exchanges with me about authors who influence his writing, he cited not only Kafka, Soseki, Hoffmann, and Popoli, but also Diop, Ben Okri (in particular his novel *Famished Road*), and Wittgenstein. I will return below to the importance of political cartoons for *Dog Days*.

2. "Pour ce qui est de mon écriture, et de son enracinement dans le terroir de chez nous, cela vient de ma conviction que nous avons, moi, vous et tous les Camerounais, l'obligation de dire notre histoire, avec les mots qui sont les nôtres, en suivant la perspective que nous lui avons donnée, sans honte, simplement comme cela, car si nous ne le faisons pas, nous aurons alors à subir les mots et la perspective des autres." Quoted in Vounda Etoa, "En Toutes Lettres: Patrice Nganang," 8. All translations are my own.

3. See the review of *Temps de chien* by André Ntonfo, a professor at the University of Yaoundé: "S'il est un ouvrage publié ces dernières années et dont on peut dire qu'il a inauguré une nouvelle ère dans le roman camerounais, c'est bien *Temps de chien* de Patrice Nganang." Ntonfo, "Le Sous-quartier élevé à la dignité littéraire," 14.

4. "La barrière de l'Adamaoua, en plus des problèmes économiques et de communication qu'elle pose, a empêché jusqu'ici le développement d'une littérature véritablement nationale au profit d'une littérature régionale du Sud, française et anglaise, chrétienne et adaptée à la vie citadine." Dehon, *Le Roman camerounais d'expression française* 16; also cited in Kom, "Littératures nationales et instances de légitimation," 67. For her part, Eloise Brière acknowledges that her study of the Cameroonian novel focuses on the literary traditions and social transformations of the country's south: "L'examen de ces questions permettra de comprendre le processus de remodelage socio-culturel actuellement en cours au Sud-Cameroun." Brière, *Le Roman camerounais et ses discours,* 7.

5. "Si un texte camerounais est sans doute spécifique par rapport à un texte français, personne ne s'est encore attaché à montrer en quoi la littérature camerounaise peut se distinguer des autres créations littéraires de la région et même du continent: Congo, Gabon, Côte-d'Ivoire, Sénégal et, pourquoi pas, Nigéria." Kom, "Littératures nationales," 65.

6. Kom elaborates these ideas in both "Littératures nationales," 68, 70, and 74, and "Writing under a Monocracy," 83–92. In "African Absence: A Literature without a Voice," he stresses the consequences of the lack of literary criticism produced and published in Africa.

7. "J'ai voulu décrire ce que cela voulait dire d'être Camerounais entre 1989 et 1990, avec la prise de parole phénominale dont j'ai été témoin et qui aujourd'hui au Cameroun semble être déjà antique!" Quoted in Vounda Etoa, "En Toutes Lettres," 9.

8. "Les noms des personnages, Massa Yo, Mini Minor, Mami Ndole, ont été imaginés par la rue. Quand je parle de Mami Ndole à Yaoundé, tout le monde sait que c'est une femme d'une cinquantaine d'années, pas si belle que ça, qui prépare la nourriture. Mini Minor est une petite femme très agitée, Massa Ya un peu dada. L'imagination et l'oralité des rues ont fabriqué ces personnages qui existent et que j'ai mis dans mon roman." Quoted in Tervonen, "L'écrivain à l'école de la rue," 104.

9. In Nganang's repeated reference to "canitude," there is both an ironic nod to the influence of Senghor's and Césaire's theories of Negritude, and an echo of Wole Soyinka's comment that Africans had as much need to proclaim their Negritude as did a tiger its "tigritude" (see Bjornson, *The African Quest for Freedom and Identity,* 172). Nganang's irony is amplified later in the novel when he describes the efforts of one of Massa Yo's regulars to set himself above his compatriots; he notes that Docta often carries a book by Césaire.

10. For a detailed overview of language policy and use in Cameroon, see the collection of essays edited by Echu and Grundstrom, *Official Bilingualism and Linguistic Communication in Cameroon*.

11. Scholars vary in the precise number of languages they recognize, although most estimate upward of 250. The "Ethnologue Report for Cameroon" lists 286, of which 279 are living languages. More important than the precise number of languages spoken, however, is their diversity. Among Cameroon's national languages, there are examples of three of the four major families of African languages: Afro-Asiatic, Nilo-Saharan, and Niger-Congo (see Bird, "Orthography and Identity in Cameroon," 134; and Biloa, "Structure *phrastique* du camfranglais," 147).

12. For an overview of Cameroon's colonial history and the creation of the current nation state, see Chiabi, *The Making of Modern Cameroon*.

13. Zé Amvela, "English and French in Cameroon," 133.

14. Echu, "Genèse et évolution du bilinguisme officiel au Cameroun," 12.

15. Zé Amvela, "English and French in Cameroon," 138, 141.

16. Zé Amvela, "English and French in Cameroon," 143.

17. Tchoungui, "Unilingual Past, Multilingual Present, Uncertain Future," 125, 118–19.

18. Feldman-Savelsberg, "Bamiléké," 37.

19. Tchoungui, "Unilingual Past," 118.

20. This episode in Cameroon's history provides the backdrop for Nganang's third novel, *La Joie de vivre*.

21. The Ethnologue Web site notes that, with some 210,000 speakers, Medumba is one of the most widely spoken of the eleven languages that form the Bamileke language subgroup. See "Ethnologue Report for ISO 639 code:bai."

22. Mbah Onana and Mbah Onana, "Le Camfranglais," 30; Biloa, "Structure *phrastique* du camfranglais," 147.

23. Biloa, "Structure *phrastique* du camfranglais," 150.

24. While the examples given here are culled from Nganang's writing, the terms also figure on the extensive lists of Camfranglais vocabulary provided by Biloa, "Structure *phrastique* du camfranglais," 160–68. For a greater sense of the structure of Camfranglais, see the two passages he reproduces as an appendix (173–74).

25. *Dog Days* gestures toward two of Chamoiseau's novels: *Texaco*, which explores the origins and social fabric of one of Fort-de-France's shanty towns, and which received the Prix Goncourt in 1992; and *Solibo Magnifique*, which focuses on the death of oral culture in Martinique. In both novels, the figure of the author/sociologist or "word scratcher," aka "Oiseau de Cham"—Bird of Ham—can be linked to

Nganang's Crow. As mentioned above, the Crow has written a novel entitled *Dog Days;* he comes to Madagascar in order to write "a story about the present, about the day-to-day, to seize history in its creation and put the reins of History back into the hands of its true heroes [. . .] 'people like all of you here around me'" (83).

26. Mbembe, "La 'Chose' et ses doubles dans la caricature camerounaise," 144.

27. Monga, "Cartoons in Cameroon," 148.

28. According to Nyamnjoh, the popularity of political cartoons led both to the establishment of several papers devoted to cartoon journalism, including *Le Messager Popoli,* and to a shift in the perceived role of the cartoonist: Nyemb Popoli, in particular, emerged as a sort of "messiah—the only one really capable of defending the interests of the people" (Njamnjoh, "Press Cartoons and Politics in Cameroon," 176). Monga also uses the term messiah to describe the cartoonists' reputation: "By the same token, anyone who challenges the government is quickly perceived as a Messiah—beginning with the cartoonists themselves" (Monga, "Cartoons in Cameroon," 154).

29. Nganang told me that one of his inspirations for examining Yaoundé through the eyes of a dog was a series of cartoons by Popoli with dogs and cats commenting on political events. In the final section of *Dog Days,* Nganang refers to *Le Messager,* a paper that carries Popoli's cartoons, as one of the sources spreading the "rumor" that brought people out into the streets, the call for Biya to step down. Finally, in the postscript to *Joie de vivre,* Nganang acknowledges the influence of Popoli's work on his own: "Ce livre, né de mon admiration pour les caricatures du *Messager-Popoli.* . . . " (399).

30. Nyamnjoh, "Press Cartoons and Politics," 179.

31. Although Mbembe contrasts the cartoons' expressive drawings with their simple text—"La richesse expressive et l'extraordinaire densité du signe graphique contrastent, très souvent, avec la pauvreté et la banalité du propos qui l'accompagne ou tente de lui prêter parole"— he also insists that the cartoons' drawings function as (verbal not just visual) language: "le signe pictographique n'appartient pas seulement au champ du 'voir'. Il relève aussi de celui du 'dire'"; and further, "En tant que figure du language, l'image est toujours un propos conventionnel, la transcription d'un réel, d'un mot, d'une vision ou d'une idée en un code visible que devient, à son tour, une manière de parler du monde et de l'habiter" ("La 'Chose' et ses doubles," 159, 143).

32. Mbembe, "La 'Chose' et ses doubles," 145, 158.

33. Nyamnjoh, "Press Cartoons and Politics," 188; Monga, "Cartoons in Cameroon," 167.

34. Mbembe first presents the paradoxical effect of the cartoonists' caricatures of Biya: "Or, le paradoxe est qu'en s'emparant du

pouvoir d'imagination publique, l'artiste amplifie l'effet de présence de l'autocrate." He then asserts that the proliferation of images of the president results in a seemingly inescapable hallucination: "[Une hallucination] dans la mesure où c'est l'autocrate qui profère la parole, commande l'écoute et l'écriture, et remplit l'espace au point où c'est encore de lui que l'on parle au moment même où l'acte créatif prétend le profaner." See "La 'Chose' et ses doubles," 160, 165.

35. Nganang, *Le Principe dissident*, 30.

Bibliography

Biloa, Edmond. "Structure *phrastique* du camfranglais: Etat de la question." In Echu and Grundstrom, 147–74.

Bird, Steven. "Orthography and Identity in Cameroon." *Written Language and Literacy* 4, no. 2 (2001): 132–62.

Bjornson, Richard. *The African Quest for Freedom and Identity.* Bloomington: Indiana Univ. Press, 1991.

Brière, Eloise. *Le Roman camerounais et ses discours.* Ivry-sur-Seine: Editions Nouvelles du Sud, 1993.

Chamoiseau, Patrick. *Texaco.* Trans. Myriam Réjouis and Val Vinokurov. New York: Pantheon, 1997.

Chiabi, Emmanuel. *The Making of Modern Cameroon: A History of Nationalism and Disparate Union, 1914–1961.* Vol. 1. New York: Univ. Press of America, 1997.

Dehon, Claire. *Le Roman camerounais d'expression française.* Birmingham, AL: Summa Publications, 1989.

Echu, George. "Genèse et évolution du blinguisme officiel au Cameroun." In Echu and Grundstrom, 3–13.

———. "Usage et abus de language au Cameroun." In Echu and Grundstrom, 113–32.

Echu, George, and Allan W. Grundstrom, eds. *Official Bilingualism and Linguistic Communication in Cameroon/Bilinguisme officiel et communication linguistique au Cameroun.* New York: Peter Lang, 1999.

"Ethnologue Report for Cameroon." <http://www.ethnologue.com/show_country.asp?name=Cameroon> (accessed Apr. 8, 2005).

"Ethnologue Report for ISP 639 code:bai." <http://www.ethnologue.com/show_iso639.asp?code=bai> (accessed Apr. 8, 2005).

Feldman-Savelsberg, Pamela. "Bamiléké." In *Encyclopedia of World*

Cultures, ed. John Middleton and Amal Rassan, vol. 9: *Africa and the Middle East,* 36–41. Boston: GK Hall, 1991.

King, Adele, ed. *From Africa: New Francophone Stories:* Lincoln: Univ. Nebraska Press, 2003.

Kom, Ambroise. "African Absence: A Literature without a Voice." *Research in African Literatures* 29, no. 3 (Fall 1998): 149–61.

————. "Littératures nationales et instances de légitimation: L'Exemple du Cameroun." *Etudes Littéraires* 24, no. 2 (Autumn 1991): 65–75.

————. "Writing under a Monocracy: Intellectual Poverty in Cameroon." Trans. Rosemarie H. Mitsch. *Research in African Literatures* 22, no. 1 (Spring 1991): 83–92.

Mbah Onana, Labatut, and Marie Mbah Obana. "Le Camfranglais." *Diagonales* 32 (Nov. 1994): 29–32.

Mbembe, Achille. "La 'Chose' et ses doubles dans la caricature camerounaise." *Cahiers d'Etudes Africaines* 36, nos. 1–2 (141–42) (1996): 143–70.

Monga, Célestin. "Cartoons in Cameroon: Anger and Political Derision under Monocracy." In *The Word behind Bars and the Paradox of Exile,* ed. Kofi Anyidoho, 146–68. Evanston, IL: Northwestern Univ. Press, 1997.

Nganang, Patrice. "La Chanson du joggeur." *Le Messager,* nos. 1919–56, July 12–Sept. 2, 2005.

————. *Elobi.* Paris: Saint-Germain-des-Prés, 1995.

————. *L'Invention du beau regard.* Paris: Collection Continents Noirs, Gallimard, 2005.

————. *La Joie de vivre.* Paris: Le Serpent à Plumes, 2003.

————. *Le Principe dissident.* Yaoundé: Interlignes, 2005.

————. *La Promesse des fleurs.* Paris: L'Harmattan, 1997.

————. *Temps de chien.* Paris: Le Serpent à Plumes, 2001.

Ntonfo, André. "Le Sous-quartier élevé à la dignité littéraire." *Patrimoine: Mensuel de la Culture et des Sciences Sociales* 38 (June 2003): 14–15.

Nyamnjoh, Francis. "Press Cartoons and Politics in Cameroon." *International Journal of Comic Art* 1, no. 2 (Fall 1999): 171–90.

Tchoungui, Gisèle. "Unilingual Past, Multilingual Present, Uncertain Future: The Case of Yaounde." *Journal of Multilingual and Multicultural Development* 21, no. 2 (2000): 113–28.

Tervonen, Taina. "L'Ecrivain à l'école de la rue: Entretien avec Patrice Nganang." *Africultures* 37 (Apr. 2001): 104–5.

Vounda Etoa, Marcelin. "En Toutes Lettres: Patrice Nganang." *Patrimoine: Mensuel de la Culture et des Sciences Sociales* 37 (May 2003): 8–9.

Zé Amvela, Etienne. "English and French in Cameroon: A Study of Language Maintenance and Shift." In Echu and Grundstrom, 133–45.

CARAF Books
Caribbean and African Literature Translated from French

Guillaume Oyônô-Mbia and Seydou Badian
Faces of African Independence: Three Plays
Translated by Clive Wake

Olympe Bhêly-Quénum
Snares without End
Translated by Dorothy S. Blair

Bertène Juminer
The Bastards
Translated by Keith Q. Warner

Tchicaya U Tam'Si
The Madman and the Medusa
Translated by Sonja Haussmann Smith and William Jay Smith

Alioum Fantouré
Tropical Circle
Translated by Dorothy S. Blair

Edouard Glissant
Caribbean Discourse: Selected Essays
Translated by J. Michael Dash

Daniel Maximin
Lone Sun
Translated by Nidra Poller

Aimé Césaire
Lyric and Dramatic Poetry, 1946–82
Translated by Clayton Eshleman and Annette Smith

René Depestre
The Festival of the Greasy Pole
Translated by Carrol F. Coates

Kateb Yacine
Nedjma
Translated by Richard Howard

Léopold Sédar Senghor
The Collected Poetry
Translated by Melvin Dixon

Maryse Condé
I, Tituba, Black Witch of Salem
Translated by Richard Philcox

Assia Djebar
Women of Algiers in Their Apartment
Translated by Marjolijn de Jager

Dany Bébel-Gisler
Leonora: The Buried Story of Guadeloupe
Translated by Andrea Leskes

Lilas Desquiron
Reflections of Loko Miwa
Translated by Robin Orr Bodkin

Jacques Stephen Alexis
General Sun, My Brother
Translated by Carrol F. Coates

Malika Mokeddem
Of Dreams and Assassins
Translated by K. Melissa Marcus

Werewere Liking
It Shall Be of Jasper and Coral and *Love-across-a-Hundred-Lives*
Translated by Marjolijn de Jager

Ahmadou Kourouma
Waiting for the Vote of the Wild Animals
Translated by Carrol F. Coates

Mongo Beti
The Story of the Madman
Translated by Elizabeth Darnel

Jacques Stephen Alexis
In the Flicker of an Eyelid
Translated by Carrol F. Coates and Edwidge Danticat

Gisèle Pineau
Exile according to Julia
Translated by Betty Wilson

Mouloud Feraoun
The Poor Man's Son: Menrad, Kabyle Schoolteacher
Translated by Lucy R. McNair

Abdourahman A. Waberi
The Land without Shadows
Translated by Jeanne Garane

Patrice Nganang
Dog Days: An Animal Chronicle
Translated by Amy Baram Reid